PROSPECT

SATAN'S FURY MC-MEMPHIS

L. WILDER

Prospect
Satan's Fury MC-Memphis
Copyright 2020
L. Wilder- All rights reserved.

L. Wilder be sure to stay connected-

Social media Links:

Facebook: https://www.facebook.com/AuthorLeslieWilder

Twitter: https://twitter.com/wilder_leslie

Instagram: http://instagram.com/LWilderbooks

Amazon: http://www.amazon.com/L-Wilder/e/B00NDKCCMI/

Bookbub: https://www.bookbub.com/authors/l-wilder

Sign up for L. Wilder's Newsletter: http://bit.ly/1RGsREL

Cover Design: Mayhem Cover Creations
www.facebook.com/MayhemCoverCreations

Editor: Lisa Cullinan

Proofreader- Rose Holub @ReadbyRose

Proofreader: Honey Palomino

Teasers & Banners: Gel Ytayz at Tempting Illustrations

Personal Assistant: Natalie Weston PA

Catch up with the entire Satan's Fury MC Series today!
All books are FREE with Kindle Unlimited!

Summer Storm (Satan's Fury MC Novella)

Maverick (Satan's Fury MC #1)

Stitch (Satan's Fury MC #2)

Cotton (Satan's Fury MC #3)

Clutch (Satan's Fury MC #4)

Smokey (Satan's Fury MC #5)

Big (Satan's Fury #6)

Two Bit (Satan's Fury #7)

Diesel (Satan's Fury #8)

Blaze (Satan's Fury MC- Memphis Book 1)

Shadow (Satan's Fury MC- Memphis Book 2)

Riggs (Satan's Fury MC- Memphis Book 3)

Murphy (Satan's Fury MC- Memphis Book 4)

Gunner (Satan's Fury MC- Memphis Book 5)

Gus (Satan's Fury MC- Memphis Book 6)

Rider (Satan's Fury MC- Memphis Book 7)

Day Three (What Bad Boys Do Book 1)

Damaged Goods- (The Redemption Series Book 1- Nitro)

Max's Redemption (The Redemption Series Book 2- Max)

Inferno (Devil Chasers #1)

Smolder (Devil Chaser #2)

Ignite (Devil Chasers #3)

Consumed (Devil Chasers #4)

Combust (Devil Chasers #5)

My Temptation (The Happy Endings Collection #1)

Bring the Heat (The Happy Endings Collection #2)

His Promise (The Happy Endings Collection #3)

✤ Created with Vellum

PROLOGUE

I'd always been overly protective, especially when it came to my little sister, Alyssa. She was polar opposite of me. Where I was six-foot-eight and weighed two-ninety, Alyssa was five-foot-six in heels, and thin. Sure, a strong gust of wind might knock her skinny ass to the ground, but don't get me wrong, the girl was far from weak. Lyssa knew what she wanted and was willing to work hard for it, whether it was getting perfect grades or making the cheerleading squad. I respected her for that. Hell, there were times when I was even jealous of the fact. It seemed there was nothing that could stand in Alyssa's way, but when it did, I was there—just like I'd been on the night of Homecoming.

It was after eleven when she came knocking at my door, still wearing her homecoming dress, but now it was wrinkled and hanging off her shoulder. She'd been crying, and a thick line of black mascara had run down her cheek. "I fucked up, Clay ... like really, *really* fucked up."

"What the fuck, Lyssa." I took her by the arm and

pulled her into my room, then closed the door behind her. "What the hell happened to you?"

"First, I need you to promise that you won't say anything." She looked up at me with her big, puppy-dog eyes filled with tears and pleaded. "This has to stay between us."

"Why do I get the feeling that I shouldn't agree?"

"Just promise me, Clay," she insisted. "I'm not saying another word until you do."

"Fine. I promise not to say anything," I grumbled. "Now, tell me what the fuck is going on."

She hesitated once again. I didn't understand why until she started, "So, you know tonight was Homecoming, right?"

"Yeah." Homecoming was just another way my sister and I were different. Even though it was my senior year, I couldn't have cared less about it, but it was the *only thing* Lyssa had been focused on for weeks. She was all excited that Lucas Brant, a senior and a varsity football player, had asked her not only to the dance but also to a big party afterwards. She was just a sophomore, so going with a senior was a huge deal—at least it was to her. Having no idea what had made her so upset, I asked, "What about it?"

"Well, the dance and all was fine," Lyssa's breaths became short and strained as she tried to explain, "until everything got all screwed up at the party at Janey Kay's house."

"Why? What happened?"

"It's hard to explain ... Everyone was there. I'd never seen so many people, and they were all dancing and drinking."

"And what about you? Were you drinking?"

Her eyes dropped to the ground as she answered, "Yeah, I was. I didn't want to be the only one who wasn't joining in, you know?"

"I get it."

"Anyway, I had a couple of beers, but Lucas ... he drank quite a lot." She inhaled a pained breath before adding, "Much more than I realized."

"What the hell is that supposed to mean?"

"It's not *all* his fault, Clay. I should've known what he had in mind when he asked me to go upstairs with him, but I just wasn't thinking." She turned to look out the window and started to sob again. "I'm so stupid."

That familiar rage started to creep over me like a wildfire. "What. Happened!"

"I'm trying to tell you," she fussed.

"No, Lyssa, you're hemmin' and hawin' around. Just tell me what the hell happened!"

"After we got upstairs, he took me into one of the bedrooms, and we started to kiss. It was nice at first, but then I could tell he wanted something more." She turned to face me, and when I saw the anguish in her eyes, it gutted me. I had a feeling I knew exactly what had happened between her and Lucas but didn't want to believe it. I wanted to stop her from saying the words out loud but didn't get that chance. Tears were streaming down her face as she muttered, "I told him that I didn't want anything else to happen, but he didn't listen."

About to come unglued, I asked, "What do you mean 'he didn't listen'?"

"No matter how many times I told him no, he just kept pushing." Lyssa dropped her head into her hands, and I could barely hear her. "I should've never gone upstairs with him. I don't know what I was thinking. I should've known what he wanted, but I was just too stupid to see it."

"Stop that shit right now! None of this was your fault. This was all on him. Every damn bit of it."

"You're wrong! This is just as much my fault as it is his. I never should've gone into that bedroom with him. I know what it means when a guy like Lucas wants to be alone with a girl, especially at a party. I knew there was a good chance that we'd be fooling around, and I think a part of me was actually hoping he'd want me like that." She wiped the tears from her eyes. "All my friends were so jealous that I was going to Homecoming with not only a senior, but with the best-looking senior in school."

"You're fucking kidding me with this shit, right?"

"Lucas could've asked a hundred different girls and not a single one of them would've given a second thought to having sex with him tonight." I couldn't believe my ears when she added, "I should've been happy that someone like him would even choose to be with me."

"Dammit, Lyssa! That asshole fucking raped you!" As I looked down at my sister, so distraught and full of heartache, I found myself thinking about a conversation I'd had with my father. He was truck driver, and it was tough on him being away from home all the time. Knowing he couldn't do it himself, he'd asked me to look after my mother and sister, to protect them in a way that he couldn't. It was up to me to fix this thing, so I didn't resist when the rage rose to the surface and took over as I grabbed my keys off the dresser. I stormed towards the door and told her, "I'm going to fucking kill him."

"Clay, stop!" she pleaded and rushed over to me.

"Don't you get it? No one can find out about this. If they do, it'll ruin me!"

"What the hell are you talking about?"

"You know how people can be ... how they twist things around and shift the blame." She ran her hand through her disheveled hair and continued, "No matter how it really played out, everyone will think it was my fault ... that I brought it on myself. I don't think I could handle that."

"So, you're just going to let this asshole get away with raping you?"

"I don't have a choice."

"There's always a choice, sis." I took a minute to consider everything she'd said, and even though I knew there was some truth in it, there was no way in hell I could let Lucas Brant get away with what he'd done to my sister. No matter what she said, there was no way I was going to let this go. I couldn't. I took a step towards her and pulled her into my arms, hugging her tightly as I whispered, "I'm going to take care of this, Lyssa."

"But ..."

"Don't worry. No one will ever know what happened," I assured her. "I'll make sure of it."

I held her a moment longer, then turned and left the room. I heard her calling my name, but I continued out the front door and towards my truck. In a matter of minutes I was on my way to Janey Kay's house, and all I could think about was that dickhead's hands on my little sister while she pleaded with him to stop. The thought sickened me, making me want to rip him apart limb from limb.

When I pulled up, the party was still going strong. The

music was blaring as I started up the steps of the two-story colonial home. There were tall white columns along the front porch and an overdone flowered wreath on the front door. As soon as I stepped inside, I couldn't help but grimace at the mess: beer cans and bottles strewn all over the place, tables and chairs turned over, and drunken teenagers wobbling around in an inebriated state as they tried to keep themselves from falling. Several were completely blistered, but I didn't give a fuck about any of them. There was only one person on my mind—Lucas Brant.

When I spotted Michael, one of Brant's friends, walking in my direction, I charged towards him, then grabbed the collar of his t-shirt and twisted it in my fist. "Where's Brant?"

"What the fuck, man?" he scowled.

"Gonna ask one more time." I gave him a hard shove, pinning him up against the wall. "Where the hell is he?"

"Last time I saw him, he was out back by the fire."

I released my hold on him, then turned and stormed through the living room. When I walked out the back door, I spotted Lucas standing by the fire, bullshitting with several of the other guys on the football team. I was filled with so much blinding rage as I headed towards him that everyone else faded from my sight. Without giving him a chance to prepare for my attack, I grabbed him by the shoulder, whipped him around to face me, and then plowed my fist into his jaw. He started to stumble back, so I grabbed the collar of his t-shirt and punched him again and again. With a *thud*, he landed on the ground, and I took the opportunity to pin him down with my knees. Once I was sure he couldn't budge, I started in on him again. A couple of his buddies tried to get me off him, but their efforts were all in vain. Nothing was going to stop me from making Brant pay for putting his fucking hands on my sister. Determined to make a lasting impression, I kept hammering away at him. It wasn't long before Lucas's entire face was bloody, bruised, and swollen, and he was barely conscious. Sensing he was about to black-out, I wrapped my hands around his throat, gripping him tightly as I leaned forward and placed my mouth close to his ear.

My voice was low and ominous as I whispered, "If you breathe a word about what happened tonight between you and Alyssa, I'll end you once and for all. You got that?"

He managed to nod, but I didn't remove my hands from his throat. I couldn't. Every time I tried to let go, I'd see Lyssa's face and the anguish in her eyes as she stood there crying in my room. I knew I should stop. I was reaching the point of no return, but I couldn't pull myself together. The rage was just too much. I kept tightening my grip, slowly squeezing the life out of him. Thankfully, Michael lunged towards me, using all of his weight to push me off Lucas and forcing me to release my grip on him. Before I had a chance to react, several of the others jumped in to help Michael—each of them kicking and punching me wherever they could land a hit. I tried to get back up on my feet, plowing away at each of them like a crazed lunatic, but I couldn't get my footing. There were just too many of them. With one hard blow to the jaw, my head reared back and everything went dark.

Just as I was starting to come around, the faint sounds of police sirens were heading towards Janey's house. I was still sprawled out on the ground by the fire as kids rushed by, scrambling to get the hell out of Dodge before the cops arrived. I knew they'd be there for me, so I tried to get to my feet, but with my head spinning, I only ended up falling on my ass. Just as I was about to try again, Michael appeared in my line of sight with two officers at his side. As he pointed in my direction, I could hear him shouting. "That's him. That's the guy you're looking for." They hardly had time to react before he started in again, "He's the one who attacked Lucas for no fucking reason, and he nearly killed him! Lucas was barely conscious when they took him to the ER."

"Okay, kid. I'm gonna need you to settle down. We've got this," one of the officers warned.

The two cops started towards me, and once they approached, one of them extended his hand. As he helped me to my feet, he asked, "You got a name, son?"

"Clay Hanson."

"All right, Clay. Why don't you tell me what happened here tonight?"

"Nothing," I snapped.

"Now, you and I both know that isn't true." He almost sounded like he was being sincere when he said, "I can't help you unless you tell me what really went down here tonight."

"Already told ya ... Nothing to tell."

"Have it your way."

Pissed that I refused to answer him, the cop reached behind and pulled out a pair of handcuffs. He turned me around and slapped them over my wrists while reading me my rights. Once he was done, I was led over to the squad car and put inside. Just as he was shutting the door, Michael yelled, "You're going down, Hanson!"

When Michael said those words to me, neither of us had any idea how true they really were. I got off easy when Brant didn't press charges, but my luck ended there. I struggled to get a grip on the anger that erupted when I went after Lucas. I couldn't suppress the rage, the need for vengeance, and all the other intense emotions I was feeling that night. Instead, they lingered on the surface like a parasite, leaving me feeling completely exposed as it waited to rear its ugly head once again.

Unfortunately, I didn't have to wait long for that to happen. Without ever knowing why I'd had the altercation with Lucas, my father's semi-truck was hit by a drunk driver, and he was killed instantly. The injustice of his death seemed to bring out the worst in me, and I started on a downward spiral. I completely lost myself. I wasn't thinking about my mother or sister. Hell, I wasn't thinking of anyone or anything. I just sank deeper into my own madness, finding trouble at every turn: drinking, fighting, and eventually more trouble with the law.

I was fucking up in every way possible, so it shouldn't have come as a surprise when Viper, my uncle and president of the Ruthless Sinners MC, decided to step in. Knowing I was making a mess of my life, he reached out to his buddy Gus, the president of Satan's Fury, then sent me to Memphis to spend some time with the brothers at their clubhouse. He hoped that I'd find my way with them. Turns out, he was right.

PROSPECT

"It's not just about knowing the brothers' names and their position in the club. You gotta know *everything* about them," Rider explained. "Their backgrounds ... where they grew up, jobs they've had, past experiences. What their life was like before joining the club ... and after—the good, the bad, and the ugly."

Rider had been chosen by Gus to be my sponsor. It was his job to guide me through prospecting and make sure I knew everything that would be expected of me during the process. Feeling overwhelmed by what he'd just informed me, I turned to him and asked, "I hear what you're saying, but I don't get why it matters so much. I mean, what difference does it make if I know what jobs Blaze had as a kid?"

"It's knowing what your family is all about," Rider answered firmly. "Knowing that Cyrus and T-Bone were here with Gus when he first started up the Memphis chapter and how they helped him find the clubhouse and build our numbers. And knowing that when our brother

L. WILDER

Runt was killed, Shadow was the one who stepped up to the plate and saved our asses, earning our vote as the club's new enforcer. It helps you understand where the brothers have been ... where they're going. It gives you some insight to what makes them tick."

"I get that, but how am I supposed to find out all this shit?"

"You listen ... not only to what they say, but what they don't say." Rider looked me directly in the eye. "You'll get it. It's just going to take time."

I hoped Rider was right. I wanted to think that I had what it took to earn my patch, but there were times when I wasn't so sure. If I wanted to be considered family to these men, I had a lot of work to do, and it wasn't going to be easy. There were over thirty members I had to learn about, all the while doing the other crazy bullshit that came along with prospecting. But I wasn't complaining. I'd finally found the life I wanted, and I wasn't going to let anything stand in my way. I gave Rider a slight nod and answered, "I'll do whatever I gotta do."

"I know you will." He lifted his beer. "I'll help where I can."

"I'd appreciate that, brother."

Just as the words left my mouth, Darcy, Rider's ol' lady, came walking into the living room. I could still remember the first time we'd met. I'd only been in Memphis for a few days when the brothers hired her to be the garage's custom painter. There weren't many women who could handle working in a shop full of strong-willed bikers, but she managed it like a pro. Darcy and Rider had grown up in the same small town and had history. It didn't take long for them to pick up where they left off, and they'd been inseparable since. Rider and I were sitting on the sofa when she walked over with a concerned expression on her face. "You know, we could go to the Smoking Gun with Murphy and the others tonight. I can hit one of Brannon's shows another time."

"I'm good with going to Neil's to see him tonight," Rider told her. "With the crowd that'll be at the Smoking Gun, it's not like they'll miss us."

"I know, but I don't want to disappoint Riley."

"I already talked to Murphy. It's all good, babe."

Looking relieved, she smiled and said, "Good. I just wanted to be sure."

"What's the big deal with the Smoking Gun anyway?"

Rider turned to me as he explained, "Riley and the owner of the bar, Grady, are first cousins and best friends, and he's having some big shindig tonight for the playoffs. I'm kind of glad we decided not to go. I wasn't looking forward to fighting that crowd."

"Okay, then I guess it's about time for us to head over to Neil's. Brannon's show starts at eight," Darcy said.

Taking our cue, Rider and I got up and followed her outside to our bikes. I waited as she got settled behind him, then we both fired up our engines and headed downtown. As we made our way towards Neil's bar, I was feeling pretty good about things in my life, and I found myself thinking of the day Viper had come to me about leaving Nashville and staying with Satan's Fury. I couldn't blame him for wanting to get me out of town. I was a ticking time-bomb. Every time something didn't go my way, I'd blow up and do something stupid—get into a fight or be laid-out drunk. When I landed myself in trouble with the law again, my mother freaked out and called Viper for help.

I KNEW *the second I walked out of that jailhouse and found him standing in the parking lot he was pissed. I wasn't surprised. I'd fucked up once again, and he was the one who'd pick up the pieces so my mother wouldn't have to.*

Once we were inside his truck, Viper turned to me with a fierce expression. "This shit has got to stop, Clay."

"I know."

"If you know, then what are you going to do about it?"

"I don't know." *I shrugged.* "I'll figure something out."

"Yeah, you've been dishing out that same bullshit ever since the night you beat the hell out of that kid, and I'm tired of hearing it," *he growled.* "I feel for you, Clay. I really do. I know you've had some rough blows, but it's time for you to make a change ... a real change."

I couldn't argue. He was absolutely right. It was time for me to change, to pull my head out of my ass and get my life back on track, but I had no idea how I was going to make that happen. "I know. I'm trying."

"You're obviously not trying hard enough!" *He paused for a moment, and once he'd collected himself, his tone was softer.* "I've got an old friend ... He's got a club down in Memphis. I think you should go down and try to prospect for him."

"Wait ... what?" *From the day he joined the Ruthless Sinners, Viper had dedicated his life to his brothers. Hell, he lived and breathed for them, so I was surprised when he'd suggested I prospect for an MC that wasn't his.* "If I was going to prospect for a club, why wouldn't I just do it for you and the Sinners?"

"I considered that, and honestly, I think you'd do well with us." I could see the sincerity in his eyes. *"But there are too many memories here ... too many things holding you back. It's time for you to get a fresh start, and I think you can accomplish that with Satan's Fury. Gus is a good man ... runs a tight ship with a good group of men."*

"So, what are you expecting me to say here?" To say that I was resistant to the idea was putting it lightly. In fact, the entire thing seemed ludicrous to me, and even though Viper was a very powerful man, I wasn't shy about letting him know exactly how I felt. My words dripped with sarcasm as I continued, *"Sure. I'll pack up my shit and move to fucking Memphis."*

"Yeah. That's exactly what I expected you to say," he said. *"Actually, I'm not taking any other answer. I've already spoken with Gus, so get yourself prepared because you're heading out at the end of the week."*

I could tell by his tone that he wasn't going to take no for an answer, so I just swallowed my pride and kept my mouth shut. I thought if I just gave him time to cool down that I could talk him out of it later. I was wrong. Viper wasn't giving up on the idea. At the end of the week, he showed up at the house, and the anger that lingered so close to the surface started to rise up once again. I was just about to blast him, tell him to go to hell and refuse to leave, but then I noticed the expression on my mother's face. The concern in her eyes hit me like a ton of bricks. My actions had hurt her, and that was the last thing I wanted to do. So, as Viper requested, I packed my shit and drove to Memphis. As soon as I walked through the clubhouse doors, a strange sensation washed over me. The hostility and heartache that had been weighing on me suddenly seemed to fade into the background.

. . .

AT THE TIME, I didn't know why. I thought it might've been because I was so focused on trying not to make an ass of myself in my newfound surroundings, but as the weeks passed, I started to realize it was much more than that.

I was still thinking about the first time I'd met Gus when Rider, Darcy, and I pulled up at Neil's. It was about half the size of the Smoking Gun, but that didn't stop the crowds from rolling in. It was a happening place. There was a stage and lighting for their live bands, a dance floor, and plenty of tables for those who just wanted to sit and drink their beer while listening to some great local talent —including this Brannon Heath guy who Darcy wanted to see. I'd never heard of him, but Darcy was a huge fan, particularly of the latest song he'd written. As soon as we were inside the bar, Darcy led us over to a table close to the stage, and it wasn't long before one of the waitresses came over to take our drink orders. She was older, maybe in her late forties, and while she tried to hide it, I could tell by the dark circles under her eyes that she'd already had a long night. With a slight smile, she looked down at us and asked, "What can I get you folks tonight?"

"A round of whatever you have on tap would be great," Rider answered.

"You got it."

When she turned and headed over to the bar, I took a quick glance around and noticed how everyone in the room seemed to be having a great time. Unfortunately, I didn't feel the same. I couldn't stop thinking about all the stuff I needed to learn about the brothers. I'd never been a stellar student and was afraid I wouldn't be able to get it all down. The fear of failure was daunting, so much so, I not only missed that the waitress had brought our drinks over, but that the band had already taken their place on the stage. A bright smile crossed Darcy's face when Heath stepped up to the microphone. "Hey ... there he is. I think they're about to start."

I nodded as I reached for my beer and took a quick sip. As much as I wanted to down the whole damn thing, I knew I couldn't—not while I was prospecting. There was always a chance that one of the brothers would need me, so like it or not, I had to keep my senses intact. Trying to make the best of it, I leaned back in my seat and listened as the band started to play. After a few songs, I could see why Heath was becoming such a big hit in the city. The guy had a good voice, and his lyrics weren't so bad either. I could've sat there and listened to the band all night, but just as I was really starting to settle in, my burner rang. I reached into my pocket with a nagging suspicion that I was being beckoned by one of the brothers. I looked down at the screen, and just as I thought, it was a message from Riggs. He was having some bike trouble and needed a hand. Knowing I couldn't keep him waiting, I motioned to Rider, letting him know that I was leaving, and headed out the door. As I got on my bike, I wasn't feeling aggravated or put out. I knew with each time the brothers called me for help, I was one step closer to becoming a member of Satan's Fury, and there was nothing I wanted more.

LANDRY

There were those girls in high school who'd always seemed to have it all—the ones with the perfect figure, perfect hair, and flawless skin. They could eat anything they wanted to without gaining a single pound, and for whatever reason, everyone on the planet seemed to absolutely adore them. Yeah, I hadn't been one of those girls. I was five-foot-ten and wore a size twelve, so I was far from little. My hair had been a curly, frizzy mess, and my complexion a total nightmare. It wasn't that I hadn't attempted to make myself look better, I did. I used all the hair mousses and gels, doctored my break-outs, and had tried every fad diet known to man. It didn't matter though. There'd been nothing I could do to make myself stand out in the crowd—at least, not while Mom was around.

My mother had been the vice principal of my high school, and a complete knockout. There wasn't a guy around who hadn't noticed her great curves, especially when she'd been wearing one of her tight pencil skirts—

and to make matters worse, the guys who I'd so desperately hoped would notice *me* were constantly telling me how hot they thought my mom was. It'd been soul crushing. No matter how hard I had tried, I was forever hidden in her shadow. If that wasn't enough, I also had to contend with my brother and his enormous popularity. Jacob was not only a big guy—six-seven and two hundred and eighty pounds—he'd also been a star athlete. He played football, basketball, and baseball, and he played them well. Everyone in town had thought he was the greatest thing since sliced bread, including my parents, and my only claim to fame had been the fact that I was his sister.

I'd hoped things would change after I graduated and went off to college. They hadn't. I never could shake those inferior feelings from my childhood. I'd gotten my degree without ever taking any real risks, figuring I wouldn't get rejected or hurt if I didn't put myself out there. As I ventured out into the real world, I never felt like I had any idea of who I really was or what I wanted out of life, but that all changed when I got my first job as a social worker. I'd finally found something I excelled at—my something— my niche.

The work was challenging, and at times, I worried if I had what it took to deal with such hard demands, but I never gave up. I was determined to do my job and help the families I was working with to the best of my ability, and after just a few weeks, my supervisor started to take notice. Recognition wasn't something I was used to, but I liked it. I liked it a lot. It gave me the drive I needed to push through when times got tough—like the day I was first assigned to the Strayhorn case.

The cases I handled were always different. Some families were poor. Some were wealthy. Some had homes that were in complete shambles, while others lived in almost mansions. There wasn't a set of criteria that marked the people in my case files, so I tried to always expect the unexpected. I kept that in mind as I pulled up to the Strayhorn home. It was a pitiful sight. The paint was cracked and peeling, and there were boards covering several of the windows. As I got out of my car and started up the walkway, I became concerned when I noticed the boards on the front porch were severely warped making me fear that I might fall through the wooden planks. Doing my best to watch my footing, I made my way up to the door and knocked.

Moments later it opened, and my heart melted when I saw her—Fiona, the youngest of the Strayhorn children. Dark corkscrew ringlets framed her angelic face, and along with the sweetest little smile, she had the biggest brown eyes I'd ever seen. It looked like she was about to speak when a pained grimace crossed her face. She brought her hand up to her mouth, covering it as she started to cough. It sounded terrible, almost strangling her as she tried to catch her breath, making me wonder if the poor thing had pneumonia. When she finally caught her breath, I knelt down to her eye level and said, "Hi there, sweetheart. My name is Landry Dawson. I've come to check in on you and your brothers and sisters."

A worried expression crossed her face as she turned and looked over her shoulder, nervously checking to see if anyone was behind her. I knew it wasn't the first time someone had come to pay them a visit. I'd read over their records, and over the past eight months, there had been several calls and four DHS home visits. After several moments, she turned her attention back to me. When she didn't speak, I gave her a little push. "Is your mom around?"

"No." She tugged at the hem of her dingy t-shirt. "She's at work."

Her sweet little voice made me want to scoop her up in my arms and hold her as if she were my own. "What about your dad? Is he here?"

She shook her head. "No. Just my brudder, *Jo-sif*."

"Oh, okay." When I read over their file, there was no mention of either parent having a job. In fact, it showed that neither of them had worked in months. They were not only on unemployment but were also receiving food stamps. This wasn't an uncommon practice in the city, and I held no judgements in regards to their working situation as long as they were using the funds to provide for their family. I wasn't so sure that was happening, especially after reading about Joseph. On numerous accounts, he'd been caught stealing food from a nearby grocery store. Most thirteen-year-old boys would be trying to lift cigarettes instead of food, but after seeing his home and the sickly state of his youngest sister, I'd surmise that he'd grabbed what he could because he and his siblings were hungry. "Do you think you could go get Joseph? I'd really like to talk to him."

"Mm-hmm."

Leaving the door wide open, she turned and ran towards the center of the house. I stood up, then leaned forward, trying to get a better view of the inside. While the furniture was sparse, it seemed fairly clean—at least from what I could see of it. I was tempted to step inside but stayed put when I heard Fiona shout, "Jo-sif! A lady's here!"

"What?" he shouted in return.

"A lady's at da door!"

"Okay." I heard footsteps approaching, and just as he was about to reach the door, I heard him whisper to her, "Who is it?"

I tried to listen to her response, but it was muffled under another round of coughing. It was then that I realized Fiona wasn't the only one who was sick in the house. My concern was rising by the second, and when Joseph finally appeared at the door, it only grew higher. While adorably cute like his sister, he was very underweight, and there were dark circles under his eyes. He tried to put on a brave front, but I could hear the fear in his voice as he asked, "Can I help you with something?"

"Yes, as a matter of fact you can." I smiled as I told him, "I'm Landry Dawson from the Department of Children's Services. We got a call about—"

"Another one?" he grumbled. "Mom's gonna be so pissed."

"So, you know why I'm here?"

"Yeah. We've had people like you here before." A resentful look crossed his face as he sighed. "You're gonna ask us all these questions, then look around our house and stuff so you can decide if we're okay or whatever."

"Yes. It's my job to make sure you and your siblings are okay."

"We're fine," he huffed. "But even if we weren't, it's not like you'd do anything about it."

"I don't know the other social workers who've come to see you and your family, so I can't speak for them." I looked him right in the eye as I assured him, "But, as for me, I'm going to make sure things are okay here, and if they aren't, I most certainly will do something about it."

I could see it in his eyes that he wanted to believe me, but he was skeptical at best as he muttered, "Okay."

"Can you tell me when your parents will be home from work?"

"They aren't working. Fiona just told you that because Mom told her to," he admitted.

"Do you have any idea where they are?"

"No." He shook his head and shrugged. "They didn't tell me where they were going."

"Did they tell you when they might be back?"

"Nope. They never do." He turned and looked down the street as he continued, "But it's getting dark, so they should be home soon."

I wanted to believe him, but I knew he was lying. The truth was written all over his face. There was no doubt that something was going on, but sadly, there wasn't much I could do about it. I didn't have a warrant, and since the kids weren't in immediate danger, I'd need the parents' consent to enter the premises. Having no other choice, I reached into my purse and pulled out one of my business cards. As I offered it to Joseph, I told him, "Please have your parents call me as soon as they get home. My cell phone number is at the bottom of the card."

"I'll give it to them, but I don't think they'll call."

"That's okay. I'll come back later, and I can speak with them then."

"Oh," he mumbled with disappointment. "Okay."

As he stood there staring back at me, he looked so defeated, like he was carrying the weight of the world on his shoulders, and it broke my heart. Before I even realized what I was saying, I asked, "Have you guys had dinner yet?"

"No, ma'am." In almost a pout, he explained, "Mom was supposed to bring us something, but she never did."

"Do you like fried chicken?"

His eyes lit up as he nodded and answered, "Mm-hmm."

"Okay, I'll be right back."

While I knew I was crossing a line, I couldn't in good conscious leave those kids without making sure they had something to eat. As I turned and headed towards my car, I scolded myself for not having a better grip on my emotions. I knew going in that that kind of situation was part of the job. I had rules to follow, protocols for every circumstance, and yet there I was, driving towards the local fast-food chain to buy a bucket of chicken. I got the order and drove back over to the house. When Joseph opened the door and saw all the food I'd brought, he looked like he'd just won the lottery. "Is that for us?"

"It sure is."

I handed him the two large sacks of food, and as he took it in his hands, he looked up at me and said, "None of the others brought us any food."

"Well, we don't normally do things like this, but let's just say ... these are special circumstances."

"Special? Why's that?" he asked with curiosity.

"It's not important." Hoping he'd accept my answer, I suggested, "You better get that inside and start eating before it gets cold."

"Okay." He turned and was just about to close the door when he glanced back over at me. "Thanks for this."

"You're very welcome, Joseph."

Once he closed the door, I went back to my car and drove over to the office to file my report. By the time I got there, it was well after dark, so I wasn't surprised to find that everyone had already gone for the day. After I got settled in at my cubicle, I pulled out the Strayhorn file and started reading back over it. I was hoping that I'd find something that might give me some insight on how to best help the children. As I flipped through the pages, it became clear that the family had struggled to keep their power and water on. They'd even gone so far as to try to hook up to their neighbor's line, which didn't end well. While there were only four home visits on record, there had been numerous calls from neighbors and teachers, reporting that the children had been left home alone for days at a time with little food and no clean clothes. One particularly disturbing call was made after a neighbor became concerned when she heard an infant—who I could only assume was Fiona—crying through the night and into the next morning. She went to the house to check on her, but couldn't get anyone to answer the door. Believing that the child had been left in the home alone, she called the police, but the parents had returned home before they'd arrived and the baby was no longer in distress.

I continued reading through each of the reports, only stopping when I came across several pictures of the kids. My chest tightened when I found an old picture of Joseph and Fiona. They were both so young and innocent, and it pained me to think of all the hardships they'd been through in their short lives. The longer I sat there studying the photos of the two as well as their three other siblings, I became more and more determined to help them. I just had to figure out how.

I peeked up at the clock and was surprised to see that it was after ten. Since there wasn't anything I could do at such a late hour, I reluctantly closed the file and put it back in my desk. As I headed out to my car, I remembered that I hadn't stopped to have anything for dinner. I didn't have anything at my apartment, so I decided to grab some takeout on my way home. I was only a few minutes from home when I came up on a burger joint that was still open. I whipped around the drive-through, grabbed my order, and continued towards my apartment. I was about a block away when a dog darted out of the alley and into the road. Trying my best not to hit him, I swerved, but knew when I heard a loud thump that I hadn't moved fast enough. Damn.

PROSPECT

"*I* don't know what the fuck I was thinking. It's been months since I've ridden her," Riggs complained. "I knew better than to take her out so late."

"Things happen." I shrugged. "No way you could've known she was gonna give out on you like this."

"No, this is on me. I should've checked her out before getting her on the road," he confessed. "Just figured I'd take advantage of this warm snap and give her a quick run."

"I can't blame you there." Since it was on the way, I'd decided to run by the clubhouse to pick up the long-bed truck and a couple of ramps. I figured it would save me some time if we weren't able to get his bike started. Turns out, it was a smart move. We'd both tried everything, but we couldn't get the engine to turn over. As I dropped one of the ramps, I looked over to Riggs and said, "If she's been sitting up for a while, it's a good chance it's just the battery."

"That's what I'm hoping, but I got a feeling it's the

27

drive chain." He started guiding the bike up the ramp. "I haven't had time to work on her like I should, and now it's gonna bite me in the ass."

"Maybe not." I waited as he got the front tire secured in the wheel chock, then grabbed the ratchet straps and started securing the bike to the rear mounts. "I'll take it down to the garage tonight so we can check it out for you in the morning."

"That'd be great." Once we had her completely secure, we both got in the truck, and I started driving towards his place. We were almost there when Riggs turned to me and said, "Thanks for coming to give me a hand."

Even though I didn't really have a choice in the matter, I nodded and said, "No problem, brother. Glad I could help."

When I pulled up to his house, he got out and gave me a small wave as he headed up to the front door. Once he was inside, I backed out of his driveway and started towards the garage. I took a quick glimpse at the digital clock on the truck's dash and groaned when I saw that it was almost eleven. I'd been going since five that morning, and I was beyond exhausted. Unfortunately, it would be at least another hour before I made it back to the clubhouse for some shuteye. Relief washed over me when I finally passed Third Street, knowing the garage was right around the corner. I flipped on my blinker and was just about to make the turn onto Second, when I noticed someone crouched down in the road.

I had no idea what the hell they were doing, and honestly, I didn't care. I just wanted to get to the fucking garage, but as I started to drive around them, I noticed it was a woman who was in the middle of the street and she was kneeling down next to some animal. My conscious got the best of me, and before I could talk myself out of it, I pulled over. As soon as I got out of the truck, I took a quick look in both directions of what was typically a very busy street, relieved to see barely any traffic around. In fact, it reminded me of a ghost town as I started walking towards the woman. I could hear her talking, but her back was to me and I couldn't make out what she was saying. Once I got closer, I could see she was speaking to a large, whimpering black dog that was sprawled across the asphalt. From where I stood, it looked like it had been hit by a car and wasn't doing all that well. Since it was dark and we were in a sketchy neighborhood, I tried my best not to startle the woman as I asked, "Hey ... Uh, ma'am. Are you okay?"

"Yes, I'm fine, but this poor dog isn't." She peered over her shoulder, and the sight of her nearly knocked me on my ass. Her long dark hair was pulled back into a loose bun, revealing the most beautiful blue eyes I'd ever seen. She was wearing a pair of black pants with a white button-down blouse that hugged her curves and a pair of black heels. I couldn't take my eyes off her as she continued, "I tried to swerve out of the way, but it was too late."

Hearing the heartbreak in her voice tugged at me, making me want to do whatever I could to help. In hopes of getting a better idea of what we were dealing with, I knelt down beside them, and starting at the base of her neck, I ran my hand along the dog's spine. She was a big dog with an enormous head and the markings similar to a Rottweiler, but her size was more like that of a Great Dane. Apparently having a good temperament, the pup never growled or nipped at me as she let me continue to check her for any broken bones. I thought she was most likely really bruised from the hit until I reached her hip. As soon as I touched it, she started to whine in pain. "It's hard to tell for sure if it's broken, but her backend is definitely bruised."

"What do I need to do?"

"I honestly don't know." I glanced back down at the dog and sighed. From the looks of her, she had the potential of being a beautiful animal, but from her frail state and her exposed ribs, it was pretty obvious that she hadn't been taken care of. "She's pretty thin. Probably hasn't eaten anything in days, and she's got no collar. If I had to guess, I'd say she's just a stray."

"Yeah, you're probably right, but I've still gotta do something. I can't just leave her like this."

"I guess we could take her to a vet or something."

"Do you know of one close by?" she asked, sounding hopeful.

"No, but give me a minute." I pulled my phone out of my pocket and started searching for a nearby animal clinic. Most of them were closed, but I managed to find a couple that were open twenty-four hours. I checked the addresses and found one nearby. "There's one on the corner of Third and Foster. It's about five minutes from here."

"Great. I'll take her there." She attempted to pick her up but quickly stopped when the dog wailed out in pain. "Can you help me get her to the car?"

"Why don't we put her in the back seat of my truck?" I could tell from the expression on her face that she was feeling a little hesitant about the idea. In hopes of easing her mind, I told her, "There's more room in my back seat.

She'll be more comfortable there, and once we get her settled, you can follow me over to the clinic."

"Are you sure you don't mind?"

"I wouldn't have offered if I did."

"Okay." She looked up at me with a soft smile and said, "I'm Landry, by the way."

"I'm Clay. Nice to meet ya."

"Likewise." Her eyes drifted back down to the dog. "I wish it was under better circumstances."

"It'll make for a great story one day." I gave her a reassuring smile, then leaned forward and carefully lifted the dog into my arms. The poor thing whimpered a bit as I started towards the truck, but she didn't try to resist or bite, which I thought was a good sign. Once I got her settled in the seat, I turned my attention back to Landry. "We're all set."

"So, I just follow you over to the clinic?"

"Yeah. It's just a few blocks away."

"Okay." As she rushed over to her car, she shouted, "Lead the way."

I gave Landry some time to get in her car. As soon as I saw that she was situated, I started my engine and headed towards the clinic. Minutes later, we both pulled up to the clinic. I got out, and by the time I'd gotten the dog out of the back seat, Landry was already holding the front door open. I was just about to step inside when one of the nurses came rushing over. She was a petite blonde with tired eyes and very little makeup, making me wonder how many hours she'd already put in for the night. Looking down at the wounded pup in my arms, she asked, "Is the animal yours?"

"No, ma'am," I answered. "I'm pretty sure it's just a stray."

"Mm-hmm," she mumbled under her breath. "And what happened to her?"

"I accidentally hit her when she ran out into the road," Landry answered. "I tried to miss her, but I just wasn't fast enough."

"It's okay. Things happen. At least, you had the decency not to leave the poor thing stranded on the road," the nurse replied. "Bring her on to the back. Once we get her into a room, I'll grab the paperwork."

We followed her through the main doors and down a short hallway. When we came up to an open room, she led us inside and motioned for me to lay the dog down on the table. As I carefully lowered her, the pup looked up at me with those big brown eyes, and I could tell that she was terrified by what was going on. I ran my hand over her head and smiled. "It's all right, girl. They're going to take good care of you."

"We sure are. We'll have you good as new before you know it." As the nurse headed towards the door, she announced, "I'll be right back with that paperwork."

As we both stood there waiting, I took a quick glance over at Landry, and it wasn't until that moment when I realized just how tall she really was. She had to be close to five-nine, and while that was still about a foot shorter than me, I didn't feel like I was towering over her like I did around most women. I liked that. I also liked the fact that she wasn't pencil thin. Landry had curves, the kind that a man could enjoy holding on to, and as I stood there studying her, I found myself wondering what it would be like to have her in my arms. The thought had my eyes drifting down to her mouth. I was staring at her full, kissable red lips when she brought me back to reality by asking, "Do you think she'll be okay?"

"Yeah, I think she'll be fine." I tried to reassure her and added, "This seems like a good place. I'm sure they'll have her fixed up in no time."

"You know, she needs a name." Landry leaned down to the dog and asked, "What do you think about Daisy ... or maybe Duchess?"

"Duchess would be cool, but you might want to hold off on that for a while?"

"Why?"

"Naming an animal has a psychological effect on people." I shrugged. "It's like subconsciously claiming it or something. That's fine if you're planning on keeping her."

Before Landry could respond, the nurse returned with a clipboard of paperwork in her hand. As she offered it to Landry, she told her, "I'll need you to fill these out before the vet comes in."

"Okay." Landry was studying the papers as she asked, "Do you have any idea how much this will cost?"

"It really depends on the patient's wounds." I could tell it wasn't the first time she'd been asked that question when she spouted off, "The office visit alone is two hundred, and if they have to operate, that'll be an additional five hundred or so. Plus, any medication she might need, so I'd say you're looking at around eight hundred dollars. Maybe more."

"Eight hundred dollars! Seriously?"

"If you aren't able to pay—"

"We can pay," I interrupted. "Just see that she gets what she needs."

"You got it." As she walked out of the room, the nurse told us, "The vet will be in shortly."

Once she was gone, Landry lowered the clipboard and sighed. "I just started my job a few months ago, and between my student loans and rent, I'm barely getting by. There's no way I can afford this."

"Don't worry about it." I took the clipboard out of her hand and started filling them out. "I'll take care of it."

"But—"

"It's fine, Landry. I've got it." I wasn't exactly rolling in it, but I was doing all right. I made a decent salary at the garage, and I still had all the money my dad had left me when he died. I had no idea what Landry did for a living, but it was clear she didn't need another bill added to her plate. "It's really not a big deal."

"No, it *is* a big deal, and I promise I'll find a way to pay you back."

I could tell from the determined look in her eye that there was no point in arguing, so I just kept my mouth shut and let her think that I'd allow her to pay me back. I started filling out the paperwork, and when it requested the dog's name, I asked, "So, are you going with Daisy or Duchess?"

"I don't know." She studied our new friend for a moment, then sighed. "I think I kind of like the name Duchess for her."

"Duchess it is."

I continued filling out the paperwork, and just as I was about to finish, the vet walked in. He was an older guy, maybe in his late sixties, and he was wearing a white lab coat and glasses. He shook both of our hands and introduced himself as Dr. Davenport, then turned his attention to Duchess. After looking her over, he turned to Landry and asked, "Is Duchess your dog?"

"No, sir. Umm ... I accidentally hit her on the way home. We checked for a collar, and when we didn't see one, we decided to bring her here."

"Well, I'm going to need to get some x-rays to be sure, but it doesn't look like it's broken. Hopefully, she's just bruised."

"Oh, okay. So, no surgery?"

"I won't know until I get the x-rays, and with the number of animals we've had in here tonight, that could take a while." He took a quick glance at his watch, then said, "It's getting late. Why don't you two head on home, and we'll give you a call when we get her fixed up?"

"That would be great."

We both gave him our numbers, then headed back out to the parking lot. I walked Landry over to her car, and as she got inside, she smiled and said, "Thank you for all your help tonight. I don't know what I would've done if you hadn't shown up."

"Don't mention it." I'd really enjoyed the time we'd spent together and wasn't ready for the night to end, but unfortunately, it was late and we both had to work the following morning. "Are you going to be all right getting home?"

"Yeah, I'll be fine. My apartment isn't far from here."

"I'd be glad to follow you."

"Thanks, but it really isn't necessary." She reached into her purse, then pulled out a business card and offered it to me. "Here's my contact information. If you hear anything about Duchess, give me a call."

"Will do."

I slipped her card into my back pocket, gave her a quick wave goodbye, and started walking towards my truck. I hadn't gotten very far when I heard Landry call out to me. "Clay!"

"Yeah?" I asked as I turned back to face her.

"It was really nice meeting you."

"It was nice meeting you too. Maybe we can get together again sometime."

"I'd really like that." A smile crossed her face. "You've got my number. Just give me a call sometime."

"Night, Landry."

"Good night!"

With that, she closed her car door and was on her way. It wasn't until I got in the truck and saw Riggs's bike in the back that I remembered I still had to stop by the garage. On any other night, I might've been aggravated by the thought, especially since it was so late, but tonight, I was actually feeling optimistic instead. It wasn't a feeling I was used to. I liked it. I liked it a lot.

LANDRY

After only a few hours of sleep, I pulled myself out of bed to check for any messages about Duchess. I grabbed my phone, and my stomach took a nosedive when there were no missed calls or messages. I had no idea if my reaction was due to the fact that the clinic hadn't informed me of Duchess's condition or that Clay hadn't tried to reach out to me. I tried to convince myself otherwise, but deep down I knew it was the latter. It turned out that my late-night rescuer had made quite an impression on me. Not only was he incredibly hot with his large, muscular build and shaggy blond hair, he was actually a really nice guy. Clay was easy to talk to, and there were times when I'd caught him staring at me that I thought he might've been interested in me. That notion came and went a hundred times, and by morning, I'd convinced myself that it was all in my head. I took his lack of texting as a sign that I was right.

Refusing to let myself be disappointed by the fact, I plodded into the kitchen and made myself a massive cup of coffee. After a hot shower, my haze of exhaustion started to fade, and I actually managed to make it to work on time. Once I got to my cubicle, I checked my messages again, and I wasn't pleased that the clinic hadn't called about Duchess. I was about to pick up the phone and call them myself when Mrs. Hawkins, my supervisor, appeared in front of my desk with another file in her hand. As usual, she was all dolled up in her favorite dark-purple pantsuit and super high heels. Her jet-black hair was pulled up into a tight bun, and she was decked out in all kinds of jewelry, making her look older than she actually was. "I have another case for you to look into. Katie Coburn. Eleven years old living with her father."

"Okay. What exactly am I looking into?"

"Child endangerment." I took the file and started looking through it as she continued, "The school's counselor called into the office. Apparently, Katie admitted that her father was drinking and driving with her in the vehicle."

I'd just started scanning over the father's history when I saw that he'd gotten a DUI in May. "Wait. He's got an ignition interlock system installed in his car."

"Yes, he does."

"So, how was he drinking and driving?"

She cocked her eyebrow as she explained, "Apparently, he got his daughter to blow for him."

"Seriously?"

"I can't say for sure, but that's what the girl told the school counselor." She shrugged as she sat down on the corner of my desk. "I'm going need you to find out if there is any truth behind the story. If there is, I'd say she needs to be removed from the home immediately."

"I'll get by there today." While I had a moment with her, I decided to use the opportunity to tell her, "I went by the Strayhorn home yesterday."

"Oh? And how did that go?"

I shrugged. "Not as well as I'd hoped. The kids were clearly sick, but neither of the parents were home."

"So, you weren't able to check out the premises?"

"No." I sighed with frustration. "And now they'll know I'm coming and will be more prepared for the visit."

"Maybe. Maybe not." A grimace marked her face. "You never can tell with people these days, but I'm really hoping you can get a handle on things over there. They've had one too many calls, and it's time for them to get their act together."

"I couldn't agree more."

"I've got some calls to make." As she stood up and started down the hall, she continued, "Just let me know if you need anything."

"You know I will!"

I turned my attention back to the Coburn file and tried to familiarize myself with all the basic details of the case. As I started reading, I saw that the father's full name was Christopher Coburn. At thirty-two, he'd already been divorced twice, and there was no mention of Katie's mother anywhere. From what I could tell, she hadn't been in the picture since Katie was born, so I assumed it was just the two of them. I took note of the police report, which stated that Mr. Coburn had been suspected of selling marijuana in his neighborhood, and he'd also been detained for a domestic dispute with an old girlfriend. None of it was anything new. In the few short months I'd been working there, I'd handled over twenty cases, and more than half of the parents struggled with some kind of addiction. It was a sad reality of the times, but I couldn't give up hope that I could help the children I worked with have a better life.

After I finished taking down some notes, I called the counselor at Katie's school to let her know I was coming to meet with them; then, I grabbed my things and walked back out to my car. Before I left, I took out my phone and dialed the number to the animal clinic. It rang several times before the answering machine picked up. Having no other choice, I left a quick message, asking them to please return my call. Once I hung up, I plugged the school's address into my phone's GPS and was on my way. Twenty minutes later, I pulled up to Berclair Elementary, one of the older schools in the city. Even though it wasn't as fancy as some of the newer schools, it had a lot of character and was very well-maintained. The lawn was mowed, the shrubs trimmed, and unlike most schools in the city, there was very little litter to be seen. I got out of my car and started up the sidewalk leading to the front door.

The secretary buzzed me in, and after she checked my credentials and had me sign in, she escorted me down to the counselor's office. I spoke with her for a few minutes, making sure that she didn't have anything new to share with me, and then I went to wait for Katie in the conference room. It was a small room, just large enough for a round table and a few chairs, with a window and a pretty picture of a pond on the wall. I pulled out one of the chairs, then sat down, and just as I was getting settled, Katie appeared in the doorway.

I quickly stood up and walked over to her, smiling. "Hi. You must be Katie."

"Yes, ma'am, I am."

"I'm Ms. Dawson." Katie was a beautiful little girl—even more so than her picture in the case file. Her shoulder-length curly hair offset her adorable round cheeks and gorgeous hazel eyes. With her mismatched clothes, she reminded me of Janice, one of my best friends when I was a little girl. I always loved the fact that Janice was brave enough to wear whatever she wanted without worrying what others thought, and I found myself wondering if Katie was the same way. Her eyes filled with worry as she listened to me say, "I'm from the Department of Child Services, and if it's okay with you, I'd like to talk to you for a few minutes."

"Umm ... okay."

"Great. Let's have a seat." I led her over to the table, and once she was seated, I sat down next to her. "You're in sixth grade, right?"

"Yes, ma'am."

"Your counselor, Mrs. Tate, said you were a good student. What's your favorite subject?"

"Math, I guess." Her voice was soft, almost a whisper as she said, "I really like Mrs. Kail."

"That's great. I was never very good at math, but I was pretty good at reading and science." I wanted to give her a few minutes to warm up to me before I dug into the hard stuff, so I asked, "What about your classmates? Do you have a lot of friends?"

"I have a few. Stacey and Isabel are my best friends." She paused for a moment, then asked, "Are you here about my father ... and what I told Mrs. Tate?"

Her question caught me off guard. I wasn't expecting her to bring the matter up so quickly. In fact, I figured it would take a lot of coaxing to even get her to talk about it. I hoped it was a sign as I answered, "Actually, I am. Would you mind if we talked about what's been going on?"

"I don't know," her voice trembled as she spoke. "He's gonna get really mad when he finds out that I told her what happened."

"I'm guessing you knew that when you went to see Mrs. Tate, so why did you tell her?"

"'Cause I want it to stop," she answered adamantly. "I love my dad, but I don't like it when he drinks. It scares me."

"How so?"

"He gets really angry. Throws things and says all these bad words, especially to Casey."

"Who's Casey?"

"She's his girlfriend. She moved in with us a few months ago." In hopes that Katie would tell me more, I didn't respond. Instead, I remained silent, and it wasn't long before she continued, "When they fight, it makes him mad, and he starts drinking."

"I see." I paused for a moment, then asked, "What do you do when all this is going on?"

"I don't like to be around him when he's like that, so I go to my room and hide." Her expression grew even more somber as she muttered, "But sometimes he comes to get me. Usually, when he needs to go to the store or something."

"What happens then?"

"He wants me to breathe into that machine so he can start his car. I try to tell him I don't want to do it, but he won't listen. He just gets really mad and makes me do it anyway." Tears filled her eyes as she continued, "He's not a good driver when he's been drinking. He can't stay on the road, and I'm always afraid he's gonna hit somebody."

"So, you've been with him when he's driving under the influence?"

"Yes, ma'am. He always makes me go with him in case something goes wrong."

Hearing the anguish in her voice made my chest tighten. "I can see why it would scare you."

"He doesn't mean it. He wouldn't hurt anyone on purpose."

"I'm sure he wouldn't, but the fact remains that he shouldn't be drinking and driving, especially with his young daughter in the car." Once my words sank in, Katie turned to look out the window, making me fear that she might start crying. "None of this is your fault, Katie. Your father is an adult, and he knows what he's doing is wrong."

"I know, but he's my dad."

"All the more reason for him to do the right thing." I leaned towards her as I explained, "You're a great kid, Katie, but even if you weren't, it's a parent's responsibility to take care of their children and make sure they're safe. It's my job to make sure your father is doing that with you, and from the sound of it, he isn't."

"So, what's going to happen?"

"I'm not sure just yet," I answered honestly. "I'll need to talk to your father, and hopefully, he and I will be able to come up with a plan."

"But what if you don't?"

Trying my best not to scare her even more, I replied,

"Let's not cross that bridge until we get there. For now, try not to worry. I know that's easier said than done, but I'm going to do everything I can to make things better for you and your dad."

"Okay."

"I'll try to get in touch with him today so we can get this thing resolved sooner than later."

"Good," she replied, sounding slightly relieved.

"While I've really enjoyed talking to you, I better let you get back to class." I stood up, and she followed me to the door. "It was very nice meeting you, Katie."

"It was nice meeting you, too, Ms. Dawson." As she started down the hall, she glanced back with a smile and waved. "Bye."

"Bye, Katie."

Once she was gone, I went back to the table and grabbed my things, then after signing out in the office, I walked back to my car. I checked my phone for any missed messages, and yet again, there was nothing. On any other day, I might've let my mind wander into a land of negative thoughts and doubts, but I was too busy with work to let that happen. I needed to get over to the Strayhorn home to see about things there, and as soon as I was done there, I had to get back to the office so I could call Mr. Coburn. I wasn't looking forward to either task, but the thought of seeing either Fiona or Joseph helped motivate me to leave the school's parking lot and head in their direction. Their house was on the opposite side of town, and with lunch-hour traffic, it took me almost an hour to get there. When I pulled up, there was an old, four-door car parked in the driveway, so I took that as a sign that someone was actually home.

With my satchel in hand, I rushed up to the front door and knocked. Moments later, a woman with long wavy hair and coal-black eyes, wearing her bathrobe, opened the door. She was the perfect mix between Fiona and Joseph, leaving me no doubt that she was their mother. "Yes?"

"Hi. My name is Landry Dawson." I lifted my ID, showing it to her as I asked, "Are you Aniya Strayhorn?"

"Yes. What can I do for you?"

"I'm from the Department of Child Services. I'm here about a call we received regarding the children in the home," I replied.

"What kind of call?"

She was playing dumb, like she'd never been through this kind of thing before, but I wasn't buying it. "Actually, it was more than one call. It seems there are several people who are concerned that your children aren't getting the proper care."

"What the hell are you talking about? I take care of *my kids*!" she argued.

"Okay. Well, here's a chance for you to prove that." Hoping to keep her from losing her temper, I kept my voice calm and nonthreatening. "I just need to ask you a few questions and have a quick look around."

I could see the wheels turning in her head as she stood there mulling over what I'd said. After several moments, she let out a slow, defeated breath. "Give me a minute."

She closed the door in my face, leaving me alone on the porch. It wasn't a good sign. A messy house was one thing, but something told me there was more than just a few dirty socks on the floor or trash that needed to be collected. Unfortunately for her, it would take more than

45

a couple of minutes to hide all the secrets she had lurking in that house. One minute rolled into the next, and I was starting to grow impatient. Hoping for a distraction, I reached into my bag for my phone, and when I checked the screen, I was pleased to see that the clinic had left me a voicemail. As I listened to it, I was relieved to hear Duchess had no broken bones, just some heavy bruising, and would be cleared to go home later in the afternoon or early the following morning. At that moment I realized I had to figure out what I was going to do with her. As much as I wanted to keep her, I couldn't. My apartment didn't allow pets, and even if it did, my place was simply too small for a dog her size.

I was trying to come up with some options when the front door opened and Aniya appeared. The bathrobe was gone, and now she wearing jeans and a t-shirt. She opened the door a little wider as she told me, "Come on in."

I nodded, then followed her into the living room. Like I'd noticed the day before, the furniture in the room was sparse, but clean. I turned my attention back to Aniya. Her unwelcoming glare was a little intimidating, but I did my best not to let it get to me as I asked, "Do you mind if I take a quick look around?"

"Just do what ya gotta do."

It was clear from her demeanor that she wasn't happy about me being there. I couldn't blame her. It was definitely an invasion of privacy, especially for the innocent, but I had to be sure that the kids were safe. She stood rigid, skeptically watching as I entered the kitchen and jotted a few notes down on my clipboard. Again, there wasn't much to it, just your basics with a small table in the corner, but it was clean. After I checked the bathroom, I went back into the living room with Aniya. "Where do the children sleep?"

"Upstairs." As she pointed to the staircase, she explained, "Joseph and Thomas are in the bedroom to the left, and Fiona is on the right."

"What about Denise and Phillip?"

"They moved out a few months ago." They were only seventeen, so technically they were her and her husband's responsibility. I was about to ask her about it when she continued, "We had a disagreement about them both dropping out of school, and since then, they've been staying with my mother."

"Oh ... So, they both dropped out?"

"I tried to tell them it was a mistake, but they wouldn't listen." I wanted to take it as a good sign that she'd tried to talk them out of it, but after reading their case file, it was still hard to tell. "You know how kids can be."

"Yes, ma'am. I do."

As I headed up the stairs, I didn't see any sign of the kids, so I assumed they were at school. I was wrong. When I opened the door to Fiona's room, I found her lying down on the bed. The walls were painted a deep purple, and over the old wooden plank floor, there was a small round rug. There were a few stuffed animals scattered amongst several piles of clothes, but other than that, there wasn't much else in the room. I stepped further into the room, and Fiona's eyes lit up when she saw me walking towards her. "You're back."

"I am." I smiled as I walked over to the edge of the bed. "So, what are you doing home today? I thought you had pre-school."

"They made me come home."

"Why's that?"

"I had a fee-fer."

"I'm so sorry to hear that. It's no fun having a fever." She started coughing, sounding even worse than she had the day before. Once she was done and had caught her breath, I said, "Sounds like you might need to go to the doctor."

"I'll be o-tay."

Getting medical attention wasn't something she could control, so I decided to change the subject. "I like your room. Purple is my favorite color."

"Mine, too." She lifted one of her stuffed animals, a tiny gray elephant with green eyes, as she said, "Bel-wa loves pur-pel, too."

"Well, Bella has great taste." Remembering her mother was waiting downstairs, I smiled and said, "I guess I better let you get some rest. I really do hope you get to feeling better soon."

"I will."

As much as I hated to leave her, I didn't have a choice. I needed to check the other rooms upstairs before I spoke with Aniya. I left Fiona's room and walked to the other bedroom. Inside, I found a set of bunk beds with several matchbox cars on the floor. Like Fiona's room, there were clothes piled on the floor, and I wasn't sure if they were dirty or clean, but I'd seen rooms in much worse condition. I wrote down a few more notes, then headed downstairs to speak with Fiona's mother. When I got to the living room, she was sitting on the sofa with a concerned look in her eyes. "I know what you're thinking."

Having no idea what she was talking about, I didn't

respond. Instead, I waited for her to continue. "I know this place isn't much, but I'm doing the best I can. Things have been really tough lately, and I've made some mistakes ... but I want you to know, I love my kids. I'd never do anything to intentionally hurt them."

I wanted to believe her, I truly did, but I'd read the file. I knew I wasn't the first DCS agent to visit the Strayhorn home. There had been too many calls made to our office about this family, and it was time to get some answers—some real answers. "If that's true, I'm going to need you to be open and honest with me. I need to know what's really going on here. If you can do that, then maybe we can find a way to make things better ... not just for the kids, but for you and your husband as well."

Her expression softened as she replied, "Okay, I'll do whatever you need me to do."

As I sat there looking at her, I noticed something hidden behind her pretty hazel eyes. This woman wasn't just carrying around old memories of heartbreak and disappointment, it was more than that. Something had happened in her life that had broken her, and I wasn't sure she even knew exactly how broken she really was. With my satchel in hand, I stood up, and as I slipped the strap over my shoulder, I smiled and said, "That's what I was hoping you'd say."

PROSPECT

My father was always big into life's little lessons. He'd say there wasn't any situation, good or bad, in our lives from which we couldn't learn something. Maybe I was too young or just too damn blind, but I never really got it. Whenever I was pissed off or aggravated, I never saw it as anything more than that. I certainly didn't think about it being an opportunity for me to learn something about patience or tolerance. It was no different when I felt alone or abandoned. While I would want to wallow in self-pity, my dad would try to tell me it was life's way of teaching me how to stand on my own two feet. From being flat-ass broke to winning the fucking lottery, he truly believed that there a lesson in everything, but I thought it was all bullshit until the day my life completely crumbled around me.

At first, I was too wrapped up in my own world to see it, but as I worked to put the pieces of my life back together, I started to feel stronger, more confident in the choices I'd made. I hadn't done it on my own. The brothers of Satan's Fury had taught me to push through the hard times and not give up, and eventually, I'd find myself on the other side. With them, I'd found the life I really wanted, one that I was willing to fight for. I just had to prove to them and myself that I had what it took to earn a Satan's Fury patch. It was one of the reasons why I'd gotten to work early that morning. I wanted to get Riggs's bike up and running before the rest of the guys came in, so it wouldn't interfere with all the other jobs I needed to finish. No such luck. I was still draining the fuel lines when T-Bone walked up behind me.

"Looking a little rough around the edges, Prospect. You all right?"

"I'm good. Just had a long night."

"Mm-hmm." He slapped me on the back and chuckled. "Get used to it."

When he headed over to his station, I turned my attention back to Riggs's bike. I'd already checked the battery, but when I found that it wasn't the issue, I drained the gas tank, checked all the fuel lines, and changed the oil. Just to be sure, I decided to check the voltage regulator and the alternator. Thankfully, they just needed some minor adjustments, so it didn't take me long to get them sorted. I was just wrapping it up when Blaze came over and asked, "Whose bike?"

"An old one of Riggs's." Blaze was in charge of the garage, and there was no doubt that he took his job seriously. He kept tabs on every project, making sure they were done to suit him, so I wasn't surprised that he noticed a bike not on his inventory. "Broke down on him last night, so I brought it here. I came in early to get her going again."

"Having any luck?"

"I was just about to find out."

I threw my leg over the side of the Harley Sportster, and to my relief, she started up the second I hit the ignition. Blaze leaned towards me and said, "Give her a little gas."

I nodded. As I revved the engine a couple of times, I remembered what Rider had told me about getting to know all the brothers. With that in mind, I tried to piece together everything I knew about Blaze. He was with Kenadee, a trauma nurse from Memphis Regional, and he had a son named Kevin from a previous marriage. Kevin had once been diagnosed with cancer, but at the moment, he was in remission. Blaze's parents were still in the picture, and understanding how important it was to him, they were both actually pretty supportive of the club. I revved the engine once more, then killed it. Hoping he thought it sounded as good as I did. "What do you think?"

"She sounds pretty damn good. Proud of you, brother." He slapped me on the back as he headed back to his office. "Now, get your ass busy on the Ford. Needs an oil change and new wipers, and don't let me forget ... I've got some parts I need you to drop off at Riley's after work."

"You got it."

I was feeling pretty damn good as I got off Riggs's bike and headed over to the Ford. When I first started working at the garage, I didn't know much. With my father always on the road, he wasn't around to teach me the basics, but the guys didn't give me a hard time about it. Instead, they put in a lot of hours teaching me everything I needed to know, especially Rider. Without even asking, he took me under his wing and made sure that I knew what I was doing. His efforts hadn't gone unnoticed by Gus, and it was one of the many reasons he'd chosen him to be my sponsor. Normally, an older veteran brother would've taken on the role, but Gus believed he was the best fit and I didn't disagree. In fact, I couldn't have chosen better myself. Rider was a good guy, a brother through and through, and I felt better knowing he had my back. I was just finishing up the Ford's oil change when he came over and asked, "How did things go last night?"

"It went okay." I closed the hood, then told him, "Went a little longer than I'd planned."

"Why's that?"

"On the way to the garage, I came up on a lady who'd hit a dog, and I stopped to help her out. Dog was hurt pretty bad, so we ended up taking it to the vet."

"Wait." Rider seemed surprised when he asked, "You went with her to the vet?"

"Yeah." I shrugged. "She was pretty shaken up, so I figured she could use the hand."

"Mm-hmm." A smirk crossed his face. "*Sooo* … was this chick hot?"

"She was all right."

"Yeah, I bet she was." With a chuckle, he continued, "Nothing like giving a hand to a beautiful woman in distress."

"Whatever," I grumbled as I started to remove the windshield wiper blades. "I was just doing what I could to help."

As Rider started back to his station, he chuckled. "Yeah, keep telling yourself that, brother."

I'd done good to stay focused on my work, but at just the mention of what'd happened the night before, my mind drifted to Landry and I was done. I couldn't stop thinking about her blue eyes, her full lips, and those fucking curves. I tried to think of anything else, but as I finished installing the wipers and moved on to the next vehicle in line, I found myself thinking about the way she'd twist one of her curls around the tip of her finger when she spoke. It was clear that Landry Dawson had made an impression on me. I just didn't know what to do about it. It wasn't like I was at a place where I could start a new relationship. Between prospecting and managing my job at the garage, I barely had time to take a breath, much less date. Like it or not, I couldn't get involved with her. I'd make good on my promise to pay the vet bill for Duchess, but after that, I'd have to put Landry behind me.

With a newfound resolve, I pushed all thoughts of her from my head and put all my focus into my work. The next thing I knew, it was after five, and the guys were starting to clear out. I worked a few more minutes, then started cleaning up my station. I was just finishing up when T-Bone came over and asked, "Yo, Prospect! You calling it a day?"

"Yeah. Just wrapping things up."

"Gauge and I are about to head over to Eight Ball for a burger and a beer. You in?"

"Sure." Remembering I needed to see about the dog, I told him, "But I've got a few things I need to take care of first."

"No problem. We'll be there for a while, so just head on over when you can."

"Will do."

I finished putting my shit away, then grabbed the parts that Blaze needed me to return and headed out to the truck. After I'd put the boxes in the back, I got inside and started towards Riley's. Once I'd returned the parts for Blaze, I drove over to the animal clinic to pay the bill. When I pulled up, I was surprised to see Landry's old Volkswagen parked up front. I'd meant to touch base with her after the clinic called, but with everything that was going on at the garage, I never got the chance—at least that's what I told myself while I headed towards the front door. As soon as I walked in, I spotted Landry sitting in the waiting room. Unlike the night before, her long, curly hair was down, flowing softly around her shoulders, and she was wearing a navy pantsuit with a pale pink dress shirt. She looked absolutely stunning. As I started towards her, her lips curled into a bright smile. "Hey! I wasn't expecting to see you here."

"Figured I'd come by and see how Duchess is doing."

"Same here." She motioned her hand over to the receptionist as she explained, "I'm just waiting on one of the nurses to take me back."

"You been waiting long?"

"No, I just got here a few minutes ago."

I walked over and sat down next to her. Lost in our own thoughts, neither of us spoke, and it wasn't long before a feeling of awkwardness fell upon us. I wanted to say something, anything to break the uncomfortable silence, but the words didn't come. Thankfully, the nurse came into the waiting room and announced, "I'll take you back to see Duchess now."

"You want to come along?" Landry offered.

"Sure."

I stood up and followed them both to the back of the clinic. As we started down the hall, I could hear the different dogs barking and howling, and it only got louder as we got closer to the kennels. When we stepped inside, I was surprised to see that Duchess wasn't barking like the rest of the dogs. Instead, she was sitting quietly in her cage. The second she spotted us walking in her direction, she lifted her head and started wagging her tail. The nurse opened the door to her kennel and said, "She's still pretty sore, so it'll be a few days before she's up and walking like normal."

"Okay." Landry knelt down and reached inside the cage, gently petting Duchess on the head. "Hey there, sweetheart. You look so much better than you did last night."

From what I could see, Duchess seemed to be doing pretty well. In fact, it was hard to tell that she'd even been hit. The thought made me curious about when she might be released, so I turned to the nurse and asked, "Any idea how much longer she'll need to stay here?"

"I'm not exactly sure." She started towards the door and said, "Let me go and check with the vet."

As I stood there waiting for the nurse to return, I watched Landry with Duchess. She was smiling and whispering softly in her ear as she continued to pet her, and it was obvious from the look on her face, Duchess was enjoying the attention. Poor thing hadn't had anyone to tend to her, and now that she did, she was eating that shit up. I was still watching them both when a tall man with dark hair and thick glasses entered the holding room. If he wasn't wearing one of those white lab coats, I wouldn't ever have guessed he was the vet on duty because he simply looked too fucking young. I waited patiently as he came over to us and said, "Hi, I'm Doctor Tanner, the vet on duty for the day. My nurse said you had some questions about Duchess."

"Nice to meet you. I'm Clay." I extended my hand, and as he shook it, I asked, "We were just wondering, any idea when she'll be released?"

He lifted her chart and looked it over for a moment, then said, "Looks like she's doing well—moving slow, but she's getting there. If you're ready to take her now, she's welcome to go."

"Well, that's good news." I glanced down at Landry as I asked, "Are you up for taking her on home tonight?"

"About that …" A grimace crossed her face as she explained, "As much as I want to keep her, I can't have pets in my apartment. I really don't know what to do with her."

That was not the response I was expecting. After the way she'd taken to Duchess, named her and saw that she was cared for, I'd just assumed that Landry was going to keep her. Apparently, that wasn't an option, so we'd have to figure out something else to do with her. I was trying to think of some options when the vet suggested, "You could always take her over to the pound. She's an unusual breed. I'm sure it wouldn't take long for someone to adopt her."

"An unusual breed?"

"She's a Weiler Dane—half Great Dane, half Rottweiler."

"I knew she was a big dog, but I had no idea she was a Dane mix."

"If you think she's big now, just wait until she's full grown," he scoffed. "Right now, I'd say she's only eight months old or so. This girl still has plenty of growing to do."

"Damn."

"A dog like this is a lot to take on, but trust me, there's someone out there who will want her," he told us with confidence. "People pay a lot of money for this particular breed. Heck, I'd take her myself, but my wife would have my ass."

"I really hate the idea of leaving her at the pound." Landry thought for a minute, then said, "Maybe I could find someone who'll be able to take her."

"You're welcome to let her stay here for a couple of days," the vet offered.

"You'd be willing to do that?"

"I don't mind." He shrugged. "You'll have to cover the kenneling costs, though."

A concerned look washed over Landry's face. "And how much will that be?"

"I've got it covered." Before she could argue, I pulled one of my cards from the garage out of my pocket and offered it to the vet. "Just plan on the dog staying here for the rest of the week. If something comes up, give me a call."

"Sounds good to me." He gave us both a quick wave on his way out the door. "You two have a good night."

Once he was gone, Landry stood up and took a step towards me. "I don't know why you're doing all this, but I really do—" Before she could finish the sentence, her cell phone started to vibrate in her purse. For a second, I thought she was going to ignore it, but when it vibrated a second, and then a third time, she said, "I guess I better see what that's all about."

I waited as she reached into her purse and grabbed her phone. When she saw the messages, she let out a defeated sigh. "Is everything okay?"

"Yeah. It's just work and ... *my mother.*"

From the sound of her voice, she was more upset about hearing from her mother than whatever was going on with her work. I knew I shouldn't start something I couldn't finish, but it seemed like she was having a rough day all around. Hoping to make it better, I said, "Looks like you could use a break. You wanna go grab a bite to eat and maybe a beer?"

"You know, that actually sounds like a wonderful idea." She shoved her phone back into her purse and smiled. "I'd love to."

"Great."

After we both said our goodbyes to Duchess, I closed the door to her kennel, and we headed out to the parking lot. I was trying to think of a place for us to go that was relatively close, but since I'd only been living in the city for just a couple of months, I only knew about the places that were close to the garage or the clubhouse. As I thought about it, it crossed my mind that I was supposed to meet up with T-Bone and Gauge. I didn't think the Eight Ball was the right place to take Landry, so I pulled out my cell and sent them a text, letting them know I wasn't going to make it. I'd just shoved my phone back into my pocket when we reached my truck. Landry was about to continue towards her car, but she stopped and turned to me. "Should I follow you over to the restaurant?"

"You can." Even though it would've been nice to have her ride with me, I didn't want her to feel pressured to do so, especially since she didn't know me all that well. When she hesitated, I added, "Or you could hop in with me, and I'll drop you off at your car when we're done."

"Okay, I'll ride with you."

I nodded and walked over to open the door for her. Then, I climbed in and started the engine, still having no idea of where we were headed as I pulled out of the parking lot and onto the main road. When I started towards downtown, Landry asked, "So, where're we going?"

"I honestly don't know. I'm still not all that familiar with the area," I confessed.

"Wait ... You're not from here?"

"Nope." I glanced over in her direction as I continued, "I moved here from Nashville a couple of months ago."

"Oh, I didn't realize."

"I'll tell you about it sometime, but for now, we need to decide on a place to eat. Any ideas?"

"There's a Huey's a few blocks down on the right. It's really good."

"Huey's it is, then."

LANDRY

*I*t wasn't like me to agree to go to dinner with someone I barely knew, but there was something about Clay that made me want to get to know him better. At first, I thought my attraction to him was because he was so devastatingly handsome, but it was so much more than that. Clay was different from most of the guys I knew. I certainly hadn't known many who'd not only help take a stray dog to the vet in the middle of the night, but also offer to pay the bill when I couldn't. It meant so much to me that he was willing to help me like that, and Duchess too. I also couldn't ignore the fact that being close to him made my heart race.

When we got to Huey's, I followed him to one of the booths in the back of the restaurant. We'd sat down and placed our orders, and the waitress had just brought over our drinks when Clay said, "I noticed on your business card that you work for the Department of Child Services. That's a tough job."

"It can be, but it's not all bad. There're actually times when I really enjoy it."

"I don't think I could do it." He ran his hand through his shaggy blond hair. "If I heard somebody had hurt a kid, I'd probably end up breaking their neck."

My mind drifted to my latest case, and when I thought about Katie being forced to blow into that breathalyzer for her father, I replied, "It's definitely tempting at times, but I try to hold on to the thought that I'm helping these families, especially the kids."

"They're lucky to have you."

"I don't know about that, but thanks for saying so." He was wearing the same leather vest that he had on the night before. I remembered seeing a motorcycle in the back of his truck, but I had no idea if it was his or not. As I sat there awkwardly studying him, I noticed a small white patch on the upper side pocket that said *Prospect*. Curious, I asked, "Does that mean something?"

"What?"

"The patch on your vest. Does it mean something?"

He glanced down at his chest, and a look of uncertainty crossed his face as he answered, "I'm a prospect for a motorcycle club here in town."

"Oh, that's cool." I didn't know much about bikers or the world they lived in—only that some MCs were good and some were bad—*really bad*. An uneasy feeling washed over me as I asked, "Which one?"

"Satan's Fury."

His green eyes locked on mine as he tried to read my reaction. I didn't want him to think I was horrified by the declaration, but in truth, I was. I'd heard about their club. I knew they were involved in some pretty bad stuff, and like everyone else in the city, I'd always done my best to keep my distance. It was hard to believe that a sweet, handsome guy like Clay would be involved with men like them, but then again, I'd learned a long time ago that people aren't always what they seem. He was still watching me as I swallowed and tried to feign a smile. "What made you decide to join their club?"

"Actually, it wasn't my idea." He reached for his beer and took a quick tug. "My uncle is the one who kind of ... encouraged me to come to Memphis and try prospecting for them."

"Why would he do that?"

"I'd hit a rough spot, and he thought I could use a fresh start." Clay shrugged. "He wasn't wrong. After my father died, I was all kinds of fucked up. I was making bad decisions, and I hurt my mom and sister. I needed to get the hell out of Nashville before I got myself into a mess I couldn't get out of. I figured it couldn't hurt to come here and give it a try."

"Any particular reason why he wanted you to prospect for Satan's Fury instead of another club?"

"He's got ties with the president ... knows what a good man he is and how he takes care of his brothers." It was odd to hear him say that the president of such a notorious MC was a good man. I would've thought he'd be some kind of vicious thug to run a club like theirs, but from the way Clay spoke, he didn't agree. "I had my doubts, but once I got here and got to know the members and what they were all about, I could see that my uncle was right. This really is where I'm meant to be."

"It's really great that you've found a place that makes you feel that way, Clay."

"Yeah, I think so too."

His attention was drawn to the waitress, who arrived with our dinner and another beer. As soon as she laid them down on the table, we both started eating. After a couple of bites, Clay looked over to me with a smile. "You made a good choice. This Philly cheesesteak is incredible."

"You should try their burgers."

I offered him mine, and watched as he lifted it from my hand and took a bite. His eyes widened as he started to chew, and once he swallowed, he replied, "Holy shit."

"Told you."

He gave me back my burger, and we continued to chat back and forth as we ate. I was really enjoying myself with him, and it wasn't long before my concerns about him prospecting for Satan's Fury were forgotten. I loved hearing him talk about his younger sister, Alyssa, and how protective he was of her. I could hear the love in his voice when he spoke about her, and his mother too. I was just going to ask him about his father when my phone chimed with another message. I didn't have to look to know it was her. I was going to ignore it, but it chimed again. Annoyed, I took my phone out of my purse and groaned when I saw that I was right. It was, indeed, my mother. Noting my aggravation, Clay asked, "Is everything okay?"

"Yes, everything's fine." I sent her a quick text, letting her know that I'd message her later, then tossed my phone back into my purse. "It's just my mother. She's on one of her tears tonight."

"What do you mean?"

"I don't know. It's ... *complicated.*" I had no idea how to explain the dynamic between my mother and me, mainly because I didn't always understand it myself.

When I was growing up, we weren't exactly close. It wasn't that she didn't try. She did. I was just too wrapped up in my own jealousy and resentment to accept her efforts. It wasn't until I went off to college that I started to let my walls down and really open up to her. I'd tell her about the things that were going on in my life, and she'd give me her two cents whenever she deemed it necessary—which turned out to be often. *Very often.* I reached over and swiped a french fry from his plate. "She tends to fixate on things, especially where I'm concerned."

Clearly amused by my struggles with my mother, he chuckled. "Oh, really? How so?"

"Well, like today," I sighed. "I told her last night that I was working on a new case. I didn't give her any real details ... just that the little girl, who I happen to think is incredibly adorable, was sick. As soon as I told her about it, she started citing off all the terrible things that could happen if her cough was left untreated and how I just *had* to do something. I tried to tell her that my hands were tied, but she wouldn't listen. She kept throwing out all these ideas of what I could do to help the girl, but they were just ludicrous."

"How so?"

"She suggested that I make another call to DCS and pretend I'm a concerned teacher. I told her I could lose my job over something like that, so she suggested that I call a doctor and have him make a house call. Again ... I could get fired over something like that." I let out a frustrated grumble. "The thing is, she's a high school principal. She knows I can't do the stuff she's suggesting, but that doesn't stop her from dishing out those ideas! Over and over again. She's even worse when it comes to *my personal life.*"

Maybe it was my tone or facial expression, but my response caused him to chuckle even more than he had earlier. "Oh ... So, she likes to give input into your personal life too, huh?"

"Oh, you think that's funny?" I cocked my eyebrow as I swiped another fry from his plate and took a bite. "You obviously haven't had your mother try to give you advice on how to flirt or tell you how long you should wait before sleeping with someone for the first time."

"No, can't say that I have."

"I didn't think so." Seeing his smile, along with that mischievous spark in his eye, sent tingles down my spine. I blushed and quickly glanced down at my beer. "If I had to guess, I'd say you never needed any advice. I'm sure you have no problem getting any woman you want."

"What makes you say that?"

"Look at you," I scoffed.

"Not sure what you mean by that, but I'll tell ya this ... I think it would be kind of great to get some advice now and then." He paused for a moment, and then his smirk returned as he reached for my burger and took another bite. While he returned it to my plate, he asked, "So, how long?"

"What do you mean?"

"How long did your mother say you should wait before sleeping with someone?"

"Umm ... well." I knew he was just messing with me, but the suggestive nature of his question made my cheeks flush hot with embarrassment. I could feel the heat radiating from my face as I tried to think of a clever comeback. When it finally came to me, I smiled and said, "I guess you'll just have to wait and see."

As soon as the words came out of my mouth, his sexy little smirk faded, making me immediately regret my response. I was wishing I could take it back when he finally responded, "Well, start the timer."

Damn. That was not at all what I expected him to say. Once again, I found myself blushing with no idea how to respond. I'd never been good at flirting. To be perfectly honest, I sucked at it. In fact, I sucked at everything where men were concerned. I just never had the confidence, nor the real desire to try and entice a man—*until now*. Having no clue what else to do, I simply smiled and reached for my drink. I was just finishing it off when his cell phone started to ring. I waited in silence as he took it from his pocket and answered, "Yeah?"

He waited a moment for the person on the other end of the line before he responded, "I'll be there in twenty."

As Clay put his phone back in his pocket, he looked over to me and said, "I'm sorry, but I've gotta get going."

"Okay, I'm ready when you are."

He placed a couple of twenties on the table, more than enough to cover our bill and the tip, then eased out of the booth. He extended his hand, helping me as I did the same. Once I was standing, I expected him to release my hand, but he didn't. Instead, he held on to it as he led me out of the bar and into the parking lot. I followed him over to the truck and waited as he opened the door for me. As soon as I was settled, he walked over to the driver's side and got in. Moments later, we were on the road and making our way back to the clinic. I glanced over in his direction, and became curious when I noticed that his back was rigid and his hold on the steering wheel was so tight, his knuckles were white. Clearly something was up. "Is everything okay?"

"Yeah. I've just got some shit I need to handle that I wasn't planning on." He shook his head with a grumble. "I know that doesn't make any sense, but it's hard to explain."

"It's okay. I totally understand." Trying to hide the disappointment that was creeping up inside of me, I feigned a smile. "I hope whatever it is that you have to do won't be too bad."

"It'll be fine. Just one of those things."

Clay pulled up beside my car and parked. When he turned towards me, I could see the wheels turning in his head, but he didn't say anything. He just sat there and silently stared at me with those incredible green eyes. I tried to ignore the butterflies doing somersaults in my stomach as I smiled and said, "Thanks for tonight. I had a great time."

"I had a great time too." I could hear the sincerity in his voice as he said, "I'm sorry we had to cut it short."

"Nothing to be sorry about." I opened the door and got out. "Maybe we can make up for it another night."

"Yeah." There was something rushed in his tone, making me curious of what exactly that phone call was all about. Unfortunately, I didn't get a chance to ask. He put the truck in gear and said, "We'll have to do that. I'll give you a call or something."

"Okay, night!"

I gave him a quick wave as I shut the door. I rushed over to my car and unlocked the door, then watched Clay whip out of the parking lot in a mad dash. As I was getting inside my car, I thought back to when he said he was prospecting for Satan's Fury. I couldn't help but wonder if that had something to do with the call. I liked Clay, I liked him a lot, and it made my heart ache to think that he might be involved in something he shouldn't. I was starting to sink into a world of doubt when my phone started to ring. Without even looking to see who it was, I grabbed it out of my phone and answered, "Hello?"

"Landry? Oh my goodness. I've been trying to get in touch with you all day," my mother fussed. "I was worried that something happened to you."

"I just texted you twenty minutes ago."

"I didn't get any text from you."

"Well, I sent you one." Hoping to prove myself right, I pulled up my texts and was surprised to see that the message I'd typed out hadn't sent. "I guess it didn't go through."

"You sound upset. What's wrong?"

I don't know how she did it. Maybe it was mother's intuition or all her years working as a principal, but Mom could always tell when something was bugging me. I wasn't ready to tell her about Clay, so I lied, "I'm just tired. It's been a long day. That's all."

"You work too hard, sweetheart."

"I don't work any harder than you do, Mom," I argued. "I'm fine."

"Well, I hope you can rest when you get home. You obviously need it."

"I'm headed that way now."

I could hear the relief in her voice as she said, "Good. Take a hot bath and curl into bed with a book ... or you could check out this new show I've been watching. It's this great little series about these women who rob a grocery store, and then get all mixed up with this gangster guy ..."

I started my car and tried to keep up as she described all the different characters and the messes they found themselves in. By the time she was done, I knew every detail about the show and no longer had a need to watch it. On a positive note, I'd made it back to my apartment. I parked, and as I started to grab my stuff, I told her, "Well, I'm home. I'll check out the show tonight if I have time."

"Great! I think you'll really like it."

"I'm sure I will. Night, Mom."

"Good night, sweetheart."

After I ended the call, I went upstairs to my apartment, dropped my things on the counter, and headed to the bathroom. By the time I got out of the shower, I was ready to crash, so I bypassed watching TV or reading and crawled into bed. I just wanted to go to sleep and put an end to my long day, but as soon as I closed my eyes, my mind started working against me. Between obsessing over how to handle my cases and rehashing my night with Clay, I couldn't get settled. Thankfully, I was unaware that my entire world was about to be turned upside down, otherwise I would've been obsessing over that too.

"*Y*ou just don't get it, man," T-Bone fussed with a drunken slur. "Women are cold-hearted. They fuck with your head because they know they can."

"You're right," Gauge grumbled as he rested his head against the passenger window. "They know how bad we want their pussy, and they use that shit against us."

Even though T-Bone was a big dude—tall, muscled-up like a linebacker, and bald, he had his soft-hearted moments, especially when it came to women. The poor guy seemed to fall fast and land hard any time it came to a chick who caught his eye. It was clear he was feeling wounded as he mumbled, "They taunt us with that shit ... dangling it right in front of our fucking faces, and just when we're ready to take hold, *bam*, the bitches yank it away. And that shit ain't right."

"Well, what are you gonna do?" Gauge was single like T-Bone, but unlike his buddy, he never got too attached.

He was more of a one-night stand kind of guy, so I wasn't surprised when he continued, "We gotta just keep at it."

"Yeah, but it's always gonna be the same bullshit."

"Maybe. Maybe not. The next one might be ... *the one*." Gauge shrugged. "I guess you could say that's part of the thrill of discovery."

I chuckled under my breath as I listened to them carry on. They'd both gone to the Eight Ball for a burger and a couple of beers, but they'd gotten caught up in a game of darts and ended up getting plastered. Since neither of them could drive home, they called me to come pick them up, and their timing couldn't have been worse. Landry was just starting to warm up to me when I got the call, so I didn't have a choice but to cut things short. While I wasn't exactly happy about it, I knew deep down it was for the best, especially since Landry was starting to grow on me—really grow on me. T-Bone's call was just another reminder that while I was prospecting, I needed to keep my distance. My attention was drawn back over to T-Bone, wearing a pathetic pout on his face. "The thrill of discovery is bullshit. She wouldn't even look at me."

"Who?" I asked, opening up a can of worms.

"*Crystal*." As soon as he said her name, it all made sense. Crystal was one of the waitresses at the Eight Ball who'd taken T-Bone up on an invitation to come to one of our club parties. He was hoping to get something started with her, but it was clear to all of us that she was more interested in Rider. When Crystal discovered that he was with Darcy, her feigned interest in T-Bone quickly faded. She made an excuse to leave and had been distant with him ever since. He was clueless about the whole thing, thinking that he'd let her slip through his fingers. "I tried to call her over to our table, but she just acted like I wasn't even there. What the fuck was that?"

"That was her blowing you off, brother," Gauge answered, sounding just as drunk as T-Bone. "You don't need that shit. Fuck her, man."

"That's just it," T-Bone huffed. "I was gonna fuck her, but I never got the chance."

"Well, I guess she wasn't the one," Gauge replied with a drunken chuckle. "You've just gotta let it go."

"I've already let it go," he lied. "Hell, as far as I'm concerned, that chick has already been forgotten."

Thankfully, their conversation seemed to die there. After a couple minutes of silence, I glanced over at T-Bone. His head was tilted back on the headrest and his eyes were barely open as I asked, "You wanting me to drop you off at your place or are y'all going back to the clubhouse?"

"Clubhouse would be good," he managed to mutter.

"Same here," Gauge added. "Gonna grab a couple more beers before I call it a night."

Moments later, silence filled the truck as they each closed their eyes and started breathing heavy. I thought they'd both passed out, but as soon as I pulled through the gate, they opened their eyes and sat up. I parked, and neither of them said a word as they handed me the keys to their bikes, got out, and stumbled into the clubhouse. As much as I wanted to follow them inside, that wasn't an option. I had to get Dane and Rip, two of the other prospects, to ride back over to the Eight Ball with me to retrieve T-Bone and Gauge's bikes. I sent them both a text, and it wasn't long before they came rolling out of the clubhouse. Rip came up to the truck and opened the door. "You got the keys to their bikes?"

"Yeah, got 'em."

He nodded, then hopped in next to me while Dane got in the back. They'd both been prospecting for almost a year, so if all went well, it wouldn't be long before they both earned their Fury patches. I couldn't deny that I was a little jealous about the fact. I had a long row to hoe before I'd be sitting where they were, but I was determined that I'd get there—*eventually*. Dane leaned forward from the back seat and asked, "How've you been making it?"

"Okay, I guess." I shrugged. "You know how it is. I'm just trying to keep my head above water."

"It's not always easy, but you'll get it." He motioned his hand towards Rip. "Hell, if numb-nuts here can survive this shit, you sure as hell can."

"Fuck you, man. I've put up with more shit than you have."

"I was shot, but apparently you forgot about that shit." Dane let out a huff.

Dane and Gauge were with Kenadee when she was abducted by the Inner Disciples, a local gang. Dane tried to intervene and got himself shot in the process. The whole thing was fucked up, especially the reason why their gang leader, KeShawn Lewis, had taken Kenadee in the first place. He'd blamed her for his son's death and attempted to seek vengeance by taking her life as well. Not giving him any credit for his actions, Rip replied, "I didn't forget. I just don't put as much significance in it as you do."

"Significance?" Dane barked. "Are you fucking kidding

me? I took a bullet for the brothers. Hell, I took more than one and was lucky to survive that shit."

"Don't see what you're getting at, brother," he poked. "You knew what you were signing up for when you started prospecting. If you expected a medal or something for the shit, you might as well give it up."

"Not expecting a fucking medal, dickhead." Dane sat back in his seat as he grumbled, "Just a simple acknowledgement of the fact."

"You'll get your acknowledgment when you get your fucking patch," Rip answered with little emotion.

If I didn't know better, I might've thought that Rip was actually jealous of the fact that Dane had been the one who'd gotten shot and not him. I didn't necessarily blame him. As prospects, there's nothing we wouldn't do to show the brothers that our loyalty lies with them and the club, even if that meant putting our lives on the line by taking a bullet for them. While I hadn't been shot, I was in that line of fire as well, not long after Dane had been hit. We'd gone to the gang leader's house to get Kenadee back, and as luck would have it, I came up on Rider and KeShawn when they were in the middle of a standoff. Knowing his life was in danger, I approached KeShawn from behind and placed my gun against his head, giving Blaze the opportunity he needed to take a shot. At the time, I didn't think much of what I'd done, but that very move caught the attention of the brothers, and it's one of the reason why Gus offered me a chance to prospect. When I accepted, I knew what I was getting into—the good and the bad. None of it mattered. I wanted to be a member and was willing to do whatever was needed to make it happen.

When we got to the Eight Ball, Rip turned to me and asked, "You following us back to the clubhouse?"

"Yeah, I'll be right behind ya."

He nodded, then he and Dane got out of the truck and headed over to Gauge and T-Bone's bikes. I waited while they threw on their helmets and started up the bikes, then I followed behind as they eased out of the parking lot. As soon as we got back, I tracked down T-Bone and Gauge and gave them back their keys. Once I was done checking in with them, I started down the hall towards my room. It was still relatively early, but I was beat and looking forward to calling it a night.

The clubhouse was an old train depot that the brothers had renovated. Like the rest of the building, the halls were old and rustic with old lanterns lining the walls. They wanted the option of staying at the clubhouse whenever they saw fit, so they added twenty or so bedrooms that were perpendicular to each other. Inside, they were all basically the same. A bed with a TV mounted on the wall, a desk, and a dresser with an attached bathroom. Each of the brothers made the rooms their own by decorating them with various pictures or biker memorabilia that meant something to them. I hadn't had a chance to do anything with mine, so it looked pretty much the same as it did when I first arrived. Just as I stepped inside my room and was about to fallout on the bed, my cell phone started to ring.

I groaned, thinking it was one of the brothers with another odd job for me to complete, but when I looked down at the screen, I was pleasantly surprised to see that it was my uncle Viper calling. "Hey, Unc. How's it going?"

"I was going to ask you the same thing."

"It's going all right. Been busy as hell," I scoffed, "but I'm making it."

"Busy is good. Busy means you're keeping yourself out of trouble."

I knew he meant well, but I didn't need a reminder of the dumb shit I'd done. Worst of all? I wasn't there for my mother and sister when they needed me the most. I'd never forgive myself for hurting them like I did, but I'd turned a corner. I hoped, in time, Viper would see that I wasn't the same guy that I was when I left Nashville. "No trouble here. Just working in the garage and doing whatever I'm told."

"That's what I wanted to hear." He paused for a moment, then asked, "You thought any more about getting your own place?"

"Yeah, I want to find something, but between work and all the running around I do, I haven't had time." A couple of the guys stayed at the club most every night, but a majority had a place of their own. I didn't mind staying at the club, though. For the most part, I actually liked it, but there was something to be said about having one's own space. "But I have a couple of places I'm gonna try to check out this week."

"Let me know if you find anything, and I'll bring your mother and sister down to help you get settled in."

"That's not gonna be necessary, Viper. I can get some of the guys to help me."

"I'm sure you can, but Janice would like to see you. You know that," he argued. "Like it or not, she's missing her son."

I knew he was right. I'd been trying to do better about calling and checking in, but things had been hectic lately and I'd put it off. Hoping he'd understand, I replied, "I know, but you know how prospecting can be. Hell, I barely have time to take a piss, much less get a decent night's sleep."

"I understand better than you know, but your mother doesn't." His tone suddenly grew harsh. "She's already lost your father. Ain't right that she's gotta lose her boy too."

"You're right." I let out a deep breath. "I'll work out something to see her soon."

"Make sure that you do," he ordered. "Go get some rest. Sounds like you need it."

"Planning on it. Thanks, Viper."

As soon as I hung up, I tossed my phone on the bedside table and lay down on the bed. I was just planning on resting my eyes for a minute, but the next thing I knew, I was waking up to the sun blaring through my small corner window. I glanced over at the clock and sprang out of bed, seeing that I only had forty-five minutes before I needed to be at the garage. I rushed into the bathroom for a quick shower, then threw on some clean clothes. Without stopping for coffee or breakfast, I went straight out to the parking lot and got on my bike. It had been days since I'd actually been able to ride my Harley, so I was looking forward to getting a little *wind therapy*, especially since we were still in a warm spell. The temps were supposed to drop dramatically over the next week, so I was happy to take advantage of the warm, sunny morning.

I'd just put on my helmet when T-Bone and Gauge came barreling out of the clubhouse. By looking at them, you would've never known that either of them were shit-faced the night before. T-Bone gave me a nod, then asked, "You going to the garage?"

"Yep, headed that way now."

"Good deal. We'll follow you in."

Moments later, the roar of Harleys cranking up filled the parking lot, and we were driving through the gate. I'd actually gotten a decent night's sleep, and was feeling damn good, riding towards the garage with two of the brothers by my side. The wind was just right, just cool enough to get the blood pumping, and even though the traffic was starting to pick up, it wasn't enough to slow us down. We all made it to the garage with plenty of time to spare. Once inside, I grabbed myself a cup of coffee and got busy working on a 1950 Chevy 3100 we were breaking down to restore. The owner requested a full remodel with all new interior, bedliner, and exhaust. To top it off, he wanted it painted black with bright red flames blending in from the hood to the side panels. Knowing the kind of paintwork Darcy did, I had no doubt that it'd look badass when it was done.

As soon as we'd pulled the engine, I started getting her prepped for painting. I spent the entire day sanding and working out imperfections and, without any major interruptions from the brothers, was making some real progress. I was both relieved and surprised when the following few days held much of the same. I'd work all day on the Chevy, follow the brothers back to the clubhouse, and after a quick bite of dinner, I'd hit the sack, praying that I wouldn't get a call in the middle of the night. I didn't. While I enjoyed the breather, I knew it wouldn't last, so I used the time I had to get the Chevy done. I was just a few hours from finishing up when Blaze came over to my station and said, "Hey ... There's someone on the phone asking for you."

"Who is it?"

"Didn't say."

I nodded, then walked over to Blaze's desk and picked up the receiver. "This is Clay."

"Hey, this is Dr. Tanner from the animal clinic. You told me to give you a call if there was a problem with Duchess."

"Yeah?"

"Well, there's a problem."

LANDRY

I'd always prided myself on being a good judge of character. I'd learned that it wasn't about what a person said, or even what others had said about them. It was a person's actions that truly defined them. Anyone could say the right thing, tell someone exactly what they wanted to hear, but if they actually lived up to the promises they made, especially when no one was watching, it showed that they had a good, decent personality. As far as Aniya Strayhorn was concerned, I wanted to believe all the things that she'd told me during my visit to their home. It was clear that things hadn't been easy for her or her husband. They'd both lost their jobs due to downsizing and had struggled to find work elsewhere. Aniya had been working odd jobs like cleaning houses and filling in at the nursing home, but with so many mouths to feed, it simply wasn't enough. It would've been great if her husband had stepped up to the plate and helped out where he could, but their financial struggles became too much for him and he left.

It was difficult to hear how hard things had been for them, but it gave me some insight as to why the calls had been made about the kids. She didn't have anyone to watch them when she went to work, which explained why they had been left alone so often. I hated for her to lose her children when she was actually trying to do right by them. In hopes of helping her keep her kids, I'd been working diligently to find her a more stable job, some options for childcare, and even though she didn't like the idea of taking handouts, I'd gotten her the paperwork to sign up for food stamps. Once I had everything together, I went back over to their house to discuss everything with Aniya. The second she opened the door and invited me inside, I could tell it hadn't been a good day for her. Unlike the time before, the house was in disarray, and with the dark circles under her eyes and disheveled hair, she looked somewhat out of sorts. "Is everything okay?"

"No," she admitted. "We've had a long night."

"You want to talk about it?" She glanced over at me, and I could see the uncertainty in her eyes as she studied me for a moment. Even though I hadn't given her any reason not to, I could tell she was still trying to decide if she could trust me. Hoping to get her to open up, I reminded her, "I'm here to help, Aniya. I can't do that unless I know what's going on."

"Fiona's cough had gotten worse yesterday, and I had to take her to the emergency room. The doctor was so angry with me." Tears filled her eyes as she explained, "I knew it was bad, but I couldn't afford a doctor's visit right now. Hell, I can barely afford to buy groceries and keep the damn lights on. I tried explaining that to the doctor, but he didn't care about anything I said. He was too busy judging me, assuming that I was some piece-of-shit parent who didn't give a damn about my kids. He doesn't know me. He doesn't know what I'm going through, but he sat up there on his high horse looking down on me for not taking better care of my kid."

"I'm sure that was difficult for you, Aniya."

"How would you know? I bet you've never had to decide between buying a bottle of cough syrup or a jug of milk for your kids!" she spat.

"No, I can't say that I have, but that doesn't mean that I don't understand." I took a step closer as I tried to reason with her. "I've worked with many families that have had to deal with the same things you're struggling with right now, and I really think I have some options for you that might help ... if you're willing to hear me out."

Her rigid shoulders grew lax as she let out a deep breath. "Okay, I'm listening."

"Good." I smiled as I motioned her over to the sofa. Once we were both seated, I turned to her and asked, "First, how's Fiona?"

"Much better. The doctor gave her a shot and a breathing treatment, and she actually slept through the night."

"That's really good news."

I opened my satchel and pulled out the paperwork I'd brought for her to look over. First, I showed her the list of job openings I'd found in her area, a couple were better than others, but each of them would provide her with a steady paycheck and enable her to be home at night. When she voiced her concern about leaving the kids unattended, I explained how I'd found a church that offered free after-school childcare until six every evening. While she was receptive to that idea, it took a little more convincing to get her to sign up for food stamps. Her brows furrowed as she looked at the forms and said, "I already told you how I feel about this."

"I know and I understand your reasons why, but with these, you won't have to decide between buying the cough syrup or that jug of milk."

"Yeah, but what kind of person would I be if I took something for nothing?"

"The kind of person who'd do whatever it took to provide for her kids."

I watched as my words sunk in, and I knew I'd finally gotten through to her. We continued to talk for several more minutes, and once we were done, I asked if I could go check in on Fiona. As soon as she gave the okay, I went upstairs and eased the door open. I was pleased to see that she was awake and sitting up on the bed. Her color was much better than it had been the last time I'd seen her, and she looked less drained. "Hey there. How ya feeling?"

"Bret-ter."

"I'm really glad to hear that." I walked over to the edge of her bed and smiled as I said, "I was worried about you."

"I o-kay. Momma took me to da hos-pit-tle."

"She told me. I'm glad that the doctor was able to make you feel so much better."

Her lips pursed into a pout. "He not nice to Momma."

"I heard about that. I'm sure it's just because he was worried about you. Not that it's any reason for him to be rude to your mother." When I saw that she was holding the same little gray elephant that she'd shown me the last time I was there, I asked, "How's Bella doing?"

She glanced down at the stuffed toy and smiled, "She's ti-erd."

"Well, I'll let you two get some rest." As I started towards the door, I told her, "I'll be back in a few days to see how you are doing."

"Bye, Ms. Lan-dree."

"Bye, sweetie."

I left the Strayhorn house feeling pretty good about things. While there was still a lot of work that needed to be done, I felt like I'd made some real progress. I hoped I would have similar luck when I went to see Mr. Coburn. He'd been dodging my calls all week, but after I left a message threatening to get the police involved, he finally answered. He agreed to meet with me to discuss the accusations that had been about him, but he made it crystal clear that he wasn't happy about it. Even went as far as to say that he'd prove whoever had filed the report was lying, but I wasn't so sure. I'd seen the dejected look in Katie's eye when she told me how her father behaved when he drank. I tried to remind myself that I needed to keep an open mind as I drove towards his house. I pulled up in his driveway and spotted a man sitting on the front porch. When I opened my car door and got out, he stood and started walking towards me.

Reeking of alcohol and cigarettes, a fake smile crossed his face as he extended his hand and said, "Hello, you must be Ms. Dawson."

"I am." I studied his face as I shook his hand. He looked a little different than he had in his driver's license picture, older and heavier, and there was a large snake tattoo on his forearm, but I could tell from his short curly hair and beady brown eyes that it was, indeed, Mr. Coburn. "And you must be Mr. Coburn."

"You can call me Chris." He motioned his hand towards the house as he said, "Would you like to come inside?"

"It's such a beautiful day." I wasn't feeling too keen on the idea of being alone with him, especially after he'd been drinking, so I suggested, "Would you mind if we just talk on the porch?"

"Sure, that would be fine."

As I followed him up to the house, I noticed there was a motorcycle parked in his garage and an assortment of tools scattered around the ground. Remembering that Clay had a similar motorcycle in the back of his truck on the night we met, I considered asking Mr. Coburn about it, but decided against it when I spotted a bottle of bourbon tucked behind a dead potted plant. There was no doubt that I had, in fact, smelled alcohol on his breath, and I wasn't interested in making small talk with a man who'd been drinking at such an early hour, especially under these particular circumstances. Once we were both seated, I took my journal and a pen out of my satchel and jotted down the date and time. "As we discussed on the phone, I'm here to talk to you about an allegation that came into our office early this week."

"Yeah, I remember ... but like I told you on the phone, that shit wasn't true. I've never had my daughter blow into my breathalyzer for me, and I don't drink and drive anymore. I learned my lesson about that shit."

"Do you have any idea why someone would make a report like that?"

"I got no fucking idea. If I had to guess, I'd say it was my daughter who made that shit up," he snapped.

"And why would she do that?"

"Cause she got pissed at me and decided to make up some bogus story to get back at me."

"Okay." I did my best to keep my tone nonthreatening as I asked, "Why was she angry?"

"Well ... she ... uh ..." he stammered, "she was late coming home from school, so I grounded her."

I took a moment to write down what he'd said, then asked, "How late was she?"

"An hour or so." He cleared his throat before saying, "She had me pretty worried."

"I'm sure. Did she mention why she was late?"

"I don't know. Something about missing the bus."

I knew he was lying. I could hear it in his voice and see it in his eyes, so I kept pushing. "If she missed the bus, how did she get home?"

"I guess she walked."

As I wrote myself another note, I gave him another little nudge. "The school is over seven miles away from here. It would've taken her hours to walk from there to here."

"Then, I guess she caught a ride."

"Oh, I see." I jotted another note, then asked, "Any idea who she got the ride from?"

"I don't see what any of this has to do with anything!" he argued. "The point is, Katie is a fucking liar. Why don't you write that in your goddamn notes?"

"There's no reason to get upset, Mr. Coburn. I'm just trying to get a grasp on why Katie would make up a story like this, especially when it pertains to her father. In my experience, kids don't do that unless there's a really good reason."

"I just told you the fucking reason, lady, but you aren't listening!"

"Do you still have the smart start ignition interlock installed in your car?"

"Yeah. Stuck with that shit for another four months," he admitted. "Why do you wanna know?"

"You had it installed because you were convicted of a DUI. Is that correct?"

"Yeah."

"If you are found guilty of drinking and driving again, you could end up serving up to a year in jail, lose your license, and possibly be fined up to thirty-five hundred dollars, correct?"

I could tell he was starting to lose his patience when he snarled, "Yeah, I guess."

"I'd say that's a pretty good reason not to get caught again." I waited for a moment, and then I went for it. "So much so, a person might even get a friend or a family member to blow for them to ensure the car's ignition interlock system isn't triggered."

His eyes narrowed as he growled, "I know what you're getting at, and I done told you that Katie was lying about that. I don't even drink anymore. Haven't touched a drop since the night I got arrested."

"That's great." I kept my voice calm and steady as I asked, "Would you be willing to take a breathalyzer test to prove it?"

"Now?" he asked with surprise.

"If you don't mind. It would really help with my report." I reached into my bag and pulled out the portable breathalyzer I'd brought from the office. "It's the same kind that police officers use when they pull someone over. Once you blow, I'll record the reading, and we'll go from there."

"Fine. Just give me the damn thing."

I pressed the button to power the device, and once the indicator light came on, stating that it was ready to test, I instructed, "Okay, I need you to blow into the mouthpiece and don't stop until I tell you to."

He did exactly as I said, and when I told him to stop, he pulled his mouth away from the breathalyzer. I could feel the tension radiating off him as he waited for the results. He knew what was coming. While he'd managed to carry on a conversation with me, I'd caught a few slurred words. That, along with the fact that he reeked of the stuff, made it less of a surprise when he blew a .11 blood alcohol content. I jotted down his results, and since he'd already shown signs of agitation, I figured it was best for me to get the hell out of there. I calmly placed the test and the rest of my belongings into my bag and stood. "I appreciate you taking the time to speak with me today, Mr. Coburn. Our conversation was very insightful."

I gave him a quick smile, then started down the steps and towards my car. I'd hoped that he wouldn't come after me, but I wasn't that lucky. "Wait! What did it say?"

"I'm sure you know exactly what it said, Mr. Coburn." I opened my car door and quickly got inside. Before I closed it, I told him, "I have another appointment, but I'll be in touch."

"So, that's it?" His face grew red with rage as he roared, "You're not even going to give me a chance to explain."

"I gave you a chance, Mr. Coburn."

I closed the door and started my car, and as I went to back out of the driveway, he slammed his fist into the hood. I didn't stop moving, fully aware of what would happen if I did, and rushed back to my office. While I didn't have enough evidence to have Katie removed from the home, I did have enough to warrant a few surprise home visits. I had to make sure that Katie wasn't in any danger, but after what occurred today, I wouldn't be going back to that house alone. I'd have a police escort accompany me to ensure the safety of both Katie and myself.

When I got back to the office, I went straight to my desk and started working on my reports. Once I was done, I decided to go through my messages and cringed when I came across several missed calls from the animal clinic. I figured they were checking to see if I'd found anyone to take Duchess. I'd called everyone I knew, pleading with them to help me out, but no one was interested in taking on such a large dog. I wasn't ready to give up just yet, so I'd been dodging the clinic's calls. Sadly, it looked like my time was running out, and I'd have to take her to the pound like the vet had suggested. Accepting defeat, I picked up the phone, dialed the number to the clinic, then said to the receptionist, "Hi, this is Landry Dawson. I'm calling about Duchess."

"Okay, how can I help you?"

"I just wanted to let you know that I haven't found anyone to take her, so I'll to have to bring her over to the pound." Disappointment washed over me as I said the words. "I'll be by there after work to pick her up."

"I'm not sure I understand, Ms. Dawson. Duchess was already picked up last night."

"What? By who?"

"Memphis Animal Control shut down a big puppy mill a couple of days ago, and they brought the dogs here to seek medical attention. We were running low on space and no longer had room to kennel Duchess for you. We tried calling several times, but when we couldn't reach you, we contacted Mr. Hanson. He came and picked her up last night."

"Really?"

"Yes, ma'am. He also took care of the bill."

"Oh, I had no idea. Thank you for letting me know."

"No problem. I hope you find a good home for her. She's such a great dog."

"Thank you. I hope I do too." I was about to hang up when I realized I had no way of contacting Clay. "Hey … Do you happen to have Mr. Hanson's number?"

"I'm sorry, ma'am, but I'm not allowed to give out personal information."

"But—"

"I'm really sorry."

With that, she hung up the phone. Damn. Now what?

PROSPECT

"What's the deal with the mutt?" Rider asked as he stepped over her and made his way to my station. "She your new sidekick or something?"

"No, not exactly. Just keeping an eye on her for a friend."

He crossed his arms as he leaned back against the counter and studied me for a moment. "This *friend* wouldn't happen to be the chick you helped out the other night, would she?"

"Yeah, that'd be her."

"And this is the dog she hit?" Without giving me a chance to answer, he glanced down at Duchess and said, "Man, she's a big one."

"That she is, and she's only a pup. Still got a lot of growing to do."

"Damn. What kind of dog is it?"

"She's a Great Dane, Rottweiler mix." I glanced down at Duchess. She was lying down with her head perched high, her black coat glistening under the bright lights of the garage, and her big black eyes were staring right at me, like she knew I was talking about her. I couldn't get over it. That crazy dog was the most easy-going, trusting animal I'd even been around—something I wouldn't have expected from a stray. "Apparently, it's an expensive breed or something. At least, that's what the vet told us."

"Seriously? Why would anyone would wanna mix a Dane with a Rot?"

"Couldn't tell ya, but she's a damn good dog." I turned my attention back to the tailgate I'd been working on. "Hasn't moved from that spot since we got here."

"How long you planning on keeping her?"

"Just a couple of days ... maybe more. Depends on how long it takes Landry to find someone to take her."

"She isn't gonna keep her?" he asked, sounding surprised.

"Can't. Her apartment doesn't allow pets."

Rider leaned down and started stroking her head. "She's a pretty thing. Shame she can't keep her."

"She wanted to, but her hands are tied." I shrugged. "Maybe she can find a home for her."

"Gus okay with you keeping her at the clubhouse?"

"Yeah, he was cool with it as long as she doesn't interfere with my prospecting ... which *it won't*."

"I didn't figure he'd mind, but it was good you checked with him."

"I had my doubts, especially since she's so fucking big, but you should've seen him when he laid eyes on her for the first time." I chuckled as I went on, "He actually wanted to keep her for himself, but Samantha wasn't having it. Said between Harper and a new grandkid on the way, they had enough on their plate, but I'm hoping he might be able to talk her into it."

"Why don't you just hang on to her?" Rider stood up, but didn't take his eyes off Duchess. "You've been talking about getting a place of your own. Might be nice to have a dog around when you do."

"I thought about it, but not sure I've got the time or the patience." I took another quick glance over in Duchesses direction, and just like all the times before, she was still staring right at me. "But I gotta admit, she's growing on me."

"I can see why." Rider finally turned his attention away from the dog and over to me. "Before I forget, come by the house after work tomorrow night. Darcy's making dinner, and I've got some things to go over with you before our run on Monday."

"I'll be there."

"Yo, Rider," Blaze called from his office. "You got a minute?"

"Be right there." He turned, and as he started towards Blaze's office, Rider looked over to me and said, "You should keep her. Chicks love dogs."

"I'll keep that in mind."

Once he was gone, I tried to turn my focus back to my work, but my head just wasn't in it. I was too distracted by that damn dog. It wasn't her fault. Hell, she hadn't made a fucking peep since we got to the garage, but every time I looked at her, I thought about Landry. I should've touched base with her the night before to tell her that I had Duchess, but I knew what would happen if I heard her voice. I'd want to see her, be close to her, and finally get that kiss I'd been thinking about since I'd last seen her. I had hoped that putting a little time and space between us would've helped make things easier. It hadn't. In fact, it only made me want to see her even more. In my gut, I knew another day wasn't going to change that, but each time I went to grab my phone to call her, I found another reason to put it off. I was starting to run out of excuses.

"Yo, Clay, there's someone here to see you!" I heard Blaze call out to me.

"Who is it?" I asked as I turned and started towards the office but stopped the second I saw the scowl on his face. He was standing next to Landry, and it was clear that he wasn't happy about her coming to see me at work. I hadn't given her my number or the garage's address, so I had no idea how she'd managed to find me. I continued towards them and tried to collect myself, but I was rattled by the situation. My tone sounded harsher than I intended when I asked, "What are you doing here?"

"I was looking for you."

"But how did you know where to find me?"

"I have my ways," she answered with a nervous smile.

Before I could respond, Blaze interjected, "I take it you know her?"

"Yeah, her name is Landry." Seeing the curiosity in his eyes, I added, "She's here about the dog."

"Oh, okay. I'll let you two get to it, then."

With that, he nodded and headed back into his office, leaving us alone to talk. Landry looked amazing in her black dress pants and fitted teal sweater. It was damn near impossible not to just stand there and soak in her curves. Hell, I probably would've still been gawking at her if she hadn't finally spoken. "I talked to the animal clinic, and they said you had Duchess. Is that right?"

"Yeah. They ran out of kennel space because of some puppy mill or something. They called me when they couldn't get in touch with you." I motioned my hand over to my station where Duchess was still lying on the floor. "She's been hanging out with me ever since."

"I'm so sorry. I had no idea."

The second Duchess spotted Landry, she started wagging her tail so hard her entire body shook. I figured she'd get up and rush over, but surprisingly enough, she remained seated in her spot. I leaned down and patted the side of my leg, then called, "Duchess! Come here, girl."

Still sore from the accident, it took her a moment to get up, but once she was on her feet, Duchess trotted over to me and leaned her head against my thigh, panting as I rubbed her head. Landry knelt down beside her as she whispered, "Hey there, sweet girl."

"Have you found anyone willing to take her?"

"No, not yet." I could hear the torment in her voice as she continued, "I'm worried I might have to take her to the pound."

"I could keep her a while longer if you think that would help?"

"Really? You'd do that?"

"Sure. It's not like she's any trouble." My attention drifted to Duchess as she sat down with her rear centered on my boot. I ran my hand over her head and added, "And I kind of like having her around."

A smile crossed Landry's face as she said, "From the looks of it, she definitely likes being around you."

I was so wrapped up in Landry and our conversation about Duchess, I never noticed that T-Bone and Gauge had walked over to us until they were both standing just a few feet away. I knew what they were doing. Considering how beautiful Landry looked today, I might've done the same thing if I was in their shoes, but unlike them, I would've simply taken a quick look and kept my mouth shut. When I noticed the goofy smirk that crept across T-Bone's face, I knew I was in trouble. "Who's your friend, prospect?"

"Landry Dawson." She stood up and turned to them as I said, "Landry, this is T-Bone and Gauge."

T-Bone's eyes skirted over her as he replied, "Nice to meet you, *beautiful*."

"Nice to meet you too." Clearly nervous, her back stiffened as she shifted a little closer to me. I could easily sympathize with how she was feeling. Hell, I could still remember how intimidated I was when I met them both for the first time, but it didn't take me long to figure out that they were both good guys. I hoped the same would hold true for her. Her voice was strained as she asked, "Do you both work here with Clay?"

"We do." Gauge was dishing out the charm as he smiled and asked, "So, what brings you to our fine establishment?"

"I came to check on Duchess." Landry ran her hand over the dog's head, then turned her attention me. "And to see Clay, of course."

"Duchess your dog?" T-Bone asked.

"Technically, no." A light blush crept across her face as she continued, "I actually hit her with my car the other night, and Clay was nice enough to help me get her to the vet. I was hoping to find someone to take her, but I haven't had any luck yet."

"I can do some asking around. See if I can find anyone who'd be interested," Gauge offered.

"I'd really appreciate that." She smiled as she looked over to me and said, "I'm sure Clay would appreciate it too. He's offered to keep an eye on her until I can find someone."

T-Bone lifted his chin as he studied me for a moment, then asked, "You tell her about Friday night?"

The club was having a party Friday night. The guys had been busting their asses for weeks prepping for the next big pipeline run, and a party gave them an excuse to blow off some steam. I'd found out earlier that morning that they'd also invited my uncle Viper and his boys to come down and share in the fun, so I had no doubt that it would be a hell of a party. There were countless reasons why I hadn't mentioned it to Landry: first, I was just getting to know her; and second, I was prospecting. I knew what the club's parties were like. Big or small, everyone there would cut loose and have a big time, except us prospects. There wasn't a lot of fun to be had since we were the ones responsible for making sure shit stayed in control. Prospects had to guard the gates; keep tabs on the food and alcohol to ensure there was always plenty for the brothers, and that was just the beginning. Simply put, we had to remain on hand in case one of the brothers needed us. I wouldn't have time to blink at that party, much less entertain a guest. I didn't want Landry to think I was holding out on her, so I simply responded, "No, I hadn't had the chance."

"What's Friday night?"

"We're having a party at the club," T-Bone answered. "If you don't have plans, you should come by."

"Um ... Well, maybe. I'll see what I have going on, but thanks for the invite."

"No problem. Hope to see you there." T-Bone gave me a quick nod before he and Gauge started back over to their work stations. "It was nice meeting ya, Landry Dawson."

"You too!" Once they were gone, she turned to me and said, "They seem nice."

"Yeah, they're good guys." As much as I hated to cut things short, it wouldn't be long before Blaze got on my ass. "I guess I better get back to work."

"Oh, yeah. Of course." Landry knelt down and whispered something to Duchess before saying, "Thanks again for keeping an eye on her for me. I really appreciate it."

"It's really no problem." I reached in my back pocket and pulled out one of the garage's business cards, then took a pen off the front counter to write my number down and offered it to her. "Just give me a shout if you find someone to take her."

"Okay, I will."

When she turned to leave, Blaze stepped out of his office and said, "You just gonna let her walk out of here like that?"

"What do you mean?"

"You know exactly what I mean. A girl like that isn't gonna wait around forever, man." His eyes met mine as he continued, "If you have any interest in her at all, and from the looks of it, you clearly do, then you need to do something about it."

"Why does it matter anyway," I scoffed. "I can't be the kind of guy a woman like her needs ... not while I'm prospecting."

"Maybe. Maybe not. Only one way to find out." He motioned towards the door as he said, "Now, get your ass out there before you fuck this whole thing up."

Knowing he was right, I ran out the front door to find Landry. By the time I scanned the parking lot, she was already by her car and about to get inside. Hoping to stop her, I called out, "Hey, Landry. Hold up!"

She quickly turned and looked at me with a surprised expression. When I finally made my way over to her, she asked, "Is something wrong?"

"No, not exactly." I hadn't really thought about what I was going to say to her, and I was struggling to find the right words. It didn't help matters that she was just a few inches away. Being so close to her made it impossible to think. It took me a moment, but I finally pulled it together. "I was thinking about going to grab some stuff for Duchess after work ... I figure she needs a bed, maybe a collar, and some food. I was wondering if you wanted to come along. Maybe give me some input in what I should get."

"I'd love to."

"Great. I'll pick you up at your place around six."

"Okay, sounds good."

"All right. I'll see you after a while then."

I turned and started back towards the garage, but stopped when Landry called out to me. "Hey ... How are you going to pick me up when you don't know my address?"

"I have my ways!"

Before she could say anything more, I headed back inside. Blaze was standing at his office door, smiling like a Cheshire cat as he nodded at me with pride. Without saying a word, he walked into his office and got back to work. Knowing I needed to do the same, I called Duchess to follow and went back over to the Chevy. As I got busy, I found myself thinking of what Blaze had said about Landry. The more I thought about it, the more I realized he was right. I liked Landry. I wanted to spend time with her, get to know her better, and see how things played out. I had a lot on my plate, and it wasn't going to be easy to balance everything out, but I wasn't going to let that stop me from trying.

I continued working on the Chevy and finally finished her up just before closing time. I needed to gather my things but went to the paint room first and let Darcy know the truck was ready for her to take over. "You're already done?"

"You sound surprised."

"I figured it would've taken you most of the week to get that rust bucket ready for me. Color me impressed."

"What can I say?" I smiled with a playful shrug. "I'm awesome like that."

"I don't know if I'd go that far!"

"Maybe not." I turned and started out the door. "But I would."

I could hear her giggle as I walked back over to my station and grabbed my stuff. With Duchess in tow, I went out to the truck and rushed over to the clubhouse for a quick shower. Once I'd changed, I stopped by to see Riggs, and then Duchess and I were on our way to pick up Landry. When I pulled up at the address Riggs had given me, I was pleased to see that it was in a good neighbor-hood, and it had decent security. With a guard at the front gate, good lighting, and digital cameras at every corner, I didn't have to worry too much about Landry's safety. I made my way up to her door and knocked, then ran my hand through my hair, trying to get it out of my eyes, as I waited for her to answer. Moments later, Landry opened the door.

While she looked unbelievable in her work clothes, the sight of her in jeans and plaid flannel top nearly knocked me on my ass. I couldn't even speak. I simply stood there and stared at her, noting the way the denim clung her to body and accentuated the hour-glass curve of her waist. Then, I noticed the hint of cleavage that was showing beneath the tank top she wore underneath, and it was all I could do to keep my hands from reaching for her. I was just starting to pull myself together when I saw the way she was looking at me.

I thought it'd ease my mind to know that she wanted me too, but it didn't—not in the fucking least.

LANDRY

*W*hen I first arrived at Satan's Fury's garage, I was surprised to see that it looked like your everyday, typical garage. There were men hustling around, working on different trucks and motorcycles, which seemed odd considering the reaction I'd gotten from my co-worker when I'd asked him where I could find the place. I should've thought that it'd be filled with thugs with machine guns by the way he talked about it, but as I walked up to the main counter, I was relieved to see that wasn't the case. I'd hoped that Clay wouldn't be bothered by the fact that I'd shown up unannounced, but I could tell by his tone that he wasn't exactly thrilled. Sensing his unease, I did my best to get out of there as fast as I could, cursing myself silently all the way back to my car. I was worried that I'd really messed up, that Clay wouldn't want to see me again, so I was more than a little relieved when he'd asked me to join him tonight.

While I had no idea how Clay had located my address,

I couldn't deny that I was extremely glad that he did, especially when I opened the door and found him standing there looking so unbelievably hot. He was wearing his prospect vest with a pair of jeans and a dark t-shirt, and his shaggy blond hair was brushed back just enough to reveal his gorgeous green eyes. That in itself was enough to make me drool, but then I noticed the way he was looking at me. I knew then that I wasn't the only one feeling this all-consuming attraction. He felt it, too, and it scared the hell out of me. So much so, I didn't know what to say or do, so I just stood there, praying that he'd make the first move. Thankfully, he did just that.

"Hey, you ready to go?"

"Sure. Let me lock up." After I grabbed my things, I locked the door, then turned to him and said, "I'm ready when you are."

"All right then. Let's do this."

Like he'd done it a million times, he reached for my hand and led me out to the truck. Duchess never took her eyes off him as he opened the door and helped me inside. Once I was seated, I thought he would close the door behind me. He didn't. Instead, he stepped up close to me, slipping his hand around my waist and pulled me closer. Before I realized what was happening, he'd lowered his mouth to mine and kissed me like I'd never been kissed before. The second his lips met mine, I knew this was different. This was more than a simple kiss. It was the beginning—the beginning of something incredible.

I lifted my hand up to his face, inching my body closer to him as his tongue delved deeper into my mouth. The bristles of his beard were rough against my palm, but his lips were soft and warm, luring me in for more. Heart racing, skin itching with need, I let go of the voices telling me this could never work. I threaded my fingers through his hair and tugged him closer. Unbelievable. I couldn't remember ever being so turned on by a single kiss. The hunger for him was all-consuming, filling me with a heated desire that coursed through me like a wildfire. My hand drifted to the nape of his neck, then snaked down to his chest. He felt so good, smelled so good, and it was all I could do to keep myself from completely losing myself in him.

We were both wrapped up in the moment when Duchess started to whimper, pulling us both back to reality. Clay's eyes met mine in a lust-filled gaze, and my heart nearly leapt out of my chest when a sexy smirk crept across his face. "Sorry about that. I just couldn't help myself."

"No need to apologize," I somehow managed to reply. "I enjoyed it."

"Good. 'Cause I plan on doing it again."

He winked as he closed the door and made his way over to the driver's side. As he got in the truck, he glanced over to Duchess and me. "You girls ready?"

"Yep. All set." I reached back and gave her a quick scratch behind the ear as I asked her, "We're gonna get you a new bed and a new collar. What do you think about that?"

A loud thumping filled the truck as her tail started drumming against the seat. Clay chuckled. "I'd say she's good with the idea."

He started the truck, and it wasn't long before we were

pulling up to one of the local pet stores. They allowed pets, but neither of us had any idea what Duchess would do if she came across another animal. Since she'd been so good at the vet, we decided to take the risk and brought her inside with us. As we started towards the front door, I couldn't believe how she was walking right next to Clay. It seemed as if an invisible rope had tied her to his side, and she never budged from her spot as we made our way inside, making me wonder if we truly needed to bother with buying a collar and leash. It felt like a waste of money until Duchess spotted a large German shepherd and its owner walking in our direction. When he dropped his head and started to growl, Duchesses calm demeanor quickly changed. Her head tilted to the side, and baring her teeth, a low, threatening growl vibrated through her thick chest. With an aggressive look in her eye, she took a charging step closer, leaving no doubt that she was about to attack. Clay quickly knelt down, and with a strong, commanding voice, demanded, "Duchess, *stay!*"

She did as he ordered and stayed put, but her growling continued. He ran his hand down her neck, trying to soothe her. "Easy, girl. It's okay. You're okay."

It took a few seconds, but he managed to settle her down. Once the other dog was out of our view, I leaned over to Clay and said, "I think we should go on and get that leash now."

"Yeah, I think you're right."

I followed him over to the next aisle and watched as Clay picked up a pretty purple collar and asked, "What about this?"

"I don't know. I love the color, but I'm not sure it's big enough to go around her neck."

His brows furrowed as he stepped back and studied Duchess for a moment. Unable to tell for certain, he took the collar and slipped it around her neck. As I'd predicted, it didn't come close to fitting. A cute smile crossed his face as he said, "I think this one might be too small."

"Yeah, I was afraid of that." I reached for one that was the same color with a longer length and offered it to him. "How about this one?"

"Let me see." After Clay hung the small one back in its correct spot, he took the new collar from me and put it around her neck, checking that it wasn't too tight as he secured it. "Looks like it fits. What about a leash?"

I grabbed the matching leash and clipped it to the collar. "I think we're all set."

"Great. Now, let's see if we can find her a bed." I nodded as I followed him over to the next row. As soon as we rounded the corner, he reached up and grabbed an oversized, padded bed that had to be the most expensive one out of the bunch. He held it up to her as he asked, "What do you think of this one?"

Duchess started wagging her tail wildly as she sniffed at the fuzzy fabric. "I think she likes it, but Clay ... does she really need one that nice?"

"What do you mean?" I reached for the tag and turned it where he could see it. I thought the price might deter him, but he simply shrugged. "It's not that bad. Besides, she seems to like it."

"She's a dog, Clay." I teased. "She's gonna like anything you offer her, especially since she's been doing without for so long."

"Exactly," he replied, slipping the bed under his arm. "She deserves to have something nice."

I thought it was extremely sweet that he wanted to get it for her, so I didn't argue. Instead, I simply replied, "Okay, whatever you think."

"All right then." When he started walking towards the next aisle, I thought he was done shopping, but I was wrong. After every few steps, he'd grab something off the shelf, and as he'd lift it up to show me, he'd ask, "What do you think about this?"

It was clear that he was enjoying his little shopping spree, so I simply nodded and said, "Mm-hmm. Whatever you think."

He'd add it to the mix, and by the time we were done, it looked like he'd bought out the store. When we got up to the counter, I tried to chip in, but he refused. "I've got it."

Once the cashier had checked us out, we each grabbed a handful of bags and headed back out to the truck. After we loaded everything into the back, I helped him get Duchess in the back seat and closed the door. I was about to turn and get in myself, when I felt him reach for my arm. The next thing I knew, he was inches away from me. "I shouldn't have kissed you earlier."

"Oh, really?" I thought the kiss was incredible, and my stomach sank at the thought that he didn't feel the same. "Why's that?"

"I can't stop thinking about it." He leaned forward, wrapping his arms around my waist, and as his lips hovered over mine, he whispered, "How good it felt ... How much I want to do it again."

I was still trying to process what he'd said when his mouth crashed down on mine. The kiss was intense, filled with a passion like I'd never known, and it completely stole my breath. A slight whimper escaped my mouth when Clay's tongue grazed over mine. With a low, needful growl, he slid his hand down, gripping my ass, forcing me even closer. Hoping to steady my balance, I clutched his shirt, pressing my breasts against his chest. I couldn't deny it: I wanted him, all of him, shamelessly. It was clear from his growing erection, he felt the same about me. We were both so lost in the moment, we'd forgotten that we were standing in the middle of the pet store parking lot, surrounded by people and passing cars. That realization might've *never* dawned on either of us if Duchess hadn't started to grow impatient and begun whining. Clay pulled back with a tortured sigh. "I guess we better get going."

"Yeah." I swallowed hard, trying to get a grip on my overactive hormones, before saying, "I think you're right."

Still feeling heated from our embrace, I climbed into the truck, and it wasn't long before we were on our way. We hadn't been riding long when I glanced over at Clay and smiled as I thought about the kisses we'd shared. I was intrigued by how sweet and docile he could be one moment, only to turn so commanding and possessive the next. I won't deny that I liked it—I liked it a lot, especially when he kissed me the way he did. Damn. It was absolutely incredible, and I couldn't wait for another chance to have his mouth on mine. When I noticed that he was heading back towards my apartment, it hit me that I might get that chance sooner than later. While I liked the idea, I was enjoying my night with him and not ready for it to be over, so I was pleased when he turned to me and asked, "Have you eaten yet?"

"No, I didn't get a chance. Why?"

"I was thinking we could grab something if you had time." He glanced back at Duchess, then said, "But I'm not sure how we can do that with her tagging along."

"We could get takeout at my place."

"That could work. You sure that'll be okay?"

"Absolutely." I tried not to sound overly excited as I told him, "We just have to decide what we want to eat. I'd cook something, but it's been a while since I've gone to the grocery store."

"No problem. We'll just hit a drive-through on the way."

"Sounds good to me."

We went back and forth several times on where to stop, but eventually decided on tacos. After we grabbed dinner, we headed back over to my place. As soon as we were parked, Clay took Duchess by the leash and walked her over to a grassy area, giving her a chance to have a bathroom break before we started upstairs. Once she was done, I helped him gather our food, and we went up to my apartment. With my crazy schedule, there were days when I didn't have time to pick up like I wanted to, but thankfully, I'd had a little extra time this afternoon and was able to do the dishes and even a load of laundry. While it wasn't perfect, it was far from a mess, so I wasn't completely embarrassed when Clay took a moment to look around. "You've got a nice place here."

"Thank you," I replied as I put our food on the table. "It's small, but my neighbors are nice and I feel safe here."

"I've been looking for a place myself." He made his way over to the table and sat down. "Just haven't found what I'm looking for yet."

"And what's that?"

"I don't know." He gave me a small shrug as I put a couple of tacos on his plate, and then two on mine. "I'm kind of hoping I'll know it when I see it."

"I'm sure you will." I picked up one of the tacos as I told him, "You seem like the kind of guy who knows what he wants."

"Yeah, I guess you could say that."

He gave me a wink, and we both started eating. Clay was just about to bite into his second taco when his cell phone started to ring. He took it out of his pocket, and a look of disappointment crossed his face as he read the screen. "Sorry, I've gotta take this."

I nodded, then watched as he stood up and walked into the living room. I heard him answer, "Yeah?"

There was a brief pause, and then he replied, "Yeah, no problem. I'm on my way."

He hung up the phone and walked back into the kitchen. Before he had a chance to say anything, I stood up and began clearing the table. I felt him come up behind me, so I said, "I know, you've got to go."

"I hate to leave like this, but yeah, I do." My back was still to him as he continued, "It's part of the deal with prospecting. When they need me, I've gotta be there."

"I understand."

"You sure about that?" Clay reached for my arm, gently turning me to face him. "'Cause this is how it's gonna be until I get my patch. If you can't handle that, I need to know."

Even though I wasn't sure what I was actually saying, I nodded and said, "I can handle it."

"I'm going to hold you to that."

He leaned down and kissed me, long and hard, causing my body to melt into his arms. As much as I didn't want him to go, I knew he didn't have a choice, so I didn't resist when he pulled free from our embrace. Without saying a word, he walked over to the counter and wrote something down on a piece of paper. Once he was done, he walked back over to me and offered me the note. "Here's the address to the clubhouse. The party will start around seven on Friday night."

"Okay." I was surprised that he mentioned it, especially after the way he'd reacted when his friend T-Bone brought it up. "Does this mean you want me to come?"

"Of course, I do." He placed his arm around my waist as he inched me closer. "Just remember, there'll be things that I have to take care of, so I'm not sure how much time I'll have to spend with you."

"Is there any point in me coming?"

"I figure this is as good a chance as any for you to get acquainted with the brothers."

"Okay."

"I've gotta go." He kissed me on the forehead before turning and heading for the door. "Good night, Landry."

"Night!"

He opened the door, and with Duchess following close behind, he disappeared into the night. The door closed, and suddenly the apartment seemed oddly empty. I couldn't take the silence, so I turned on the TV and listened to an old movie play in the background as I finished cleaning up our dinner. Once I was done, I shut off the TV and got ready for bed, then grabbed my case files and lay under the covers. I grabbed the Strayhorn file and started reading it over. Just as I'd hoped, it was the perfect thing to distract me from all my crazy thoughts about Clay, and it wasn't long before I fell fast asleep. The next morning, I was up and out of the apartment before eight, and I spent the entire day working on reports and studying up on a new case. There were times when my mind would drift to Clay, but I tried to stay busy, hoping it would help keep my nerves about the upcoming party in check. Unfortunately, that didn't happen.

When I got home from work, I was looking through my closet and started to panic when I realized I had no idea what to wear. I'd never been to a clubhouse, much less a clubhouse party, so I wasn't sure if I should wear something super casual or go all out. I was staring at all the different outfits I'd laid across my bed when my cell phone rang. I was tempted to just let it ring, but inevitably, I took it off the bedside table and answered, "Hey, Mom. I'm kind of busy."

"You're always busy, dear," she complained. "What are you busy doing tonight?"

"I'm trying to find something to wear to a party."

I knew it was a mistake to tell her, but the words came out before I could stop myself. "A party! That's wonderful. What kind of party is it?"

"It's just a regular party, Mom."

"Well, you should wear that black dress you wore to your grandparents' anniversary party. You looked wonderful in it."

"I don't know. I think it might be too dressy for this kind of party."

"Nonsense. You can dress it up or down. It's all in the accessories," she argued. "Just throw on a couple of those silver bracelets you wear, a pair of cute earrings, and your boots. Oh ... and leave your hair down. It looks so pretty when you leave it down."

While I liked the black dress, I wasn't sure I had the confidence to wear it to a biker party, but I was in no mood to argue. "Okay."

"That's wonderful! You'll look great. I promise."

"Um ... okay. Well, it's getting late, and I still have some work I need to do."

"Okay," she replied with disappointment. "Let me know how the party goes."

"I will."

I tossed my phone down on the bed and spent another hour going through all my clothes. When I couldn't find anything I liked better, I decided to just wear the stupid black dress like my mother had suggested. Feeling overly anxious, I took a hot shower and crawled into bed. I was just about to turn out the light when I received a text message. Thinking it was my mother again, I was reluctant to even check my phone, but thankfully, curiosity got the best of me. A huge grin spread across my face as soon as I saw that it was from Clay.

CLAY:

Hey. It's Clay.

ME:

Hey! It's nice to hear from you.

CLAY:

I just wanted to let you know that Duchess was thinking about you.

ME:

Is that right? Well, you can let her know that I was thinking about her too. I actually think I might've found someone to take her today.

CLAY:

Really? I was kind of getting used to having her around.

ME:

It's only a possibility, but she seemed really interested.

CLAY:

Guess we'll just have to see how it goes.

ME:

I guess we will.

CLAY:

You still coming tomorrow night?

ME:

Planning on it.

Clay:

Good. I'll see you then.

Me:

Okay. Good night. ☺

PROSPECT

I don't know what the fuck I was thinking. I knew it was a bad idea for Landry to come to this fucking party. Hell, I would've never even mentioned it to her if it hadn't been for T-Bone bringing the shit up. If I hadn't known better, I would've thought the man was trying to stab me in the fucking back, but deep down, I knew that wasn't what it was all about. He was trying to prove a point—I had to learn to manage the things I could control and accept the things I couldn't. At the moment, I was struggling with the latter. When Dane sent word that she was at the gate, I rushed outside to meet her. As soon as she stepped out of the car, I knew I was in trouble. She was wearing a fitted black dress that showed off every single curve, and with her hair down around her shoulders, I was barely able to keep my hands off her. I wanted to keep her close, make sure no one fucked with her, but that wasn't an option. I had things I had to tend to, so I got her a beer and put her at a table with Darcy and

August. I'd hoped that they'd be able to keep the predators at bay, but I was wrong.

I was stocking the beer coolers when I noticed T-Bone and Gauge making small talk with her. At first it seemed pretty innocent, but when T-Bone walked off, Gauge stayed put. I could tell by the way he was looking at her that he was interested, and to make matters worse, she wasn't exactly blowing him off. Instead, she was smiling and talking to him like she was actually enjoying herself. Even though I'd seen her watching me and knew she'd come there for me, it was getting under my skin seeing them like that. Unfortunately, there wasn't a damn thing I could do about it. I hadn't laid claim to her, and even if I did, I was a prospect—a goddamn bottom dweller in the club. No one gave a fuck about any claims I might or might not have made.

I was watching them out of the corner of my eye as I cleared the tables of empty beers when Viper came over and chuckled. "You got something on your mind, son?"

"Nope," I lied as I tossed a few empties into the garbage can. "Just trying to get this shit cleaned up."

"Hmph." I'd almost forgotten how big Viper was until I found him standing in front of me with his arms crossed and his brow cocked. "So, that sour look on your face has nothing to do with the beautiful brunette sitting over there talking to one of Fury's brothers?"

I peered back over at Landry and Gauge, and my stomach twisted into a knot as soon as I found them both laughing. I was still staring in their direction when Landry's eyes met mine. She held my gaze for only a moment, then turned her attention back to Gauge. Frustrated, I tossed another couple of empty beers into the garbage and grumbled, "Fuck it. Nothing I can do about it anyway."

I grumbled several curses under my breath while Viper stood there watching me without saying a word. When I finally stopped chucking bottles into the garbage, he looked down at me with a scowl and asked, "You done with your little tantrum?"

"Yeah." I let out a slow cleansing breath as I told him, "This shit is harder than I thought it was gonna be."

"Things worth having usually are. Just keep your focus. Prospecting won't last forever." He nodded his head over in Landry's direction. "And if that girl is worth having, she'll stand by ya until this thing is done."

"Maybe she will. Maybe she won't." I shrugged. "Either way, a girl like her deserves better than what I can give her right now."

"It'll be worth it in the end."

"Yeah. You keep saying that." I took a quick survey of the packed room, and I found it odd to see so many of my uncle's brothers here at the clubhouse, especially with knowing Viper like I did. The man was protective to a fault. He trusted no one, never letting anyone get too close—not even a woman. Hell, the man was almost fifty, and he still hadn't settled down with an ol' lady. He'd say he didn't need the fucking distraction, but something told me there was more to that story. I knew better than to ask him though. Instead, I simply shrugged and said, "I guess time will tell."

"Yes, it will." A smug smile crept across his face. "I'll look forward to the day when you admit I was right."

"Mm-hmm." Even though a piece of me knew he was

right, I wasn't going to let him know that. "Don't hold your breath."

I'd barely gotten the words out of my mouth, when I felt a hand on my back, followed by a familiar voice saying, "Clay, my man. How's it going?"

"Hey, Hawk. It's been a while." Hawk was Viper's sergeant-at-arms. I'd gotten to know him, along with the other brothers, when I'd visited Viper at his clubhouse. He was a good guy and I'd always thought a lot of him, so I was pleased to have a chance to see him again. "How have you been making it?"

"Pretty good. Just staying busy. You know how it is with your uncle. He's always got us on the move." Without realizing what I was doing, I glanced back over in Landry's direction and grimaced when I saw that Gauge had gotten her another fucking beer. I wanted to be the one sitting there next to her, and it was eating at me that I couldn't. Noticing my aggravation, Hawk nudged me and asked, "What's with the chick? She your girl? 'Cause it sure looks like your buddy is trying hard to make a play."

The knot in my stomach grew even tighter as I told him, "To be honest, I don't even know. Right now, I've gotta get this shit done before the brothers have my ass."

"Well, I'll let you get to it."

I nodded and headed towards the back to meet up with Dane so we could check inventory. I hoped that it wouldn't take long, so I could look in on Landry. Unfortunately, we were running low on beer and needed to make a run. I sent Landry a message, letting her know what was up, but she didn't respond. I knew that wasn't a good sign, and I was right. By the time we'd returned, Landry was no longer sitting at the table with Darcy and

Gauge. Instead, she was at another table—alone with Hawk. Fuck. As much as I liked Hawk, I knew he was a fucking player. If there was a beautiful woman in a fifty-mile radius, you could bet money that he'd make a play on her, but I'd be damned if he was going to make a fucking move on Landry. Not on my fucking watch.

Landry's eyes narrowed when she spotted me walking in their direction. Yeah, she was pissed. Hell, I couldn't blame her. I hadn't said two fucking words to her all night, but there wasn't a damn thing I could do about it and I intended to set things straight—with her and with Hawk. I was just a few feet away when Gus called out to me, "Hey, Clay. I got something I need you to do."

"Be right there." If it had been anyone other than the president, I might've tried to put them off, but there was no way in hell I could do that to Gus. When he wanted a hand, you gave it to him. Period. I quickly turned back, and as I hurried towards him, I asked, "Whatcha got?"

"Samantha is ready to head home, so I'm gonna need you to run her to the house."

Samantha was Gus's ol' lady, and all the brothers thought a great deal of her. She was one of those truly genuine women who wasn't quick to judge, and we respected her for it. Gus and Samantha had only recently crossed paths again, so he was very protective where she was concerned. "Sure thing, Prez."

"She's waiting for you in the kitchen."

"Headed that way now."

"Be careful." He gave me a warning look as he said, "You'll be carrying precious cargo."

"Yes, sir. Absolutely."

Knowing I couldn't just walk out on Landry again, I

headed over to the table where she was sitting with Hawk and said, "Hey ... I've gotta run Samantha home. I'll be back in twenty."

"Okay. Take your time."

"Yeah, brother. Take your time." Hawk winked before saying, "I'll keep an eye on her while you're gone."

It took all I had not to knock his fucking teeth right out of his fucking mouth, but I managed to hold it together. I knew it wouldn't be good if I lost my shit with him. Not only would Gus have my ass, Viper would too. I gritted my teeth as I told him, "Don't do me any favors, Hawk. I'm sure Landry can take care of herself."

Before either of them could respond, I made my way to the kitchen to find Samantha waiting by the back door. A soft smile crossed her face as she said, "I tried to drive home myself, but Gus wouldn't have it."

"It's fine. I don't mind taking ya."

I followed her out to Gus's truck, and once she was inside and buckled up, I pulled up to the gate where Gash was standing guard. Just like earlier, Duchess was sitting in her spot right next to him. I rolled down my window and asked, "She doing okay?"

"Yeah, she's good." He glanced down at her and smiled. "Kind of nice having her around."

"Can't disagree with you there. I'll be back. Just going to run Samantha and Harper home."

"Good deal. Be careful."

I nodded, then rolled up the window and started driving towards Gus's house. As we headed into down-town, I took a quick look at the clock, and I found myself wondering if Landry was still sitting at the table with Hawk. I wondered if he was making a play for her, and if she was buying into it. The whole thing was fucking with my head. Noting my tense mood, Samantha looked over to me and asked, "Is something wrong?"

"No, ma'am. I've just got a lot on my mind."

"Oh, so your quiet mood doesn't have anything to do with the pretty girl I saw you talking to earlier tonight?"

"Maybe."

"I kind of thought so." She patted me on the arm as she said, "Have you talked to her about things?"

"Yes and no." I kept my eyes on the road as I continued, "I probably fucked ... I mean, screwed things up by not talking to her more."

"Better late than never."

"I don't know." I shook my head. "I haven't been able to spend much time with her, and if I had to guess, I'd say she isn't exactly happy about it."

"Give her time. Club life takes some getting used to," she tried to reassure me.

I knew she was right. I just hoped Landry would give me a chance to make things right. As soon as I dropped off Samantha and Harper, I rushed back to the club-house. I had it set in my mind that I was going to sort things out with her, once and for all. When I got back, I was relieved to see that things were starting to die down. I hoped that was a good sign, and I'd finally get a chance to talk to Landry. As soon as I walked in, I spotted her sitting at the bar with August and Darcy. I started towards them, but stopped when I noticed that Hawk was not only sitting with them, but he had his hand planted on the small of Landry's back. A mix of jealousy and rage surged through me as I watched her laugh at something he'd said. I'd seen enough. I walked up behind her and lowered my mouth to her ear as I growled, "We need to talk ... *Now.*"

"Okay." She turned to face me. "What's on your mind?"

"Not here."

I took a hold of her hand and led her out of the bar. As we walked down the hall towards my room, she asked, "Wait ... Where are we going?"

I didn't respond. Instead, I opened my door and guided her inside. Once the door was closed, Landry pulled her hand from mine and walked to the center of the room. With her arms crossed, she glared at me with a scowl on her beautiful face. A million thoughts were racing through my mind as I stood there staring back at her. She looked incredible in that black dress. Fuck. My dick got hard just seeing how it hugged her curves, and all I could think about was how much I wanted to take the damn thing off. I wanted to take her right against that goddamn wall and show her exactly what she'd been doing to me all night long, but the second I thought about Hawk's hands on her, my carnal thoughts were quickly replaced with anger. "You seemed to be enjoying yourself tonight."

"I did." Her eyes drifted to the corner of the room as she muttered, "I would've enjoyed it more if you'd been around."

"Yeah ... right," I replied, my words dripping with sarcasm.

"What's that supposed to mean?" She tucked a loose strand of her hair behind her ear as she muttered, "Wait ... are you mad at me right now?"

When I didn't respond, she shook her head in disgust and muttered, "You do remember that you're the one who left me alone out there tonight? You basically threw me to the wolves and left it up to me to figure things out. And to make matters worse, you barely said two words to me all night long."

"You said you could handle the fact that I was prospecting!"

I could see from the scowl on her face that my words stung, but they didn't stop her from coming at me again. Without hesitating, she snapped, "I can, and I did. Did I bail on you when you were busy? I stuck it out and handled things the best way I knew how."

"Flirting with my brothers wasn't handling it, Landry."

She placed her hand on her hip as she continued, "Have you ever heard the saying, 'perception is reality'?"

"Yeah. What does that have to do with this?"

"Well, from where you were standing, it might've looked like I was flirting with those men, but I wasn't." Her expression softened as she continued, "I was just trying to be nice ... I wanted to make a good impression and get to know your brothers and their ol' ladies because I know this club thing is important to you."

"Ol' ladies?" I scoffed. "For someone who didn't know anything about MCs, you seem to have figured out a few things."

"I just spent four hours talking to them. I picked up on 'a few things'," she argued. "Regardless, I was just trying to make a good impression on them."

She was telling the truth. I could hear it in her voice, but that didn't stop me from saying, "Well, you certainly made an impression."

"You know what?" A wounded expression crossed her face. "Just forget it."

Regret washed over me as I watched her turn towards the door. I should've just let her leave. Nothing good would come from having her stay, but the thought of her walking out that door had me calling out to her. "Landry … Wait."

She stopped but kept her back to me as she said, "You got it all wrong, Clay. Yeah, I was upset that I didn't get to spend much time with you, but I wasn't trying to punish you by flirting with your brothers. In fact, we spent the entire time talking about you." Damn. I'd really fucked up. I let my frustration and jealousy cloud my judgement, especially where Gauge and Hawk were concerned, and I'd hurt Landry in the process. She turned to face me, and her pained expression gutted me. "I really like you, Clay, and I want to see where this goes between us. If you don't feel the same, then just let me walk out of here."

I didn't have the words to tell her, so I did the only thing I could. I showed her. I stepped closer, gently placing my hand on the nape of her neck, and pulled her full mouth to mine. The touch of her lips set me on fire, and I knew there was no going back, no more keeping my restraint. Consequences be damned, I needed her. I'd never felt such a hunger for a woman, and from the way she kissed me, there was no doubt she felt the same. It was like I'd waited a lifetime to feel her in my arms, and now that I finally had her, I was afraid I'd never be able to let her go. She felt too good, too right. The scent of her skin and the warmth of her mouth seduced my senses, making me want her even more.

I trailed kisses down her neck as I whispered, "I should've let you walk out of here, but I can't. I want you too fucking much."

I slipped my hands behind her back and slowly unzipped her dress. I gently lowered it down her shoulders, revealing her black silk bra and perfect round breasts heaving up and down. Through the thin, smooth fabric, I could see her nipples tighten beneath my gaze. She was so damn perfect—just like I knew she'd be. "I want you, too, Clay. I want you so much."

My cock stirred in response and my mouth moved to her collarbone. I kissed her skin softly, teasing her, wanting her wet and aching for me. After I dropped her dress to her ankles, I pulled off her boots, then I made quick work of unhooking her bra, sliding it down her arms before lowering my lips to her breasts. Goosebumps prickled her skin as I took one nipple in my mouth and the other between my index finger and thumb. I circled my tongue around one taut peak as I firmly squeezed and rolled the other between my fingertips. Her hands moved to my hair and her fingers wound themselves in the strands as a moan escaped her. When that voice reached my ears, I was lost. Her heart, her body, everything called out to me, like she was made just for me.

Heat filled her gaze as she hooked her thumbs in her black lace thong and slid it seductively down her tan legs. She stepped out towards me, running her hands along my chest and under my cut.

"Your turn," she whispered. She looked up at me tentatively and when I didn't stop her, she carefully slid my cut off and laid it on the bed. I yanked my t-shirt over my head and pulled her against me. Her skin was warm and soft, and a jolt of need surged to my cock. I heard her gasp as my growing erection pressed against her. She gazed up at me wantonly, biting her lip, before moving her hand to my crotch and slowly stroking me through my jeans. That was all the restraint I could muster. I slid my hand to the nape of her neck and pulled her mouth to mine. A soft whimper escaped from her lips as they parted, allowing me to kiss her deeper. With my other hand, I unfastened my belt and jeans, letting them drop to the floor. Her hands instantly flew to the waistband of my boxer briefs. She pulled back from our kiss for a moment, her eyes flashing as she tugged my boxers down and saw my arousal. Her mouth opened with a little gasp and I couldn't take it anymore. I pulled her to me, walking her backward until we reached the wall.

My tongue caressed her soft lips and tongue, teasing and tasting her. She was absolutely incredible. I wanted every fucking inch of her. I knelt down in front of her and lifted one of her long legs to hook over my shoulder. I heard her breath catch in anticipation as she leaned back against the wall … waiting. Landry squirmed and groaned as I slowly touched my lips to her ribcage and trailed kisses down her stomach. I pulled back, appreciating her soft, smooth skin before lowering my head between her legs. A hiss escaped through her teeth as I raked my tongue against her inner thighs. Each lick, each kiss, each and every tiny taste made me hungry for more. Her hips jerked forward as I pressed the palm of my hand firmly against her center, rhythmically rubbing her clit. With two fingers, I slid through her folds and delved deep inside her. I smiled when I felt that she was already soaking wet. The anticipation of what I was going to do to Landry was getting to her just as much as it was getting to me. As much as I wanted to be inside her, my dick was going to have to wait.

I started slow and steady, teasing her clit with my mouth. Her little moans and whimpers filled the room, and I reveled in the effect I was having on her. As I sucked on her tender flesh, I moved my fingers in and out in a punishing rhythm, curving them forward to hit her most sensitive spot.

"Yes!" she chanted over and over as her hands wound in my hair, pulling me more tightly against her. After just a few more flicks of my tongue, her orgasm took hold, causing her entire body to quiver and shake uncontrollably.

As she leaned against the wall in a blissful haze, I grabbed a condom from the pocket of my jeans and stood. She gazed at me with lust-filled eyes as my mouth came down on hers. I pressed my bare flesh against hers, pinning her to the wall before sliding my hands underneath her firm ass and lifting her to my waist. Her legs immediately wrapped around my hips as her arms wound around my neck, holding my mouth to hers. I could feel her heart hammering against mine. We had both thought about that moment, dreamt about it, and it almost felt too good to be true. She looked up at me with eyes full of desire as I brushed my throbbing cock along her entrance. She tightened her legs around me, urging me forward.

A deep growl vibrated through my chest as I sank deep inside her. I paused, giving her time to adjust to me and allowing me to savor the delicious warmth of her wrapped around me. Slowly and deliberately, I began to move. I wanted her to feel every inch of me pushing inside her.

"You're so fucking tight," I growled as I ground my hips against her.

I was determined to keep up my slow rhythm so that I didn't hurt her, but as her nails dug into my back and her heels spurred me on, I found myself craving more, so I drove deeper ... harder. She threw her head back as her moans echoed around us. Her legs tightened around my waist as her hips rocked against me, begging me to give her more.

"Clay, please!" she cried out. My resolve weakened at the pleading in her voice, and I thrust deep inside her, again and again, gradually increasing my pace. Her eyes clenched shut as she panted and moaned her pleasure. My fingertips dug into her ass, pulling her harder onto my cock, each move more intense than the last. I could feel her body beginning to tense around me, and her thighs held me tight against her G-spot. I watched in awe as her mouth opened wide into an O and her eyebrows knitted together in concentration. Her breath quickened as she clamped down around my cock, making it damn near impossible not to come. A low groan vibrated through my throat as I continued to drive deep inside her. I could feel her imminent release, could see it on her face, so I thrust harder and faster, forcing her over the edge. Her fingertips dug into my shoulders as her orgasm took hold once more. I tried to fight it, but the clenching waves of her muscles contracting around me felt too damn good. My mind went blank as my body took control, and I finally gave in to my own release.

I felt her shudder against me as my own orgasm took hold. I held Landry tight against the wall and buried myself further inside her, savoring the intensity of the moment. I felt her body start to slowly relax against mine, and I looked up to see her eyes close as her breathing slowed.

I carried her over to the bed and carefully lay her down. Then, I quickly disposed of the condom, sat down on the bed, and tugged off my boots before lying next to her. Without a word, she immediately curled into my side. After I pulled one of the covers over us, she settled in the crook of my arm and rested her head on my shoulder. Without looking in my direction, she whispered, "Oh, my god. That was incredible."

"You're incredible." I leaned over and kissed her on the forehead as I continued, "But I've known that from the first time I laid eyes on you."

"Oh, really?" She glanced up at me with those blue eyes and smiled. "And how did you know that?"

"Let's just call it a gut instinct." I had to bite back my smile as I thought of something she'd mentioned a few days prior. "So about a week, huh?"

"What?"

"Was that how long your mom told you to wait before having sex?"

"*No.* Not even close," I scoffed. "She told me to wait at least three to six months."

Before I could respond, there was a knock on my door, followed by Dane shouting, "We've got trouble! Get your ass out front!"

LANDRY

"Coming!" Clay shouted as he jumped out of bed and started throwing on his clothes. "I'm sorry, baby, but I've gotta—"

"I get it. Don't worry," I assured him. "Go do what you have to do. I'll be here when you get back."

"Just so you know, it won't be like this forever." He sat down on the edge of the bed as he pulled his boots on. "Once I get patched in, I'll have more time ... Hell, I'll actually have my life back."

"I know. Gauge explained it to me."

A pained expression crossed his face. I knew he felt bad for misreading the situation.

Once Clay was dressed, he kissed me and rushed for the door. "I'll be back as soon as I can."

Just as he was about to charge into the hall, I remembered to ask, "Wait, where's Duchess?"

"She's out front with Gash."

That's all I got before he darted out of the room and closed the door behind him. Once he was gone, I sat up in the bed and took a moment to look around. It actually reminded me of a small hotel room. There was a queen-sized bed, a TV mounted above the desk in the corner of the room, and a small bathroom. No personal pictures or mementos were sitting around, so other than his scent on the sheets, there was nothing that would have identified the space as Clay's. As I lay there studying my surroundings, I heard a startling sound, causing me to sit up on the bed in a panic. Moments later, the music rumbling from the bar suddenly stopped, and in the midst of silence, the hairs stood up on the back of my neck when I heard a woman scream. Frantic, I got up and threw on my clothes.

As soon as I stepped out the room, a nervous chill ran down my back. From where I stood, the place looked like a maze with all the different hallways. Clay was in such a rush when he brought me down here, I hadn't really paid attention to where we were going, and without the sound of the music to lead me, I wasn't sure how to get back to the bar. I just stood there, hoping that something would spur me in the right direction, but there was nothing. I finally decided to take a chance and started to walk towards a light at the end of the hall. When I reached the end, I noticed a door that led outside. I eased it opened, and that's when I heard a man's voice yell, "Where did the motherfucker go?"

"He's headed towards the gate!" another man shouted.

I could hear feet pounding against the pavement as several of the guys started charging towards the front gate. Curious to see what was going on, I stepped outside and started walking between all the different motorcycles and cars. As I got closer, I spotted Clay tackling a guy to the ground. Several of the others circled around them, watching as Clay straddled him, using his weight to keep him pinned down. The man was rendered helpless as Clay started punching him, over and over again. It wasn't long before his face was bleeding and he was barely conscious. I couldn't understand it. Clay looked like a wild animal as he continued his assault on the stranger. I thought for sure that he'd stop when the guy passed out, but he didn't. He just kept pounding away at him. He didn't even stop when Gauge shouted, "Clay! That's enough!"

Terrified that he might actually kill the guy, I rushed over and pushed my way through the crowd as I shouted, "Clay! Please stop!"

His body froze as he turned to look at me. I don't know what terrified me more—the state of the man he'd just beaten half to death or the wild look in Clay's eyes as he sat there staring at me. His eyes were still locked on mine when T-Bone and Gauge lifted him off the guy. I couldn't move. I could only stand there and watch as the crowd of men gathered in closer, making it impossible for me to see what was going on. Moments later, Hawk came up next to me, and as he took a hold of my arm, he whispered, "Come on. Let's get you back inside."

"What was that all about?"

"Some guy decided to get rough with one of the club hang-arounds." Hawk looked down at me with concern in his eyes as he replied, "Roughed her up pretty good before she could get away from him."

Hawk was a handsome man, tall and muscular with short blond hair and striking eyes. I noticed his biker vest was different than Clay's. Instead of a prospect patch, his sported one that said Sergeant-at-Arms, and a large Ruthless Sinner's logo was embroidered on the back, letting me know he and Clay weren't in the same club. "Was he a member of Satan's Fury?"

"No." Hawk shook his head. "Just a friend-of-a-friend kind of thing."

I couldn't think straight. All I knew was I needed to get the hell out of there. Hoping he would help me out, I looked up at Hawk and said, "I really need to go. Would you mind walking me to my car?"

"I'm not sure that's a good idea. It's late and with all that's gone down—"

"Hawk, please," I pleaded. "I really just want to go home."

"Okay, but I'm going to follow you ... just to make sure you get there safe." When I nodded, he asked, "What about your keys and stuff?"

"I left them in my car."

"All right then. Let's do this."

I was thankful that the crowd was still gathered around the back gate, so no one seemed to notice as Hawk followed me over to my car. Once I was settled inside, he ordered, "Wait for me to pull around, and then I'll follow you out."

"Okay."

I waited as Hawk got on his motorcycle, and once he'd pulled up behind me, I drove out of the parking lot and out onto the highway. My mind was still reeling as I started towards my apartment. I'd never seen a fight, not like that, and I couldn't get it out of my head. I found myself wondering if I'd been wrong about Clay. Maybe he wasn't the nice guy I'd thought he was. I just didn't know anymore, and the thought sickened me. I was still struggling to come to terms with things as I pulled up to my apartment. When I got out of my car, Hawk called out to me, "You okay?"

"I don't know. I'm still trying to figure that out."

"Can I offer some advice?"

"Sure. I could definitely use some."

"Club life isn't for everyone. Take some time ... think about things, and don't make any rash decisions." He looked me dead in the eye and said, "You're a smart girl. You'll figure out what's best for you."

"Thank you, Hawk." I held my keys in my hand as I added, "And thanks for following me home."

"No problem." He gave me a quick nod. "I hope I haven't seen the last of you."

Without giving me a chance to respond, he whipped out of the parking lot. Once he'd disappeared into the darkness, I went inside and took a long, hot shower. I was hoping it would help clear my head, but it didn't. My mind was still running a mile a minute as I crawled into bed. As I lay there, I thought back over everything that had happened while I was at the clubhouse. The was no denying that the fight was bothersome. No, it was more than bothersome. It made me question everything, especially where Clay was concerned. I couldn't believe that the man who'd been so good to me, who'd just made love to me, could be so brutal, so out of control.

I rolled to my side, and as I closed my eyes, my mind drifted back to the party. While I was disappointed that I didn't get to spend more time with Clay, I'd really enjoyed being there. Clay was right when he said they acted like they were family. They laughed and carried on like they'd known each other their entire lives, and even though we'd never met, they included me in the fun, making me feel at home with them. It was that thought I held on to as I drifted off to sleep.

The next morning, I woke up in a foul mood and struggled to get out of bed. It had been ages since I took a day for myself, so I decided to just stay put. I'd made up my mind that other than getting up for coffee and random snacks, I was going to stay in bed and binge-watch Netflix. I was actually pretty excited about it. I had several shows I'd been wanting to catch up on, and I was finally getting my chance. Like a kid playing hooky, I turned on the TV and snuggled up with my favorite blanket. I was just starting to get wrapped up in one of my favorite series when my cell phone started to ring. I glanced down at the screen and groaned after I saw it was my mother. I wasn't in the mood to talk to her or anyone else for that matter. I just wanted a little time to escape into my show and not think about the outside world or the people in it, so I flipped the ringer and tossed my phone on the other side of the bed. I kept it off the entire day, hoping it would be enough to keep the wolves at bay. Unfortunately, it didn't.

Just as it was starting to get dark, there was a knock at my door. It wasn't like my mother to show up unannounced, but after not returning her calls, I wouldn't put it past her. I eased out of bed, and I'd almost made it to the kitchen when another round of knocking ensued, only this time it was more frantic. I rose up on my tiptoes and grumbled curses under my breath when I found my mother standing on my doorstep. I unlocked the deadbolt, then opened the door and fussed, "Mom, what are you doing here?"

"I came to check on you!" A grimace crossed her face

as her eyes scanned over my disheveled hair and wrinkled pajamas. As usual, she was looking great in her black, scoop-neck t-shirt and jeans. Her makeup was on and her freshly colored hair was styled perfectly, making me even more aggravated that she'd intruded on my free day. She reached out to touch my forehead as she asked, "Are you sick?"

"No, Mom. I'm fine."

"Then why didn't you answer any of my calls?" she shrieked. "I was worried something was wrong."

"I turned off my ringer."

Her brows furrowed. "Why did you do that?"

"I don't know," I scowled as I dropped my hand to my hip. "Maybe it's because I didn't want *to be disturbed*."

"Why, is something wrong? Did something happen with that guy who helped you with the dog?" She dropped her keys and purse down on the table, letting me know that she wasn't just checking to see if I was alive. She wanted to know all the juicy details of my night out, but that wasn't going to happen. I wasn't ready to discuss it, not with her or anyone else. When I didn't immediately respond, she kept at it. "Was he at that party last night?"

"*Mommm*, stop!" I dropped my head into my hands and groaned. With my hands still covering my face, I told her, "The party was fine."

"Then, what's wrong?"

"Everything ... and nothing." I looked up at her, and guilt washed over me when I saw the anguished expression on her face. "I just needed a bit of time to figure some things out."

"What kind of things?"

"Mom ... I need you to stop pushing. I'll talk to you about it when I'm ready."

"Fine. I won't say another word." That was something I'd heard many times from her and knew it wasn't true, so I wasn't surprised when she said, "Just tell me ... Did you wear the black dress?"

"Yes, Mother. I wore the dress."

"Good." With a proud smirk on her face, she reached for her purse and keys. "I'll let you get back to whatever it was you were doing."

"Thank you." I gave her a quick hug and walked her to the door. "I'll give you a call tomorrow."

"Okay. Enjoy the rest of your night." As she started towards the door, she called, "Don't forget to turn your ringer back on."

"Yes, ma'am."

I closed the door behind her, then went over to the refrigerator to grab something to eat. After I made myself a sandwich, I carried it back into my room and turned my show back on. I was just about to start eating when I spotted my phone at the end of my bed. Curious to see if my mother's calls were the only ones I'd missed, I reached for it, and my chest tightened the second I saw that I had a message from Clay.

CLAY:
We need to talk.

THOSE FOUR SIMPLE words made me want to crawl back under my covers and hide. I knew he was right. We did have things we needed to talk about, but as I stared down at my phone, I couldn't make myself respond to his message. I don't know why I was being such a coward. It wasn't that my feelings had changed for Clay. I still thought he was an amazing guy, and when we made love, it was unbelievable. I'd never felt such passion with any man, and while I wanted to experience that again, I needed to be sure that I was thinking with my brain and not my hormones. I was trying to think of a good response to his text when my phone started to ring with a number I didn't recognize. Thinking it was probably a telemarketer, I was hesitant to answer, but after several rings, I took a chance and answered.

"Hello?"

"Is this Ms. Dawson?" a young girl asked.

"Yes, it is. May I ask who's calling?"

With a slight tremble in her voice, the child answered, "It's Katie ... Katie Coburn."

"Oh, hi, Katie. How are you?"

"Not good. It's my dad." I'd given her my number in case of an emergency, but I was hoping that she wouldn't have to use it. Sadly, that wasn't the case. "He's ... uh ... been drinking ... *a lot* a-and he's trying to make me blow in that thing in his car again so he can drive. I don't want to, Ms. Dawson, but he's getting really mad."

There was an awful commotion in the background while she spoke, and I began to panic. As I got out of bed and started to remove my pajamas, I asked her, "What's that noise?"

"That's him." Hearing the terror in her voice gutted me. "I locked myself in the bathroom, and he's throwing stuff at the door and yelling."

"Where's his girlfriend?"

"She's gone." Her voice cracked and she started to cry. "They got in a fight, and he kicked her out."

Hoping to keep her distracted, I asked, "Do you know what they were fighting about?"

"The gas bill or something. They're always ..." As she explained how the argument began, I pulled up my messages and sent a text to Danny, an officer down at our local precinct who I'd worked with on several different cases, letting him know about the situation. When he asked for the address, I was too rattled to remember offhand, so I rushed into the kitchen and grabbed the Coburn file out of my bag. Once I had the information, I sent it over to him, then sent another message to Mrs. Hawkins, my supervisor, to fill her in on the situation. I'd just completed the message when Katie asked, "Are you still there?"

"Yes, honey. I'm right here." I didn't want to scare her even more, so I tried to keep my tone calm and reassuring as I told her, "I'm sending someone over to the house so they can check on you."

"Wait ... you're not coming?"

"Yes, but he can get there a lot faster than I can," I explained, as I pulled my hair up into a messy bun. "I just need you to try and hold tight until he gets there. Okay?"

"Yes, ma'am. I'll try." Mr. Coburn started screaming Katie's name along with a long stream of curses as he pounded on the door. "He's right outside the door. Can you stay on the phone with me until you get here?"

"Of course." I jerked my shoes on, and as I grabbed my purse and keys, I told her, "I'm leaving my house now. Just keep talking and let me know when the police arrive."

"Okay."

As much as I loved my job, it was moments like this that made me question if I was strong enough to handle all the suffering that came along with it, especially when the kids were so young and defenseless. As I got in my car and headed towards the Coburn home, I wasn't thinking about anything except getting Katie to safety. With my mind so preoccupied with her, I didn't think about Clay or the text he'd sent. I'd soon find out that the same didn't hold true for him.

PROSPECT

"*Y*ou did what?"

"I followed her home," Hawk answered. "I knew you'd want to know that she made it home safe."

"Yeah, but it would've been nice if I'd had a chance to do that myself." I'd seen the look on her face after she saw me plowing into that fuck-up. Hell, it'd been burned into my memory, and I hoped I'd be able to explain what had gone down. That didn't happen. As soon as the dust settled, I set out to find her, but she was already gone. It didn't help matters that she wasn't answering my calls or my texts. I shook my head as I continued, "Or at least gotten to talk to her before she hightailed it out of here."

"Sorry, brother. I tried to get her to stick around, but she was set on leaving."

"You'll get your chance to sort things out." Viper patted me on the back. "She'll be back."

"You sound pretty sure of yourself."

"That's because I am." He smiled. "I saw the way that

girl was looking at you. Just trust me when I say, give her time. She'll come around."

I watched as some of the other Sinners started loading up. They stayed longer than they'd planned, but after a long night of partying, it took them some time to recover. Viper looked none the worse for the wear. In fact, it looked like the man had gotten a full night's rest and was ready to take on the day. I, on the other hand, felt and looked like complete shit. I certainly wasn't in the right frame of mind to be patient the way I needed to be with Landry. I wanted to set things straight with her sooner rather than later, but decided that I would do what I could to take a step back and give her some time like Viper had suggested. I gave him a nod, then replied, "I don't exactly like it, but I guess you're right."

"I usually am." A knowing smirk crossed his face as he patted me on the back. "The sooner you learn that, the better off you'll be."

"Mm-hmm. Whatever you say, boss."

"We're about to roll out." He gave me a sidelong, man-hug, then started towards the others. "Keep in touch!"

"You know I will."

I watched as Viper walked over to Gus, and after he said his goodbyes, he and the rest of the Sinners hopped on their bikes. They started up their engines, the sounds blaring, and one by one, they pulled out of the gate. Once they were gone, I leaned down and rubbed my hand over Duchess's head. "How ya doing, girl? You ready for something to eat?"

When she stood up and started wagging her tail, I knew I'd gotten my answer. I strolled towards the club-house and she followed right behind me. We were just about to head inside when I heard T-Bone shout, "Yo, 'Crusher'! Where ya running off to so fast?"

The brothers had yet to come up with a road name for me, so they usually called me "prospect" or simply by name. Crusher wasn't one I'd heard around the clubhouse before, so I wasn't sure who he was actually talking to. Curious, I turned around and was surprised to find T-Bone and several of the others behind me. At that moment, I realized he was talking to me. "Crusher?"

"Yeah, Crusher. After the way you crushed that guy's skull last night, I'd say the name suits ya." T-Bone turned to the others as he asked, "What about y'all?"

"Crusher ... Yeah, that could work, or 'Hammer.'" Blaze chuckled as he explained, "'Cause he hammered him pretty good."

After being called prospect for the past couple of months, I was eager to finally get a road name, but I knew better than to get my hopes up. The guys were always fucking around, especially with the prospects, so I tried to keep a level head as Shadow looked down at my hands. His eyes were fixed on the various gashes and bruises. "Could call him 'Knuckles.'"

"Knuckles ... yeah." Riggs nodded. "The kid definitely knows how to throw a fucking punch."

"That he does," Gauge agreed. "After that asshole put his fucking hands on Jasmine like that, I'd say he gave that piece of shit what he deserved."

"Hell yeah, he did," Blaze replied. "Had to know he couldn't get away with that shit, especially not here. I would've fucked him up myself, but Bruiser here beat me to it."

"'Bruiser.' I like it."

T-bone was about to continue but stopped when Gus walked up, parting the group as he looked at me with a serious expression. My hopes of acquiring a road name quickly dashed when he announced, "Prospect, you and I need to have a word."

"Yes, sir."

I could tell by his tone that he wasn't happy with me. I just wasn't sure what had set him off. The group fell completely silent as they watched Duchess follow Gus and me into the clubhouse. Knowing they were just as clueless as I was made me even more apprehensive as we followed Gus down the hall. When we got to his office door, I ordered Duchess to sit in the hall, then followed him inside. My mind was racing, and it didn't help matters that Gus was being so fucking quiet. Hell, he didn't say a word as he walked over to his desk and sat down. He motioned his hand to the chair in front of his desk, so I quickly took the cue and sat down. Still, Gus said nothing. He just sat there, staring at me with those dark eyes.

Even at my size, it was hard not to feel intimidated by him. It wasn't just his broad, bulked-up chest and thick biceps that were getting to me. It was much more than that. Power and strength radiated off the man, making him a legend among bikers, and the last thing I wanted was to piss him off. I would never purposely do anything to jeopardize my chance of earning a patch, and I prayed that his displeasure was something I could fix.

After several long, torturous moments, Gus finally said, "You're a regular Dr. Jekyll and Mr. Hyde. Here I was thinking you were just a good ol' boy, but after last night,

I got all the confirmation I needed to know that there's another side to you."

I could tell by the look in his eye that he was just getting started, so I didn't respond; instead, I just sat back and listened. "Saw it first during our encounter with the Disciples. When all hell broke loose, you'd been ordered to return to the clubhouse, but you hadn't listened. Instead, you put everything on the line and stayed behind. Good thing you did. Things might've ended differently for Rider if you hadn't, but the fact remains—the guy who'd always done what he was told didn't follow orders. Then, last night ... Hell, you were a completely different person while you were beatin' the shit out of that guy."

"Yes, sir." I knew I'd lost control. It wasn't something new to me. It seemed I had a bad habit of not knowing when enough is enough, and beating that man to an inch of his life was no different. "I lost it when I saw what he'd done to Jasmine, but I didn't mean to take it that far."

"I know you didn't. That's the problem." He grunted under his breath as he shook his head. "Let me make this clear. I wouldn't have cared if you put a bullet in that motherfucker's head. As far as I'm concerned, he had it coming after what he'd done to Jasmine, but it's what happened to you that concerns me. You *blacked out.* You let your rage take over, then slipped into Mr. Hyde."

I couldn't argue. Everything he'd said was spot on. A feeling of defeat washed over me as I ran a hand through my hair and said, "You're right. I did."

"I need to know what was going on in your head when you went after him."

"Alyssa ... my sister."

I spent the next few minutes telling him about the

night she'd come to me after Homecoming. Once I was done, he leaned back in his chair and crossed his arms as he asked, "You ever share that story with anyone?"

"No, sir. Not even Viper knows what happened to Lyssa that night."

"So, you kept your promise to your sister, even when it would've been easier to divulge her secret?"

"Yes, sir. I gave her my word, and I intend to keep it." I looked him straight in the eye. "Today is the first time I've ever broken a promise between us."

"Her secret will never leave this room," he assured me. "How's she dealing with what happened?"

"The best she can." I lowered my head and studied the floor. "It hasn't been easy, but she's always been tough. She'll figure it out."

"And you? Are you going to be able to figure this shit out?" Before I had a chance to respond, he continued, "Being a brother of this club means more than wearing a patch, son. You've gotta be able to keep a level head, *maintain control*—even when it feels like there's none to be had. You also need to follow fucking orders. You think you'll to be able to manage that?"

"Yes, sir. I give you my word."

"Good. That's what I was hoping to hear." He stood up and said, "Met your friend last night. Seems like a nice girl."

"Yes, sir. I think so."

"She have any luck finding a place for the dog?"

Hoping he might've been able to convince Samantha to keep her, I answered, "No, sir. You wanna take her off my hands?"

"Wish I could. She's clearly a smart dog, but she's just

too damn big." He chuckled as he made his way around his desk. As I stood up, he continued, "You're looking for a place of your own, aren't ya?"

"I am."

"Maybe you should consider keeping her. Not often a dog like her comes around."

"I'm thinking about it."

"Good." He slapped me on the back, "Rider said you were heading over to his place to discuss Monday's run."

I'd been on runs before but hadn't had the opportunity to be with the guys during a pipeline run. Along with our own, we'd be hauling cargo from four other chapters down to Mobile, so there was no room for any mistakes, especially from me—not after I'd already fucked up. I nodded as I replied, "That's the plan."

"All right. Let me know if you have any questions when he's done."

"Will do."

With that, I walked out of his office and, with Duchess in tow, down the hall to my room. After I fed her and filled her water bowl, I fell back on the bed and stared up at the ceiling. While I was lying there and thinking about everything that'd happened over the past twenty-four hours, I caught a hint of Landry's perfume. And just like that, all I could think about was how good she'd felt in my arms. I hated to think that I might've lost her, especially when I hadn't had the chance to explain myself. The thought had me reaching for my phone. Noticing that she hadn't returned my calls, I sent her a text, telling her we needed to talk but there was no response. I tried not to let it fuck with my head, but it did, nonetheless. Hoping a distraction might help get my mind off things, I got up, then Duchess and I headed towards the bar. After last night's party, I needed to double-check the inventory and finish cleaning up anyway.

By the time I was done, I needed to get over to Rider's place. I let the guys know where I was off to and, with Duchess in tow, ran out to my truck. Once I got her loaded up, we were on our way. Rider's place wasn't anything over-the-top, just an older two-bedroom home in a good neighborhood near the center of downtown. As I pulled up in his driveway, I wondered if I could find something similar for myself. Something with a backyard for Duchess and enough room for a family down the line. I was surprised that the thought of having a family had even crossed my mind. It seemed Landry had had more of an effect on me than I'd realized. Before I had a chance to really consider the notion, Rider stepped out the house and motioned for me to come inside. "Come on in. I've got a cold one waiting on ya."

"Good!" I replied as Duchess and I got out of the truck and walked up the steps. "I could use a cold one. Hell, I could use about a dozen."

Rider chuckled. "Get your ass in here and quit the whining."

"Just telling it like it is." I was about to enter with Duchess when I stopped and asked, "It gonna be all right if she comes in, or should I tie her up out here?"

"She'll be fine as long as Scout doesn't spot her." While I'd never seen either of them, I'd heard many stories about Darcy's cat and her dwarf rabbit. For small animals, it sure seemed like those two were always into something. Rider held the door open as he waved us both forward. "Bring her on in."

As soon as I stepped inside, the scent of home cooking made my stomach start to growl. "Damn. Something's smelling awfully good."

"Darcy made lasagna. Let's get to the kitchen and I'll fetch you that beer." I followed him through the small entryway towards the kitchen, and Rider grabbed a beer out of the fridge and offered it to me. "How you making it today?"

"I've been better, but nothing a little sleep won't fix. How you doing, Darcy?"

"I'm just fine, thanks. Maybe a good dinner will help too." Darcy was standing at the stove, finishing up the garlic bread. She turned and looked over her shoulder with a smile. "It's almost ready. Just need to put the bread in the oven and make up the salad."

"Smells great." It seemed strange to see her standing there at the stove looking like a typical housewife. Normally, I only saw her at the garage. Cussing like a sailor in her painters suit, she seemed more like one of the guys than an ol' lady. Darcy was a pretty girl, but she was tough and didn't take shit off of anyone. I liked that about her. We all did, and if I had to guess, it was one of the reasons why Rider had hooked up with her. "You need a hand with anything?"

"No, I'm good." She used her hand to motion us out of the room and ordered, "You two go discuss your club stuff, and I'll call you when it's done."

Even though Darcy worked at the club's garage, she wasn't privy to any of the club's business. While it wasn't always easy for them to understand that it was for their own protection, the brothers' women had become accustomed to the fact that there were certain elements of their men's lives that they'd never truly know or understand. Rider walked over and kissed her on the cheek, then popped her on the ass. "Thanks, babe."

I hit my thigh, signaling Duchess to follow as Rider and I walked outside onto the porch. As soon as I sat down, Duchess settled in next to me, resting her head on the tip of my boot. Moments like that made it difficult not to get attached to her. Unable to resist, I leaned down and gave her a quick rub on the head, then rested back in my seat and took a sip of my beer. Wasting no time, Rider turned to me and said, "You've been on a run before, so you might think you've already got the gist of things. You need to know this one's gonna be different. Very different. There's a lot on the line, but if things go as planned, there'll be a hell of a payout."

He took some time to explain how the shipments were carried in two different horse trailers. The crates were hidden beneath the trailer floor in secret compartments that Gus had installed to help throw off the cops, or anyone else for that matter, if they happened to run into any trouble. "Blaze and Shadow will lead in the trucks. You'll follow behind with me and T-Bone. It'll be our job to keep an eye on things, and when we get to the dock, we'll go in first. We'll survey the area ... check for any signs of trouble."

"Got it. And if all's clear?"

"We'll meet up with Ronin, our distributor. He and his crew should be at the dock waiting on us so they can help load everything onto the yacht."

"The yacht?"

"Yeah. They originally used a barge to move the shipments, but after some fuck-up, Ronin purchased the yacht," Rider explained. "It's a little unconventional, but there's not much about all this that isn't."

"I can't disagree with you there," I scoffed.

"Just remember. There's a lot weighing on this." His expression turned fierce as he said, "No mistakes. Got it?"

"Got it."

"Now, that we've got that out of the way ... How's it going with the brothers? You getting a sense of what they're about?"

"Yeah, I'm getting there." I leaned back in my chair as I told him, "There's a lot to get down. Hard to keep it all straight in my head, especially with all the running there is to do."

"I remember." He shook his head and sighed. "There were times when I thought I'd never get it right, but I did and you will too."

"I sure as hell hope so."

"So ..." From the look on his face, I figured he wanted to hear about my conversation with Gus, but instead, he asked, "How'd things work out with your girl?"

"Got no idea." I took a chug of my beer. "I haven't talked to her yet."

"Don't sweat it too much. Things have a way of working themselves out."

"Yeah, maybe."

The back door opened, and Darcy stuck her head out. "Okay, guys. Dinner's ready when you are."

"Coming!" Rider answered before turning his attention back to me. "Let's go eat. I'm starving."

I nodded, then Duchess and I followed him up to the back door. We were just about to head inside when I stopped Rider. "So, you aren't gonna ask about what went down with me and Gus today?"

As he opened the door, he glanced back at me, and with a typical Rider response, replied, "Nope. That's between you and him."

Without any further discussion, we went inside. Duchess and I made our way into the kitchen, and Rider started helping Darcy get everything on the table. I went over and gave them a hand, and it wasn't long before we were all seated and making ourselves a plate. Everything smelled incredible, and it tasted even better. While I managed to leave there with a full stomach, I didn't leave with a clear head. Instead, I had even more on my mind than I did when I'd arrived. I needed to focus on the upcoming run, and *only* the run, but I knew that wasn't going to happen until I resolved things with Landry. I was on my way back to the clubhouse when I found myself driving in a completely different direction. Twenty minutes later, I was pulling up to Landry's apartment door. When I looked around, I didn't see her car in the parking lot. I still took a chance and knocked on her door, but there was no answer. It was impossible not to feel frustrated. I needed to set things straight with her, but that wasn't going to happen—at least not tonight.

LANDRY

*I*t was after two in the morning when I finally pulled into my parking lot. I was mentally and physically exhausted and just wanted to get into bed. I could barely keep my eyes open, much less think straight, as I got out of my car and started towards my apartment. I was just about to unlock the door when I heard, "Landry?"

Even though I recognized Clay's voice, he'd startled me by coming up behind me in the dark. With a terrified gasp, I whipped around and shrieked, "Shit! You scared the hell out of me, Clay!"

"Sorry. I figured you heard me walking up."

"Well, I didn't," I fussed. "What are you doing here anyway?"

"You haven't returned my calls."

"Yeah, well ... I've been busy." A disapproving look crossed his face, but he said nothing. He just stood there waiting for some explanation as to where I'd been. I was too tired to argue with him, so I unlocked my door and went inside. He followed me into the kitchen and waited patiently as I placed my things on the table and removed my coat. When I was done, I walked over to the sink and poured a glass of water, trying to collect myself. Sadly, it didn't stop my voice from trembling as I turned to him and said, "I had to remove a girl from her home and put her into protective custody tonight."

"Why? What happened?"

"The girl's father decided to get plastered after getting into an argument with his girlfriend. It's not the first time this guy's had issues with alcohol, but this time ... he really screwed up, and it could quite possibly cost him his daughter."

"Fuck." Clay ran his hand through his shaggy hair, brushing it back out of his eyes. "She gonna be put in foster care or something?"

"Yes. At least, temporarily." I shrugged with defeat. "It'll be up to the judge to decide if we need to put her somewhere more permanent."

He took a step towards me and placed his hands on my hips. "It'll sort itself out."

"I know." Tears filled my eyes as I whispered, "It's just hard to see kids being mistreated, you know? I just want to bring them home with me and keep them safe."

As soon as the words left my mouth, I started to cry. Normally, I wouldn't have been so emotional, but I was simply too tired to keep myself together. Clay wrapped his arms around me, holding me close as I leaned my head on his shoulder and sobbed. After what had happened the night before, I should've resisted, pushed him away, but I felt so safe there in his arms. Without saying a word, he just stood there holding me until the tears finally stopped falling. My head was still resting on Clay's chest when he knelt down and lifted me into his arms, cradling me close to his chest as he carried me into the bedroom and lowered me down on the mattress. After he helped remove my jeans, he leaned down, kissed me on the forehead, then pulled the covers over me and whispered, "Get some rest."

Not wanting him to leave, I pleaded, "Wait! Don't go."

"Are you sure?"

"Yes, I want you to stay."

"Okay, I'll stay, but I've gotta get Duchess out of the truck."

I nodded, then watched as he walked out of the room. When he returned with Duchess, she trotted over to the edge of the bed, licking me hello and wagging her tail wildly as I rubbed her on the head. After several moments, Clay snapped his fingers and ordered, "Okay, girl. Make a spot."

With that, Duchess gave me one last lick before walking to the foot of the bed and lying down with a thud. While I couldn't see her, I could hear her tail thumping against the floor as Clay slipped off his boots, socks, jeans, and t-shirt, leaving him only in his boxers as he climbed into bed next to me. He slipped his arm around me, easing me closer. As I nestled in next to him, I draped my arm across his chest and rested my head on his shoulder. He felt so good lying there next to me that I practically melted into him. He started to trail the tip of his finger up and down the length of my arm as he whispered, "I know you've had a long night and aren't up for a big talk, but I have something I need to share with you."

"Okay."

His voice was low, almost a whisper, as he started, "I

made a promise to my sister that I'd never repeat the story she'd told me on the night of Homecoming, so out of respect for her, I can't tell you much ... just that ... after hearing what she told me, I ended up beating the hell out of her date. Damn near killed the guy."

"Oh God, Clay." My stomach drew up into a knot. I'd heard countless stories of boys taking advantage of young girls—drugging them, even raping them—and the thought of that happening to Clay's sister made my heart ache for him. Even though I felt certain that he did, I asked, "Did that guy hurt your sister?"

Clay didn't answer. Instead, he said, "I'll never forgive myself for not being there to protect her. She's my little sister. I should've been there watching out for her."

"There's no way you could've known anything was going to happen."

"Maybe not, but that doesn't change the way I feel." He turned and looked down at me as he said, "That guilt is one of the reasons I lost it last night. That guy was trying to force himself on one of our hang-arounds and ended up hurting her when she didn't give him what he wanted. As soon as I saw her face, all bruised up and bleeding, I lost it."

"Oh, Clay ... I had no idea."

"I know you didn't. That's why I told you." He leaned down and kissed me once more. "I hadn't had a chance to tell you sooner."

"That was my fault. I shouldn't have bailed on you like that." Feeling guilty, I glanced up at him and said, "I'm sorry."

"Nothing for you to apologize for, Landry."

I snuggled up a little closer and whispered, "Thank you for coming here tonight. It really means a lot to me."

"Good, cause *you* mean a lot to me." He rested his head back on the pillow and closed his eyes as he said, "Now, get some rest, beautiful."

I was tempted to argue, especially when having him so close brought up all those hot memories from the night before, but I was just too exhausted. And from the looks of it, he was too, so I did as I was told and quickly drifted off to sleep. The next morning, I awoke to not only an empty bed, but an empty apartment as well. I lay there a few more minutes before I forced myself out of bed and into the kitchen for a cup of coffee. When I spotted a note from Clay sitting on a little pink box, a huge smile crossed my face. I rushed over to read what it said:

MORNING, *Beautiful,*

Sorry I wasn't there when you woke up. I had to get back to the clubhouse, but I'll give you a call in a bit. Take it easy today.

CLAY

ENJOY YOUR BREAKFAST!

STILL SMILING, I opened the pink box and found it filled with muffins, croissants, and various other baked goodies. It seemed that Mr. Clay Hanson was full of surprises, and I couldn't deny that I liked it. I liked it a lot. After I made myself a cup of coffee, I grabbed one of the chocolate croissants out of the box. I leaned against the counter as I took a bite, and a small groan of pleasure vibrated through me as I stood there savoring the decadent treat. Once I was done, I headed to the bathroom for a shower. As much as I hated to go into the office on a Sunday, I didn't have a choice. I needed to get my reports on the Coburn case sent over to Mrs. Hawkins. The emergency hearing for foster placement would be the following morning, and I wanted to make sure I had everything ready for the attorney who would be handling the case. I had a lot I wanted to get done, so I wasted no time getting dressed and out the door.

When I got to the office, I picked up the phone to call Danny down at the precinct. As soon as he answered, I asked, "How you making it this morning?"

"I'm here. That's gotta count for something, right?" he scoffed. "What about you? Have you recovered from all of last night's excitement?"

"No, but I'm working on it." Danny had been on the force for years, so last night wasn't anything new for him. He'd seen it all before, and even worse. The same didn't hold true for me. I was still trying to wrap my head around everything, and seeing Katie in danger didn't help matters. I thought back to the moment when I pulled up at the house.

Danny had just arrived and was talking to Coburn, who was pacing back and forth on the front porch. I couldn't help but notice the almost-empty bottle of tequila sitting on the table as I got out of my car and started walking towards them. Coburn lost it as soon as he saw me. "What the fuck are you doing here? Are you the reason why this fucker just showed up at my house?"

"I already told you," Danny barked. "A call was made about a possible domestic disturbance. We're here to make sure everything's okay."

"Done told you everything's fucking fine, so the both of you can get your sorry asses off my goddamn property," Coburn slurred.

"I'm sorry, Mr. Coburn. That's not going to happen until we speak to your girlfriend, Casey Michaels, and your daughter." Danny continued towards him as he said, "Where are they now?"

"Casey's gone. I done got rid of her sorry ass," he shouted.

"And Katie?" I asked nervously.

"She's in the house," Coburn answered. "She's fine."

Coburn had scratches on his face, and when I glanced down at his hands, I noticed that his knuckles were all scratched and bloody as well. Seeing his wounds terrified me, making me wonder what he might've done to Katie. It was like he was reading my mind when Danny growled, "I'm going to need to see that for myself."

Without asking for consent, Danny walked past Mr. Coburn and barged into the house. "Hey! Where the fuck do you think you're going?"

As Danny entered the house, I could hear him shout, "Katie! It's Officer Reed. Where are you?"

Coburn raced in behind him, and when Danny reached the bathroom door, Coburn lunged at him, trying to prevent him from getting to his daughter. Thankfully, Danny was stronger than he looked and was able to tackle him to the ground. After he got Coburn restrained, Danny put him in a pair of cuffs and led him out to the patrol car. As he started out the door, I heard him call into the dispatcher and request backup. Once they were outside, I turned my attention to the bathroom door. I cringed when I noticed that the wood was covered in dents and blood stains. I reached for the handle, and when I saw that it was locked, I tapped on the door. "Katie? Are you in there?"

"Ms. Dawson?" she cried.

"Yes, sweetie. It's me. Can you open the door for me?"

Without answering, Katie eased the door open, and my chest tightened when I saw that she was still crying. She rushed towards me, wrapping her arms around me as she sobbed, "You came!"

"Of course, I did." I hugged her tightly. "I'm just sorry I couldn't get here sooner."

"I've never seen him this bad. I was so scared."

"Everything's going to be fine, Katie." I looked down at her as I said, "Your father really messed up tonight, so he's being arrested. I need to know if you have any family in the area who might be able to look after you for a while."

"No, ma'am. Not that I know of."

"Okay, then we'll have to figure something else out." I stood up and asked her, "Do you think you could gather some clothes for me?"

Her lips trembled as she asked, "I'm not going to stay here?"

"No, Katie. It's not safe here, but I promise I'll get you to a place that is. Okay?"

She nodded while she wiped her tears. "Okay."

I followed her into her bedroom and helped gather some belongings, then Katie and I went outside to check on things with Danny and Mr. Coburn. As always, Danny was wonderful with Katie. He helped set her mind at ease as he explained the situation with her father, relieving her of any blame she might be feeling, and I could tell it meant a great deal to her. His soft *side was one of the reasons why I enjoyed working with him, especially in situations like these.*

I was pulled from my thoughts when Danny said, "Thankfully, the asshole hasn't been able to post bail yet."

"I wonder what will happen to him."

"I figure the judge will slam him this time. The charges are stacking up against Coburn: domestic disturbance, domestic violence, child endangerment, assault of an officer, and resisting arrest. I wouldn't be surprised if the judge throws the book at him." He paused for a moment like he was reading over something, then said, "But you know how the court system works. It'll be at least a month or two before he goes to trial."

"Do you think he'll stay in jail until that happens?"

"Doubt it. If I had to guess, I'd say it won't be long before that bat-shit-crazy girlfriend of his comes to get him out."

"You're probably right." I sighed. "You gotta wonder why she'd ever want to be with a guy like that."

"Can't ever tell. Probably 'cause she can mooch off his ass instead of actually getting a damn job of her own."

"Probably so." Thinking back to the reason why I called, I asked, "Would you mind getting me a copy of your report when it's done?"

"Sure thing. Just give me a few minutes to wrap things up, and I'll send it your way."

"Thank you, Danny. You're a sweetheart."

"Anything for my favorite DCS agent."

As soon as we ended the call, I turned on my computer and started filling out my reports. It took hours, but thankfully, I managed to get everything written up and emailed over to Mrs. Hawkins. Thinking I would get a little more work done once I was back home, I put my files in my bag and headed back to my apartment. When I walked in, the box of goodies Clay had brought me for breakfast were still sitting on the counter, taunting me with all their yumminess. Unable to resist, I opened the box, and smiling like a goofy kid, reached inside for a donut. I took a bite, and just as I expected, it was just as amazing as the croissant I'd had earlier. Once I finished, I decided to send Clay a message and thank him for the sweet gesture.

ME:

Just wanted to say thanks for the breakfast. You didn't have to do that.

CLAY:

Hated to leave without saying goodbye, but I knew you needed the rest.

ME:

I figured you had to get back.

CLAY:

I did. Had to help get things ready for tomorrow.

ME:

What's tomorrow?

.   .   .

CLAY:

Going out of town for the day.

ME:

Just for the day?

CLAY:

Yeah. Leaving early. Back late.

ME:

Okay. Well, I hope it goes well.

CLAY:

Thanks. I'll see you when I get back?

ME:

I'd like that.

CLAY:

I'll touch base tomorrow.

ME:

Okay. Talk to you then.

. . .

WHILE I WAS a little disappointed that I wouldn't be seeing Clay again any time soon, I was glad that he'd come over the night before. I still had my apprehensions, but seemingly less bothersome than before, I was able to focus on other things—like work and catching up on chores around my apartment. After I threw a load of dirty clothes in the wash, I cleaned the dishes in the sink and stripped the bed. After a little dusting, I took a break from straightening up to do a little work. It didn't seem like I'd been at it for long when I looked over at the clock and saw that it was after ten. Knowing I had a full day ahead, I decided to call it a night and went to bed.

The following morning, Katie's case was brought before the judge. As expected, he agreed to place her into foster care until the official hearing, which would be in a couple of weeks. Hoping that would be the case, I'd already started searching for the perfect home to place her in. Mr. and Mrs. Hopkins were younger than some of the families I'd worked with, but both were extremely sweet and I liked the fact that they lived in a nice neighborhood close to Germantown. The house was a traditional four-bedroom home with plenty of room for them to foster Katie for the next few weeks. I hoped it would be a good situation for her. From the excited way the foster mother spoke about wanting another child in the home, it was clear that she was happy about taking Katie, which in turn set my mind at ease. She and her husband were even interested in keeping Katie full-time if the courts decided her father was unfit.

On my way back to the office, I found myself thinking

about Clay. As soon as he entered my mind, a smile crossed my face and butterflies fluttered in my stomach. I wished he was near so I could share the good news with him, but then I remembered that he and his brothers would be out of the town for the day. Now that I'd actually had time to really think about it, I found myself curious about not only where they were going, but what they would be doing.

PROSPECT

The brothers and I had been up and moving since well before sunrise. We had to double-check all the crates and get them loaded into the secret compartments of the horse trailers. It was one thing to hear Rider explain how this whole thing worked, seeing it all in action was something else entirely. These men took nothing for granted, taking every precaution necessary to ensure our safety as we headed to Mobile. I was worried that I might fuck something up, but Rider and Murphy were both watching me like a hawk, making sure that I did everything exactly the way it needed to be done. Once we got all the different crates loaded onto the trailer, T-Bone and Gauge brought over the horses and secured them inside. As I stood there looking at the white, seven-foot-wide trailer with two of Gus's beautiful black mares inside, it was hard to believe that there were hundreds of illegal weapons hidden in it. The same held true for the second trailer parked right next to it. I had no idea how Gus came up with the idea, but it was fucking brilliant.

I could tell the guys were getting anxious to get on the road, but no one was moving until Gus gave the word. Since he was nowhere in sight, I decided to run inside the clubhouse for a quick piss-break. I was just making my way back outside when I heard Jasmine call out, "Hey, Clay! You got a second?"

I stopped, and when I turned around, she was standing behind me. As soon as I caught sight of her wicked black eye and busted lip, I wanted to track down the mother-fucker from the other night and have another go. Jasmine was one of many club hang-arounds, but unlike the others, she'd been there a while. She understood how things worked, respected the club, and did her best to be there for the brothers whenever they needed her—and she did it without trying to sink her claws into one of them. I liked that about Jasmine. Hell, we all did, and it was one of the reasons why I'd gotten so angered by the situation the other night. "Sure. What's up?"

"I just wanted to say I was sorry about the other night." A dark red blush crept across her face as she continued, "I tried to handle things myself, but ..."

"Nothing for you to apologize for, Jasmine. That guy was a complete douche, and what happened is entirely on him," I assured her.

"Yeah, but I should've known better. I should've seen that he was a dirtbag from the start and steered clear."

"We all make mistakes." I might've said more, but when I heard Murphy shout that it was time to roll out, I knew I didn't have time. "Sorry, I gotta run."

I turned, and by the time I made it back over to the others, they were all loaded up and ready to head out. Wasting no time, I got in the truck with Rider, Gunner, and Gash. We waited patiently as Shadow and Blaze pulled their trucks out of the gate, then followed behind. With the two large horse trailers, it took some maneuvering to get through downtown, but we finally made it to the Interstate. With over six hours of driving ahead of us and only one quick stop for fuel, I did my best to settle in for the long drive. I glanced over at Rider and Gunner, and just as I expected, their total focus was on the two horse trailers in front of us. It was impossible not to be moved by their commitment to the job at hand. As I turned my attention back to the trailers, I felt good knowing I had them both at my side, and I hoped one day there would be a brother who'd feel the same about me.

By the time we made it to the dock in Mobile, it was already after one. I'd never actually been at a loading dock with all the different cranes, barges, and cruise liners. It was a lot to take in. With everything that was going on around us, I wasn't even sure what we were supposed to be looking out for, but thankfully, Rider and Gunner were able to determine that the coast was clear and signaled to the others, letting them know it was safe to proceed. As soon as they'd parked, Murphy got out of the truck and headed over to a black SUV. Moments later, an average-sized guy with dark hair and black sunglasses stepped out with three other dudes and shook Murphy's hand. While they talked, the rest of the brothers gathered around and took a moment to stretch their legs. I was taking everything in when Rider walked up behind me and asked, "How ya making it?"

"Good." I cocked my head to the side and popped my neck. "My ass and back may never be the same, though."

"Good." He chuckled and gave my shoulder a pat.

"We'll take our time heading back ... grab something to eat and fuel up."

"Sounds great." I motioned my head over to Murphy and the guy he was talking to. "That Ronin?"

"Yeah, that'd be him."

"For some reason, I thought he'd be bigger," I scoffed.

"Don't let his size fool ya," Rider warned. "Ronin isn't a man to be messed with."

Our conversation came to an abrupt end when Shadow opened one of the horse trailers and said, "Come on, boys. Let's get this thing done."

Rider motioned for me to follow as he stepped inside the trailer. He took ahold of the mare's reins and walked her down the ramp, then looked over to me. "You get the other one and follow me."

"You got it."

Following Rider's lead, I took ahold of the second mare's reins and carefully led her out of the trailer and over to Rider. We tied them both to the fence, then went over to the second horse trailer and did the same with the other two. As soon as we had them sorted, we started helping the guys unload the wooden crates, one by one, onto the dollies. When it was my turn, I reached for one of the larger boxes and carried it over to the others. As soon as we had both trailers all unloaded, Blaze turned to me and Gash, "You two get the dollies down to the dock."

"You got it."

Gash and I took control of the dollies and followed the others. When I saw which boat we were headed to, I nearly stopped dead in my tracks. I remembered him mentioning a yacht, but I never imagined that it would be a brand new seventy-foot, high-performance yacht with all the bells and whistles. I tried to keep my surprise under wraps, but when I noticed T-Bone smirking at me, I knew I hadn't done a good job. "It's pretty badass, isn't it?"

"Yeah, it's pretty fucking sharp." I took a quick glance around as we made our way to the lower deck. "I sure wouldn't mind having one of these for myself."

"You and me both."

Once we got below deck, Blaze reached for one of the crates, and as he started to put it in one of the storage compartments, he looked over to T-Bone and asked, "What the hell would you do with a boat like this?"

"It's a chick magnet, brother." T-Bone chuckled. "I'd have so many women, I'd have to shake them off with a stick."

Riggs stepped up to grab a crate, and as he lifted it, he looked over to Blaze and said, "As I recall, he was supposed to win the lottery ... was gonna use the money to buy him a yacht just like this one."

"You're right." Blaze nodded with a snicker as he turned to T-Bone. "Let me guess ... You never bought a ticket."

"Nope." I grabbed a crate, and as I placed it with the others, I heard T-Bone boast, "But when I do, I'm gonna win that motherfucker and get me a yacht just like this one. You'll see."

"Mm-hmm"

The guys continued to joke back and forth, riding each other as they finished stacking the rest of the crates in various storage compartments. Once T-Bone and Blaze made sure that everything was secured, we headed back to the trailers. While Murphy wrapped things up with

Ronin, Rider and I took a moment to walk the mares around for a bit before loading them back into the trailers. By the time we had them secured, Murphy was ready to roll and we were on our way. I hadn't had a bite to eat all day, so I was relieved when they pulled off at a roadside diner for a late lunch. Not wanting to draw any unwelcome attention during the run, none of us were wearing our cuts as we entered the small café, but we still got plenty of stares as our large group made our way to the back of the restaurant. Once we were seated, a waitress came over to get our orders. She was in her late twenties, maybe early thirties, with bleach-blonde hair that was pulled up on top of her head and makeup that was a shade too dark, making her look older than she really was. While she was attractive, it was clear from the scowl on her face that she wasn't in the best of moods. She feigned a smile as she said, "Hi, guys. I'm Layla, and I'll be your waitress. What can I get for you today?"

In typical T-Bone fashion, he looked up at her with a smirk and said, "You could get me your number."

"How about I get your drink order instead?"

"How about both?" Clearly unfazed by her soured expression, he continued to smile as he told her, "I'll make it worth your while."

Ignoring him, she turned her attention to the rest of us and said, "We have tea, soda, and beer. What'll it be?"

We each gave her our order, and once she was gone, Blaze glanced over at T-Bone and said, "You don't ever give up, do you?"

"Never have. Never will."

The corner filled with laughter as the brothers started giving T-Bone a hard time for being turned down once again. They kept at it until the waitress returned with our food. As soon as the plates hit the tables, the group fell silent as we all began stuffing our faces. We were just about to finish up when Riggs leaned over to me and asked, "You still looking for a place?"

"I guess you could say that. I really haven't had much time to look."

"Well, there's a house that just came up for sale a few streets over from me and Reece. Heard the husband got a new job out of town, so they're eager to get it off their hands." He took a quick drink of his tea before continuing, "It's got a fenced-in backyard, so you'd have a place for Duchess if you decided to keep her."

"You got the address?"

"Yeah, I'll text you all the info, but don't wait around. I got a feeling it's gonna go fast."

"Thanks, man. I'll see if I can go by there tomorrow."

"Good. I hope it works out for you." He cocked his eyebrow and added, "If today's run was as good as the last, you should have plenty for a down payment on whatever house you want."

Before I could respond, Blaze stood up and announced, "It's getting late. We better get a move on."

He tossed a couple of hundred-dollar bills on the table —more than enough to cover our bill and a healthy tip for our sullen waitress, then started towards the door. Knowing better than to keep him waiting, we all got up and followed him out to the parking lot. Even though we had a long ride in front of us, the run had gone off without a hitch, and spirits were high as we all headed home.

It was late when we made it back to Memphis, and

by the time we got the horses and trailers put away, it was even later. We were all exhausted, and I was relieved when the guys decided to skip drinks at the bar and head on home instead. I hoped it meant that none of them would need me in the middle of the night, and I would have a chance to get more than a couple hours sleep. When I got to my room, my entire body was aching from the ride, so I decided to take a hot shower, hoping it was ease the pain. Thankfully, it did the trick, and by the time I got out, I was able to walk without being in agony. By the time I'd dried off and put on a pair of boxers, it was almost midnight. Since it was too late to call Landry, I decided to just call it a night and crashed.

The following few days were pretty much a blur. Word had started to get around about Darcy and her expertise in custom painting, and orders were beginning to pile up, which meant we all had to bust our asses to keep from getting behind. But on a good note, the guys were so busy at work, they had little time for anything else, leaving me with a small amount of free time—something I hadn't had much of since I'd started prospecting. Knowing it wouldn't last, I made the best of it and spent as much time as possible with Landry. I even took her to see the house that Riggs had told me about. I enjoyed every second I spent with her, especially those times when we were alone.

"You're going to have to stop looking at me like that."

Landry was sitting at the edge of the bed, and she looked all kinds of sexy in my old Vols hoodie. She twirled a strand of her hair around her finger as she smiled and asked, "Like what?"

"Don't play innocent with me. You know exactly what I'm talking about."

"Are you saying *you don't like* the way I'm looking at you?" With her eyes trained on mine, she stood up from the bed and pulled the hoodie over her head, revealing her black lace bra and panties. "Because I can stop if you want me to."

"Never said I didn't like it." I let my eyes drift over her curves as I growled, "And no, I don't want you to stop ... Not now. Not ever."

"Good." She held my gaze as she reached her arms behind her, slowly removing her lace bra. A mischievous smirk crossed her face as she sassed, "'Cause I can't seem to help myself whenever you're around."

Between the sexy-as-hell smile and the provocative tone of her voice, I could barely keep it together, and it certainly didn't help matters that she was standing just inches away wearing nothing but her lace panties. Damn. I wanted to play it cool, but the woman was killing me. It was all I could do to keep myself from losing it right then and there. I stepped towards her, dropping my hands to her waist as I slowly lowered her onto my bed. Impatient for more, her hands quickly dropped to her hips. Her eyes never left mine as she slowly lowered her panties, inch by inch, down her long legs. She lay there, her naked form sprawled across the bed just waiting to be taken. As I let my eyes drift down her body, I couldn't believe such an incredible creature was mine. Her delicious curves called me as I lowered myself down onto the bed next to her. "Damn, woman. Do you have any idea how beautiful you are?"

I watched her squirm beneath me as I began to trace

the slope of her breast with my fingertips. "Just looking at you makes me fucking hard."

I lowered my mouth to her neck, kissing and nipping at her soft skin as I made my way down her collarbone to her breast. I nipped and sucked her delicate flesh as my fingers worked their way across her abdomen. Heavy pants and low moans filled the room as I made my way further down between her legs; my fingers grazed across her center, circling her, teasing her. Unable to contain herself, she rocked her hips forward, pleading for more. Fuck. Seeing her so worked up had my cock throbbing for attention.

I wanted to make her come undone. I wanted to hear all of her little gasps and whimpers again and again as I pushed her to the edge of her release. Damn. Everything about her had me burning for more. I eased my fingers inside her, searching for the spot that drove her wild. Her hips jolted forward, letting me know the second I'd found it. Landry's breath quickened as her hands dove into the sheet, twisting them tightly in her fingers as her orgasm surged through her body like a bolt of lightning. "That's it, baby. Come for me."

Panting, she muttered over and over again, "Oh, my God."

Hearing her pleasured moans filled me with need, and I couldn't wait a moment longer to have her. I stood up and removed my jeans and boxers before slipping on a condom. A flash of desire crossed her face as I eased down on top of her and raked my throbbing erection against her. "Do you see what you do to me, Landry?"

"Clay," was the only word she could muster.

I knew right then that I would never get tired of

hearing her say my name in that breathy, wanton tone like she wanted me just as much as I wanted her. She pressed her lips to mine in a possessive, demanding kiss as she used her legs to pull me forward, and I felt her tremble beneath me as I slid deep inside her, giving her every aching inch of my cock. Fuck. She was so tight, so warm and wet. After pausing for several breaths, I started to move, slowly rocking against her. I watched as she started to writhe beneath me, her neck and chest flushed red with desire, and her eyes clenched shut. Seeing her so lost in the moment was the sexiest thing I'd ever seen. Hell, I couldn't take my eyes off of her.

Our fingers laced together as I pulled back and thrust inside of her again. I lowered my mouth to hers, kissing her deep and rough before placing my hands on her hips and rolling her over onto her stomach. I lifted Landry up, positioning her on her knees, and relished in the sight of her perfect ass before driving into her once again. After several slow, steady thrusts, I started to increase my pace. Needing to be deeper, I placed my palm on the small of her back, pushing her down slightly to adjust her angle, and she moaned in pleasure when I buried myself inside her once again. She tilted her head back, and I reached for her hair, gently tugging it as I drove into her again and again with a hard and relentless rhythm. The headboard pounded against the wall as she rocked her hips back. Landry wasn't holding back. Instead, she met my every move with the same fevered pace, letting me know without words exactly what she wanted.

When she started to tighten around me, there was no question that she was getting close. I could feel the pressure building myself, forcing a growl from my chest.

Unable to resist, I began to drive deeper, harder. I couldn't wait to see her orgasm take hold once again, to hear those little sounds she made over and over. "I'm going to keep fucking you until you come all over my cock."

Her body grew rigid, and she started gasping for air as the muscles in her body grew taut and her climax took hold. After a brief moment, her muscles began to quiver and a rush of air escaped from her lungs. With my impending release quickly approaching, I continued to drive into her with the sounds of my body pounding against hers echoing throughout the room. With one last deep-seated thrust, I buried my cock inside her as I found my own release.

After several deep breaths, I lowered myself down onto her chest and rested there for just a brief moment, then rolled onto my back, slid off the condom, and tossed it in the basket by my night table. When I pulled her over to me, she rested her head on my shoulder with the palm of her hand on my chest and a satisfied smile on her face. After a few moments of recovery, I was pleased to see that Landry was more than willing to have another go, and then another. In fact, we spent the entire night tangled up together, and would've continued on even longer if my burner cell hadn't started to ring.

LANDRY

I couldn't believe how good everything was going. The Coburn case was finally about to go before the courts. I'd been working day and night, trying my best to be prepared. My major concern was Katie. After all she'd been through, the kid deserved to find a little bit of happiness, and after seeing her with her new foster family, I truly believed she'd found it. I just hoped that after reviewing all the charges against Mr. Coburn, the judge would allow Katie to stay there with them. Things were also great with Aniya and the kids. The last time we'd talked, Aniya seemed to be in much better spirits, especially where her new job was concerned. The hours were much more tolerable, and the pay was better than she'd ever expected. Fiona and Joseph were both on the mend from their colds, and they were both loving the new after-school daycare at the church.

As well as things were going at work, they were even better with Clay. Unlike when we'd first started dating, the two of us were actually getting to spend a bit more time together, and I was loving every minute of it. He had a way of making me feel so beautiful and adored. It wasn't a feeling that I was used to, but it was growing on me. In fact, everything about Clay was growing on me—his smile, his touch, and his protective nature. I knew it was much too soon to be falling for him, but as I curled up next to him in bed, I simply didn't care.

The sun was just starting to peak through the blinds when I leaned over and kissed him softly on the cheek. "Good morning."

"Morning, beautiful." He yawned, then gave me a quick squeeze. "What time is it?"

"From the sounds of it, it's time for you to get moving."

Confusion marked his face as he mumbled, "Huh?"

"Your cell phone ... It just went off again."

"What?" He shot up in bed and reached over to grab his phone off the side table. "Damn, I didn't hear it."

"It's only gone off a couple of times."

As soon as he looked down at the screen, he groaned and pulled himself out of bed. "*Damn it!*"

"What's wrong?"

"The alarm is going off down at the garage."

"Someone was trying to break in?"

"Doubt it." Clay grabbed a t-shirt out of his bag, and as he put it on, he explained, "Riggs checked the cameras and didn't see anything, but since I'm closer, he wants me to go check it out."

"Okay." Trying not to sound too hopeful, I asked, "Will you be coming back?"

"I wish I could, but I've got a crazy day ahead." He

slipped on some socks and a pair of jeans, then started pulling on his boots. "But I should have some time later. You good with that?"

"Yes, I'm definitely good with that." Once he was dressed, he looked down at me with an odd expression. Having no idea what he was thinking, I asked, "What?"

"Do you have any idea how hard it is for me to leave here when you look so damn good lying in that bed?"

"I'll have you know, it's no easier watching you go." I smiled. "But, I'll see you later tonight."

"That you will."

He leaned down and gave me a kiss, but not just any kiss. It was one of those kisses that sent a spark of desire burning through my entire body. Just as I was about to reach that point of no return, he took a step back to release himself from my lips, leaving me all kinds of hot and bothered. When he caught sight of my flushed cheeks and neck, a sexy little smirk crossed his face. "I saw that!"

"What?" he asked innocently.

"You know exactly what!" I teased. "You did that on purpose!"

He was still sporting that same sexy smirk as he put on his cut and started for the door. "Maybe ... you can get me back tonight."

"You can count on it!" I laughed as he and Duchess headed down the hall.

Moments later, I heard my front door open and close, letting me know they were both gone. I lay there for a few minutes and tried to fall back asleep, but failed miserably. Giving up on the idea of more rest, I got up and started getting ready for work. After a quick shower, I got dressed and fixed my hair and makeup, then went into the kitchen for a bite to eat. As soon as I filled my tumbler full of coffee, I tossed a protein bar into my bag and headed to work.

It was still early when I made it to the office, too early for most, so I used the quiet time to drink my coffee and go over the Coburn file. Once I was completely certain that I was ready to testify, I put the Coburn case to the side and started going over a few of my other cases. When I came across the Strayhorn file, I couldn't help but smile. They'd come such a long way since my first visit, and I took pride in knowing I'd helped make a difference in their lives. I just needed to make sure everything was still going well so I could update Aniya's file. I grabbed my things and started out to my car.

I could've just called Aniya instead of driving out to the house, but I was hoping I might get to see Fiona and Joseph since it was a school holiday. When I pulled up to their house, I spotted an old Ford pickup in the driveway that I'd never seen before. I thought it might've belonged to someone in her family or maybe a friend who'd dropped by. I'd soon discover it was neither.

Completely oblivious that I was about to find myself in a precarious situation, I went up and knocked on the door. Just as I'd hoped, Fiona opened the door. She looked absolutely adorable in her purple leggings and unicorn sweatshirt. Her corkscrew curls were pulled back out of her eyes, so there was no hiding the expression on her face. Unlike the times before, she didn't look happy to see mc. Instead, she seemed completely terrified and didn't even speak. She just stood there with a panicked expression when I said, "Hey there, sweetie. How are you this morning? Are you feeling better?"

I was hoping for a verbal response, but she simply nodded. Sensing something was terribly wrong, I asked, "Fiona, is everything okay?"

"Who's at the door!" a man's voice roared.

Fiona's breath quickened as she glanced over her shoulder and whispered, "He's back."

"Who's back?"

Before she could answer, the man shouted, "I asked a goddamn question, and I expect a fucking answer!"

I could hear the loud, storming thud of footsteps approaching, and Fiona's little brown eyes widened as a large man with overgrown curly hair and a thick beard came up behind her. He was a fierce creature, tall with bulging muscles and tattoos covering his body, and his eyes were cold and menacing. I could hear the fear in Fiona's voice as she glanced up at him timidly and muttered, "It's Ms. Dawson."

"Ms. Dawson? Who the fuck are you?" His eyes met mine in an angry glare. "And what the fuck do you want?"

"Hello." I tried my best to sound unfazed by his gruff behavior. "I'm from the Department of Child Services. I'm here to have a word with Aniya."

"Is that right?" he growled. "And why the hell would she want to talk to you?"

Before I could answer, Aniya came up behind him, and my stomach sank when I saw her black eye and the bruises that covered her wrists and arms. It looked like she'd been in a hell of a fight, and it had gotten the best of her. The strong, determined Aniya I'd seen several days prior had been replaced with a meek, terrified soul that reminded me of a wounded animal. I could see the hesitation in her eyes as she placed her hand on his shoulder and whispered, "Stephen, please."

It took hearing his name for me to finally realize that the man was Aniya's husband, the one who'd run out on her and the kids just a few months ago, leaving them to fend for themselves. From the looks of it, his return wasn't exactly a pleasant one. I could see that she was hoping to defuse the situation when she told him, "Ms. Dawson has been really helpful. She's the one who found me that job down at the coffee shop."

"Well, now that I'm back, you're not going to need her fucking help anymore," he sneered. "You got that?"

"But—" she started, but quickly stopped when he raised his hand to her, threatening to hit her once again. "Okay, whatever you say. I don't want to argue."

As he lowered his hand, Stephen turned his attention back to me. "You heard her. She don't need your help no more."

"Yes, I heard her." I was furious, but I tried my best to hide it. "And that's fine, but I'll need to see the kids and make sure they're okay before I leave."

"You got a court order?"

"No."

"Then, you can get your ass off my property!" he barked. "'Cause you aren't welcome here."

"Stephen," Aniya muttered, "You might as well let her come in. She'll just come back with a police escort if you don't."

"I don't give a fuck!" Rage flashed through his eyes as he took a threatening step towards me. "I'm not saying it again, lady. You aren't welcome here, and if you come back with the cops, I'll slit that pretty little throat of yours."

It wasn't the first time I'd been threatened. It was actually fairly common in my line of work, but it was the first time that I actually believed it was more than a simple threat. This guy was off his rocker, and if given the opportunity, he'd make good on his word. I knew better than to push the situation any further than I already had, so I simply nodded and said, "Thank you for your time, Mr. Strayhorn."

I turned and hurried to my car. I was just about to get inside, when I heard him shout, "You best not be back. You'll regret it if you do!"

Without giving him a response, I got in my car, slammed the door, and backed out of the driveway. Once I'd gotten a few miles from the house, I pulled over and made a call into the office, letting Mrs. Hawkins know what had taken place. I became madder and madder as I told her about the threats he'd made. I should've been terrified that a man of his stature had threatened me, but I was too angry to see that my life might've been in danger. I'd worked so hard to help Aniya get back on her feet. I wanted her to be able to provide for her children and give them a stable home environment, but it was clear that wasn't going to be possible as long as he was around. The whole thing weighed on me, making it difficult to think about anything else, so I was relieved when she gave me the rest of the day off.

I'd hoped that some time away from work would help me clear my head, but it didn't. Clay had to cancel because of something going on at the clubhouse, so I ended up spending the entire night alone thinking about Aniya and the kids. I hated seeing the terrified look in Fiona's eyes and those bruises on Aniya's arms. When I wasn't obsessing over them, my mind was on Katie and her hearing the following morning. Everything was still weighing on me the following morning as I headed into the courthouse. As soon as I walked in, I spotted Katie sitting with Vicky, her guardian ad litem. She was wearing a dark, purple dress, and her hair was pulled back in a braid, making her look even younger than she really was. I could tell from her shaking knee and the tense expression on her face that she was nervous, and rightly so. Replaying to the judge what had happened at her home would be difficult for her, but thankfully, she wouldn't have to do it inside the courtroom with her father and everyone else watching. Instead, she would talk to the judge alone in his chambers.

I walked over, and as I sat down beside her, I smiled. "Hey there, kiddo. How ya doing?"

"I've been better."

"I know this whole thing is hard, but it'll all be over soon."

"I hope so." Her eyes drifted to the floor with a sigh. "'Cause I'm really tired of all this. I'm tired of my dad drinking all the time ... scaring me and knocking me around ..." she paused for a moment, then looked up at me, "I love him, I do, but I don't want him to be my father anymore. I want to have normal parents like my friends at school."

In most cases, children didn't want to leave their home, even when they were physically and mentally abused. It was just part of the vicious cycle they'd found themselves in. Having their parents approval was ingrained in them, and they sought it out even when it could never be attained. Katie, on the other hand, had come to the point where she'd detached herself from her father, and I hoped that it would make things a bit easier if she was taken from the home permanently. "Honey, I can't make any promises, but I will tell you this ... Things will get better." I placed my hand on her knee. "Just be honest with the judge, and he'll do what he can to make things right."

"Okay." As she glanced over at the courtroom doors, she asked, "Do you have to go in there?"

"I do, but it shouldn't take long. I just have to answer a few questions."

"Are you nervous about it?"

Even though the thought of testifying had my stomach tied up in knots, I didn't want her to worry, so I replied, "Umm ... a little, but it'll be okay. Like I said, I shouldn't be in there very long."

"Okay."

It was almost time for the hearing to start, so I stood and said, "I better get in there, but I'll see you when it's over."

She nodded and watched as I turned and headed into the courtroom. There were several other cases on the docket, so I wasn't surprised that the room was filled to capacity. When I spotted Danny sitting in the back row, I went over and sat down next to him. "You ready for this?"

"Yeah. Just ready to get it over with," he grumbled as he glared over at Mr. Coburn. "Hell, just looking to see this guy get what's coming to him."

"You and me both."

The room fell silent when the court officer ordered us

all to rise. The judge walked into the courtroom, and in a matter of minutes, court was in session. I was thankful when the clerk announced that our case would be the first to be heard. Both attorneys stood, and just as the proceedings were about to begin, Coburn's lawyer shocked us all by asking for a continuance. The judge gave him a disapproving look as he asked, "On what grounds?"

"The defense needs a little more time to gather evidence. We're still missing some reports from social services, and we'll need those in order to properly present Mr. Coburn's defense."

"Mm-hmm." He cocked his eyebrow with a disgruntled sigh. "And how long are you going to need to gather this *evidence* for Mr. Coburn's defense?"

"A couple of weeks, maybe a month at most."

The judge turned to the opposing counsel as he asked, "Do you have any objections?"

"No, sir. I don't have a problem with agreeing to a continuance as long as the child in question, Katie Coburn, remains in her current foster home until we can proceed with the hearing."

"Understood."

"We'd also like to request a no-contact order."

As soon as the words left the lawyer's mouth, Mr. Coburn started mouthing off to his attorney. It was clear that he wasn't happy about the stipulation, but that didn't stop his attorney from replying, "Mr. Coburn agrees with the terms."

"Then, the continuance is granted. Get the paperwork filed with the clerk and set up a date for the hearing in thirty days."

"Yes, your Honor."

With that, the attorneys started gathering their files, stuffed them into their briefcases, and headed out of the courtroom. Shocked, I turned to Danny and asked, "So, that's it?"

"That's it for now. Looks like we'll be back in thirty days, but at least for the time being, the kid gets to stay put."

"That's definitely a plus."

When we noticed that the next case was about to start, Danny and I got up and slipped out of the courtroom. Considering how things had turned out, I was hoping to get a chance to speak with Katie, but when we stepped out into the hall, she and Vicky had already gone. Since there was no reason for either of us to hang around, Danny and I headed out to the parking lot. As soon as we stepped outside, I spotted Mr. Coburn talking to his lawyer, and it was clear from their expressions that the conversation was heated. When Coburn turned and glared over at me, Danny reached for my arm, stopping me in my tracks. "Hold up ... Let's just wait here for a minute."

"Why?" An uneasy feeling washed over me when I saw the cold, hateful expression on Mr. Coburn's face. "You don't think he'd actually try and do something, do you?"

"Never know, especially with guys like him." Danny glanced over in Coburn's direction. "I just have a bad feeling about the guy."

"Well, hopefully it won't be long until he's behind bars."

We both watched as Coburn shouted once more at his lawyer, then stormed off to his car. Once he was out of sight, Danny and I continued down to the parking lot and over to my car. We said our goodbyes, and as he started to walk over to his patrol car, he waved and said, "Until next time."

I got in my car and pulled out of the parking lot with every intention of driving back to my office, but instead of heading downtown, I found myself going in a different direction entirely.

PROSPECT

I got the fact that Landry couldn't tell me much about her work, just some trivial details here and there. It was her job to keep things under wraps and protect the privacy of the families she was working with, but that didn't mean I liked it, especially when some motherfucker had threatened her. I might've never known about it if I hadn't overheard her talking on the phone with her boss. I'd never heard Landry so upset when she told her, "I would've never gone there if I'd known he was there. You know that?"

There was a pause as she waited for a response. "Yes, but you didn't see the bruises on her face and arms. It was obvious that he'd hurt her, and I needed to make sure that he wouldn't do the same to the kids. I wouldn't be able to live with myself if something happened to them."

Another long pause. "Yeah, he lost it. He got up in my face and reamed me up one side and down the other. The cussing and screaming was one thing, but he said he had people that would do things to me ... really bad things.

Then, he followed me out to my car, took a picture of me and my license plate. Not only that, but I'm pretty sure someone followed me back to my apartment."

At this point, I was ready to blow. I wanted to hunt down this motherfucker and handle him my-goddamn-self, but I knew nothing about the guy. Hell, I didn't even know which coffee shop she was talking about. I should ask Landry about it, but even if I did, I knew she wouldn't tell me. I had no other choice but to stand back and listen as she continued, "No, I didn't actually see anyone, but I just got the feeling someone was watching me."

Moments later, Landry explained, "Yes, ma'am. I'll file a report right now and get it over to you. I'll also give Danny a call and let him know what's up. Maybe he knows something about the guy that can help."

I didn't want Landry to know that I'd been eavesdropping, so I stepped away from the door and went over to Duchess in the living room. I knelt down, and I'd just started to pet her when Landry came walking out of the guest bedroom. Her eyes and nose were red from crying, and she was still sniffling as she made her way over to me. I stood and walked towards her as I asked, "You okay?"

"No, but I will be."

"Anything I can do to help?"

"No, I've got to handle this on my own." She wound her arms around my neck and forced a smile. "But thank you for asking."

"Well, at least let me get you out of here for a little while." If there was even a slight chance that someone had followed her back to the apartment, I didn't want her to be alone, so I suggested, "We could grab some dinner and head over to the clubhouse."

"Okay, but I need to send in my report to Mrs. Hawkins before I can go."

"That's fine. I can wait."

She leaned up on her tiptoes and pressed her lips to mine, before saying, "You're kind of awesome."

"Kind of?"

"Okay, you're a lot of awesome, but don't let it go to your head," she teased.

"I'll do my best."

She kissed me once more, then turned and walked over to her bag. I watched as she sat down at the kitchen table and opened her laptop. I didn't want to disturb her while she worked, so I reached for Duchess's leash and led her over to the door. As I headed out the door, I looked over to Landry and said, "We'll be waiting outside when you're done."

"Okay. I won't be long."

I nodded, then followed the sidewalk down to a grassy area near the parking lot. As usual, as soon as Duchess's feet hit the dirt, she started searching for a place to take care of business. I stood still, trying not to distract her, and used the time to scan Landry's parking lot. I was hoping something would catch my attention, and I could get a clue about who might've been following her. I didn't see much. Just a few empty cars, and a sizable pile of cigarette butts between two parking spaces. At first, I didn't think much of it, but as I stood there staring at it, I realized that someone had to have been sitting in their car smoking for quite some time to make such a big pile of butts. I led Duchess over to the spot, trying to see if they would've had a good view of Landry's apartment. Just as I feared, I could not only see all of her front door, but through her windows, I could see parts of her kitchen and bedroom. Damn.

It didn't take a genius to know that Landry was right about someone following her. From the looks of it, they'd spent a good bit of time watching her as well. Fuck. I was really working myself up into a rage when Landry stepped out of her apartment. With her overnight bag in tow, she started towards me with a smile. "You two ready to go?"

"Absolutely." Easing past the mound of cigarette butts, I made my way over to the passenger side of the truck and opened the door for her. "You got everything?"

"I think so."

"Good deal." I closed her door, and after I got Duchess settled in the back, I hopped inside and started the truck. "So, you have two choices: I can pick something up on the way to the clubhouse, or I can order us a couple of pizzas when we get there."

"I'm good with whatever." When I glanced over at her with a disapproving look, she sighed. "I really don't care."

"Then, it shouldn't be hard to choose one. "

"Okay, fine. Let's just order pizza."

"Perfect." As I pulled out of her parking lot, I chuckled. "See, that wasn't so hard now, was it?"

Landry just shook her head and smiled. On the way to the clubhouse, she barely said two words. I knew she was worried, and I hated that she couldn't talk to me about it. I hoped that I could help take her mind off of things, but I wasn't having much luck. I got us a couple of pizzas and rented a movie, but as we sat there snuggled up together, she seemed a million miles away. I hoped it would pass, but even when we got into bed, she seemed completely lost in her own thoughts. When I couldn't take it a moment longer, I looked down at her and said, "I'm gonna need you to talk to me, Landry. I need to know what's going on in that head of yours."

"I'm sorry. I know I've been off tonight, but work really got to me today. I can't get into all the details, but I screwed up. I screwed up big, and it's making me feel like a complete failure."

"Why would you ever feel like a failure?" While I didn't hear her entire conversation with her boss, I'd heard enough. From what I could tell, it was the husband that had been the one who'd fucked up, not Landry. "You work harder than anyone I know, and if you ask me, you're amazing at what you do."

"Not today. Today I overstepped, and I'll be lucky if I don't get a huge reprimand for it." She brought her hands up to her face, hiding behind them as she muttered, "I should've never gone to her work like that. It will be my fault if she loses that job."

"Why would she lose her job?"

"Because her husband got furious that I showed up there and …" Realizing she was saying too much, her voice trailed off as she groaned. "Let's just say it's complicated."

I was just about to push her to tell me more when her cell phone started to ring. "Don't worry. It's probably my mother."

She eased up out of bed and grabbed her phone off the bedside table. When she looked down at the screen, her brows furrowed with bewilderment. Concerned I asked, "Not your mother?"

"No, it's not." She quickly answered. "Hello?"

There was a brief pause before she said, "Yes, this is Landry Dawson. Can I help you?"

Moments later she continued, "No, not that I'm aware of."

As she listened to the person on the other end of the call, a look of utter panic crept over her beautiful face. She was still listening when she jumped out of bed and started changing out of her pajamas. "Thank you, Mr. Evans. I'm on my way there now, and don't worry about calling the police. I'll call them once I've had a chance to check things out."

As soon as she hung up the phone, I asked, "What's going on?"

"That was Mr. Evans. He manages my apartment complex, and he thinks someone broke into my apartment."

I got up and started to get dressed along with her. "Thinks?"

"Well, he said my door was wide open, and it looked like someone had been poking around. Not sure what he meant by that, but he left things the way they were and locked the door. Regardless, I need to get over there and check it out."

"Absolutely."

As soon as I grabbed my cut and keys, we were out the door. When we pulled up to her building, Landry jumped out of the truck and raced towards her apartment. I got out of the truck and rushed after her, barely catching up before she got to the door. "Hold up, Landry. Let me and Duchess go in first."

"Okay." She stepped out of my way, and after I unlocked the deadbolt, she said, "Be careful."

I stepped inside, and right away I could see that Evans was right. Someone had definitely been riffling through her shit. Not only were chairs knocked over and drawers opened, her work files were scattered all over the table and floor. It didn't look like the asshole took anything, so I could only assume he was trying to scare her. I wanted to clean it all up, protect her from the fear this would bring on, but it was too late for that. Without my realizing it, Landry had slipped into the apartment and was standing in the doorway in complete shock. "Oh my god! Why would someone do this?"

"I don't know, but I have every intention of finding out."

She reached into her back pocket and took out her phone. When she started dialing a number, I asked, "Who are you calling?"

"The police."

"Wait ..."

I started, but stopped when she held up her hand and said, "I get why you and your brothers might not want to deal with the cops, but this is me and my place that's been broken into, so like it or not, I'm calling them."

Even though I'd never discussed club business with her, Landry had her suspicions, and she was right about the cops. The club never got tangled up with them. It just wasn't worth the risk. While I didn't like the idea of her calling them now, I understood why she found it necessary, especially with her line of work. I didn't say a word as she made the call, and it wasn't long before two officers showed up at her door. I was unaware that she actually knew one of the cops until she told him, "I bet when you said until next time you weren't thinking it would be this soon."

"No, I can honestly say I didn't." He took a quick glance around her apartment as he asked, "Do you have any idea who might've done this?"

"A few come to mind, I'm sure the same ones that come to your mind, but I really can't say for sure."

When he finally made his way over to me, he extended his hand and said, "I'm Officer Daniel Michaels, and who might you be?"

Before I could answer, Landry replied, "This is Clay. Clay Hanson."

"Oh, so this is the guy you were telling me about."

A light blush crept over her face as she said, "Yes, this is him."

"Nice to meet ya, Clay." As we shook hands, he continued, "I hope you know you've got quite a girl here."

"Yes, I'm fully aware."

With that, he released my hand and got down to business. He reached into the front pocket of his coat for his notepad and jotted down a few things before asking, "Have you noticed if anything has been taken?"

"Not that I know of."

"And this is how you found the place when you got home?"

"Yes."

He asked a few more questions and took several more notes, and once he started wrapping things up, he looked over to Landry and said, "Okay, I'll get with your security guard and see if he noticed anyone snooping around. If we're lucky, they'll have some camera footage that might help us identify who did this."

"And what should I do until then?"

He glanced over at me as he asked, "I don't feel good about you staying here. Do you have somewhere you could stay tonight?"

"I could stay—"

"You're staying with me," I interrupted. "And don't even think about trying to argue. This isn't up for debate."

"All right then. Now, that *that's* settled, we'll be on our way." Michaels snickered. "I'll check with the guard on our way out."

"Thank you, Danny."

"No problem." He glanced over at me as he said, "You be sure to keep a good eye on her. We don't want anything to happen to our girl."

I didn't like the way he called Landry "our girl." I didn't like it one fucking bit, but I bit back my displeasure as I replied, "You don't have to worry about that."

He and his partner quickly said their goodbyes, and then they were out the door. Once they were gone, I helped Landry gather her files off the floor and pick up the chairs that were strewn in the living room. I could tell she was upset, but knowing she had a lot on her mind, I didn't push her to talk about it. I knew she'd open up to me when she was ready. After I helped her gather a few of her things, we locked up her apartment and drove back over to the clubhouse. She was still painfully quiet as she undressed and got back into bed. When I crawled in next to her, she curled up beside me, resting her head on my shoulder as she whispered, "Thank you."

"What exactly are you thanking me for?"

"For everything. I know this has all been a hassle, and I'm really sorry you got dragged into it."

"Let me make this clear once and for all: I want to be involved in all aspects of your life ... the good and the bad. I wouldn't be here if I didn't want to, so don't ever apologize for that."

"You sure make it easy to like you. If you aren't careful, I might end up falling for you."

"Might?" I scoffed. "Hmmm ... Looks like I'm gonna have to step up my game."

"Just remember what you're getting yourself into."

"I know exactly what I'm getting myself into." I leaned over and kissed her on the forehead. "And I'm not going anywhere."

"Good."

Landry nestled in closer, and it wasn't long before she drifted off. I looked down at her face, watching her as she slept, and there wasn't a doubt in my mind that I was falling for her. She'd opened my eyes to a world of new possibilities—a future, a family—and my chest tightened at the thought of something happening to her. While I had no idea what I could do, I knew I wasn't just going to lay there and do nothing. I had to find some way to protect her. Being careful not to wake her, I gingerly got out of bed and threw on my clothes. Once I was dressed, I eased the door open and slipped out into the hall. I didn't want to get the brothers involved, but I'd need their help to get some answers. When I stepped into the bar, I was relieved to see that Rider and Riggs were still here. They were sitting at one of the back tables drinking a beer when I walked up. Rider looked up at me with a smile as he ribbed me. "What's up, prospect? You needing a job to do?"

"No, I'm needing a favor."

"What kind of favor?"

"The kind you might not wanna give, but I'm asking all the same."

I sat down next to them and explained the situation with Landry. Neither of them spoke as I told them all about the phone conversation I'd overheard, and all of my concerns about what happened at her apartment. When I was done, Rider looked over to me and said, "I get that you want to do something, but it's not a good idea to get involved."

"I can't just sit here and do nothing." I looked him straight in the eye as I asked, "What would you do if this was August we were talking about?" Then, I turned to Riggs. "Or Reece?"

"I get what you're saying." Riggs leaned forward as he continued, "But I don't get what you're wanting us to do here?"

"I need some help finding out who's doing this shit ... I need to know who I'm supposed to be looking out for, you know?"

"And how do you suppose we find that out?"

"I was hoping you might be able to hack into the social services database and go through her case files. Maybe we could find some answers there."

"Yeah, I could do that." Seeming much more open to the idea than I expected, he stood up and said, "I just need a few minutes on my laptop."

"Thanks, man. I really appreciate."

Rider and I stood up and followed Riggs out of the bar. We were just about to head into Riggs's room when Rider reached for my arm, stopping me as he said, "Before we do this, I'm going to need your word on something."

"Okay." Curious what that could be, I asked, "What's that?"

"If you decide to make a move, any move at all, you discuss it with Gus first."

I wasn't crazy about the idea. I knew Gus well enough that he wouldn't want me getting involved in this shit, especially if there was any chance it could blow back on the club, but Rider left me with no chance. If I wanted answers, I had no choice but to agree. I nodded as I told him, "You have my word."

"Good. I'm going to hold you to that."

By the time we made it into Riggs's room, he was already sitting at his desk, typing away at his computer. Rider and I stood behind him, watching in awe as he worked his magic, and it wasn't long before he'd made his way into Landry's work database. A few minutes longer and Landry's name popped up on his screen. After a few more keystrokes, Riggs shook his head and said, "Damn ... she's got a hell of a case load. There are over thirty active files on here. You got any idea which one we're looking for?"

"I only know about two. One has to do with a girl who was taken out of the home, and the other is a woman who has a bunch of kids. I think Landry just got her a job or something."

"Okay, I'll start with her most recent entries." Seconds later, a report with a young girl's face popped up on the screen. Riggs scrolled through it for a moment, then announced, "I think we've found the first one. Kid's name is Katie Coburn. She was taken out of the home a couple of weeks ago, and from the looks of it, they had a hearing earlier this morning."

"Yeah, that's her." I leaned forward to get a better look. "Can you find anything on the father?"

Seconds later, a man's face appeared on the screen. I was surprised when Rider said, "Wait ... I think I might know that guy. What's his name?"

"Chris Coburn."

"The name sounds familiar. I just can't remember where I've seen him," Rider replied.

"Well, the dude has a hell of a rap-sheet. Looks like he's had more than a few domestic violence charges, a DUI, and recently got charged with assaulting an officer and resisting arrest."

"Does it say where the guy is from?"

"He lives here in Memphis now ... not far from downtown, but he used to live in Oakland. Maybe that's where you know him?"

"Yeah, he was a few years older than Darcy and me."

Riggs looked over to me as he said, "I'll print this all off for you so you'll have it."

"Thanks, man."

"And you said we were looking for a lady with several kids?"

I nodded. "Yeah. One's a little girl that Landry took a liking to... I got the impression she was younger. Four or five, maybe?"

"This might be her. Aniya and Stephen Strayhorn." Riggs opened another file and quickly started reading. "Looks like they've got two kids who are no longer in the home, but two others who still live with them—Fiona and Joseph. Do those names sound familiar?"

"I'm not sure." I shrugged. "She never told me any names, and the details were vague at best."

"Gotcha." Riggs continued reading for several moments, then said, "The mother's name is Aniya. Says she started working at a coffee shop a couple of weeks ago. Hold up ... Landry just filled a report this afternoon. It's a full description of the altercation between her and the husband, Stephen Strayhorn. Damn. He didn't just threaten her, he took a picture of her ... and her license plate."

"Yeah. That has to be the guy she was talking about on the phone this afternoon. I bet that's how he found out where she lives. "

"Maybe, if he knows someone who could run her tags," Rider replied.

When Riggs pulled up his picture and I saw the menacing expression on the asshole's face, my blood ran cold. I wanted to kill that motherfucker for threatening Landry like he had, and from the looks of him, he was more than capable of breaking into her apartment. "So, this guy lives there with the mom and the two kids?"

"I'd say so, but I'd have to read through all these reports to be sure." Riggs grumbled, "I gotta say, your girl is thorough. There's a mountain of paperwork here."

He started typing once again, then seconds later the printer started shooting out one page after the next. Once it was done, Riggs grabbed them and handed them over to me. "This should be enough to get you started. If you need something more, just let me know."

"Thanks, Riggs. I owe you one."

"No problem."

"I guess I better get back to the room before Landry realizes I'm gone."

"Let her know we're here if she needs anything," Rider

told me as I started for the door. "And don't forget. You gave your word that you'd talk to Gus before you made any moves on this."

"I know, I will."

I stepped into the hall, and as I headed back to my room, I scanned through all the papers Riggs had given me. I stopped when I got to the photograph of Stephen Strayhorn. I thought back to the phone call and the state of Landry's apartment, and it was all I could do to keep myself from hunting him down. I knew that wasn't an option, not yet, but I found solace in knowing that I was one step closer to getting this guy. When I made it back to my room, I shoved the papers in my top drawer under my clothes, then quickly undressed before easing back into bed with Landry. She was exhausted and didn't even notice when I settled in next to her. Even though I was just as beat, I couldn't sleep. Every time I closed my eyes, all I could see was Strayhorn, and I kept imagining all the different ways I could find him and take him down.

I was still lying there thinking it all over hours later. Realizing sleep wasn't gonna come, I rose out of bed and got dressed. After taking the papers out of my dresser drawer, I left Landry a quick note, letting her know that I had something to take care of, then headed for the door. Twenty minutes later, I was sitting in a chair on Gus's front porch, watching the sunrise. I don't know how long I'd been perched there when he finally opened the door and said, "What are you doing here, son? Something wrong?"

"Yeah, I guess you could say that." As he walked over and sat down in the chair next to me, I told him, "I have something I need to discuss with you."

"All right, let's hear it."

He listened intently as I told him everything that had taken place with Landry, including the fact that Riggs had hacked into her database. He didn't say a word. He just sat there listening to me with a blank expression. Once I was done, he leaned back in his chair and shook his head. "Looks like Hyde might be back."

"Maybe, but I can't just sit here and do nothing. I love her, Prez." Hoping he'd get my need to protect her, I looked at him and asked, "If this was Samantha, what you would you do?"

"I'd probably go after the guy," Gus admitted. "But I'll be honest with you, son. I don't think it's a good idea for you to get involved in this, especially with the cops investigating it."

"You and I both know the cops aren't going to do shit. Hell, she'd have to get her ass killed before they even consider taking these threats seriously." I growled in frustration. "I just want this guy to leave Landry alone."

"Fine. Do what you gotta do." Gus stood, and his voice was full of warning as he ordered, "Just make damn sure that whatever you do, it doesn't blowback on my club."

"You have my word."

I'd gotten what I'd come for, so I stood up and headed back out to the truck. I pulled out the papers that Riggs had given me, checking the address one last time, and once I'd figured out exactly where I was going, I started the engine and pulled out of Gus's driveway. Half an hour later, I pulled up to an old, shabby blue house with white columns on the front porch that were more chips of paint than anything else. The floor boards and steps leading up to the front door were sagging, barely holding together, and there was an old, beat-up truck and an even older Nissan car parked in the driveway. I eased up to the curb, parking close enough to see who was coming and going, and killed the engine. Since it was still early, I was hoping I'd get a glimpse of the guy taking his kids to school or something, so I just sat back and waited.

Just as I hoped, around seven fifteen, the front door opened and two kids came rushing out. One of them was a cute little girl who looked to be about four or five. Her curls bounced right along with her as she raced in front of her big brother. It was easy to see why Landry had taken to her. As they got closer, I noticed several dark discolorations around her left wrist. I leaned forward and tried to get a better look, but I already knew that they were bruises. I was so focused on the little girl that I hadn't noticed their mother had come outside along with them. She didn't catch my attention until I heard, "Fiona! Let's go, sweetie. Momma can't be late today."

"Okay, Momma. I'm coming."

The little girl rushed over to the car where her mother was standing, and my stomach turned when I noticed that the woman not only had a fierce black eye and busted lip, but there were also bruises covering her wrists and arms, much like the ones her daughter had. I didn't want to jump to conclusions and assume that the husband had been the one to beat her, but the cards were stacking up against him, especially after he came barging out of the house like a mad man. He was a big guy, muscled up with various tattoos and an earring. The veins in his neck pulsed as he stepped off the porch and shouted angrily, "Fiona!"

The little girl stopped dead in her tracks and her face turned white as a ghost as she answered, "Yes, sir?"

He stormed over to her, grabbing her roughly by the arm, and lifted her up with her tiptoes barely touching the ground as he snarled, "What did I tell you about leaving your shit in the living room?"

I'd almost forgotten that Duchess was sitting in the back seat until I heard her start to growl. I turned my head and found her standing with her face just inches away from the glass with her teeth exposed like she was ready to attack. Not wanting her to draw any attention, I reached behind and placed my hand on her back. "Easy girl. I've got this."

She stopped growling but never took her eyes off Strayhorn. I turned back around just in time to hear Fiona say, "I'm sorry, Daddy."

"You're gonna be sorry!" He slung her forward as he ordered, "Get your ass in there and clean that shit up."

And just like that, all the rage that I tried to keep at bay came creeping over me, and it was all I could do not to get out of my truck and kill that motherfucker. My anger continued to rise as I glanced over at the mother, watching as panic washed over her when the guy started walking in her direction. He immediately got in her face, grumbling a stream of curses that I could barely make out, and when she opened her mouth to respond, he back-handed her across the cheek. She quickly dropped her face into her hands and started crying. Without even considering an apology, he barked, "Worthless. The whole fucking lot of you!"

He turned and headed back towards the house, and I was relieved to see that Fiona had made her way back out before he reached the front door. She raced past him and over to the car with her mom and brother. Before she got in the car, the brother put his arm around her shoulder, whispering something in her ear that almost made her smile. Once they'd both gotten in the car, their mother backed out of the driveway, and they disappeared into traffic. I knew I'd just end up getting arrested or worse if I barged into the house, so I had no other choice. I had to wait for him to leave the property.

When I woke up to find myself in bed alone, I was disappointed, but not surprised. With prospecting, it seemed like every time I turned around, Clay was on the go, but without fail, he'd always found a way to be there when I needed him. It was one of the many reasons I'd found myself falling in love with him. With everything that was going at work, I didn't have time to lie around and daydream about Clay, so I forced myself out of bed and into the shower. I wasn't looking forward to the long lecture I'd be receiving from Mrs. Hawkins, so I took my time getting dressed. I was also in no rush as I made my way down to the kitchen for some coffee. When I walked in, I was surprised to find it completely abandoned. I didn't get it. Normally, there were at least a few of the brothers and a handful of hang-arounds having breakfast. I didn't have much time on my hands, so I made my coffee and quickly walked back to Clay's room to grab my things. I'd just stepped out into the hallway when I heard voices coming from the family room. I got the feeling that something was going on, so I went down to check it out.

When I walked in, I found several of the guys, along with Darcy and August, standing in front of the television, watching the news. The familiar blue banner scrolling across the top of the screen caught my attention and had me walking towards them for a better look. When I saw Katie's face flash across the screen, I stopped dead in my tracks and gasped, "Oh, my god."

I couldn't move. I could barely breathe. I was overcome with panic and guilt, and I didn't know how to respond when August rushed over to me and asked, "Are you okay?"

"That's Katie Coburn."

"Yeah ... They just issued an Amber alert for her."

Without responding, I walked past her and headed over to the TV. I stood there and listened as the reporter stated that Katie's father, Chris Coburn, had gone into her foster parents' home, and after assaulting the father, he kidnapped Katie. No one has seen or heard from her since. I couldn't believe what I was hearing. It just didn't seem possible. We were so careful. I couldn't imagine how he'd managed to find her. "Dammit! I can't believe he did this!"

August stepped back over to me and asked, "I take it that you know her?"

"Yes, I do." I tried my best not to cry as I continued, "I've been working with her for the past month or so. That kid has been through so much. She must be absolutely terrified."

"I'm not sure if there's anything to it," August said while turning back to Rider and Darcy, who were both now staring directly at me, "but when the news showed a picture of the father...Rider thought he might know him."

"You do?"

"Yeah... Darcy and I grew up in Oakland with Chris," Rider answered. "There was a time when he was pretty good friends with Darcy's brothers, Danny and Eddie."

"And?"

Rider looked over to Darcy as he continued, "We're not sure if they're still in touch with him, but if they are, they might be able to give us some idea of where he might be hiding out."

"Could you call them or something?"

"I already did." I could tell from Darcy's expression that she wasn't thrilled about the idea. "They were just a few blocks away, so they're on their way here. But, don't get your hopes up. Like Rider said, I'm not sure if they're even still friends with the guy. It's been a while since I've spent time with my brothers."

I had a feeling there was a reason why she hadn't spent time with them, but I didn't push. I was just relieved that she and Rider were willing to try and talk to them. Hopefully, they might know something that could help find Katie before Mr. Coburn did something we'd all regret. "Even if they don't know where he is, I really appreciate you asking them to come. It means a lot to me."

"Of course."

"I really should call into the office and let them know that I'll be late."

"Okay. Do whatever you need to do," Rider replied. "It'll be a few minutes before they get here."

"Great. I'll be right back."

I left the family room, then rushed down to Clay's

room to get my things. When I reached for my phone, I saw that I'd already missed a ton of calls. Several from the office and Mrs. Hawkins, and even more from Danny. I listened to their messages, and it was clear that they were just as distraught by Katie's kidnapping as I was. Knowing how she hated to be put off, I called Mrs. Hawkins first. As soon as she answered, she snapped, "Where have you been? I've been trying to reach you for over an hour."

"I know. I'm really sorry. I didn't have my phone with me."

"Considering what happened yesterday with the Strayhorns and the break-in to your apartment, that's simply unacceptable, Landry," she fussed.

"I know, Mrs. Hawkins, and I apologize. With everything that's going on, I didn't get much sleep last night."

"I'm sure you didn't." Her tone softened as she asked, "Did you see the Amber alert for Katie?"

"Yes, ma'am. I just can't believe it!" I swallowed hard, trying to push back the tightness in my throat. "I just don't understand how he could've found her."

"I've been wondering the same thing myself and we will figure that out, but right now, we need to focus on getting Katie back."

"Yes, ma'am. I completely agree."

"Good," Mrs. Hawkins clipped. "So, when will you be getting to the office?"

"Shortly. I need to return some phone calls, and then I'll be on my way."

"Be sure to call Officer Michaels. He's called here twice looking for you."

"Yes, ma'am. I'm about to call him now," I assured her.

"Okay, I'll see you soon."

I knew I needed to call Danny back, but I was eager to get back to the family room to see if Darcy's brothers had arrived. I wanted to be there when Darcy spoke to them, so I grabbed my things and headed that way. When I walked in, even more of the brothers were there, and they were all standing around talking to one another. It was difficult not to feel a little overwhelmed, especially since Clay wasn't around. Considering all the guys seemed to be here, I found myself wondering where he might be. The thought quickly slipped my mind when I spotted Rider talking to Gunner. As soon as I walked up to them, I asked Rider, "Did Darcy's brothers make it yet?"

"Yeah, they just pulled up. Darcy went out to get them."

"Okay, great." I glanced over at the door. "Is she bringing them back in here?"

Rider glanced around the room at all his brothers standing around talking as he said, "Yeah, but we should probably go somewhere a little more quiet so we can talk."

"Yeah, you're probably right." A feeling of urgency washed over me as I stood there staring at the door. "Do you really think they'll know something about Chris?"

"Won't know until we ask them."

Damn. That wasn't the answer I was hoping for. Thankfully, it wasn't long before Darcy walked in with two men following close behind. They all made their way over to us, and I could tell Darcy was feeling uneasy as she said, "Hey ... They made it."

"I see that," Rider answered. "Why don't we head into the kitchen where we can talk a minute?"

"Sounds good."

While I wasn't sure I was supposed to be included in

this conversation, I followed them all out of the family room and down to the kitchen. When we walked in, I was relieved to see that it was still empty. I glanced over at Darcy's brothers, and while they had their similarities, they looked quite different from her, like they'd lived a rougher life or something. Their clothes were more rugged and worn and somewhat disheveled, making me wonder if they'd fallen on hard times. I was still trying to make sense of them when Rider turned to the two men and said, "Eddie ... Danny, this is Landry Dawson."

"Hey," Eddie replied. "Nice to meet ya."

"It's nice to meet you as well."

Eddie looked over to Darcy as he asked, "You wanna tell us why you called us here or what?"

"Yes, Eddie. I was just about to get to that," Darcy grumbled, clearly displeased with his abruptness. "You both were pretty close with Chris Coburn back in the day, and I was wanting to know if you've seen or heard from him lately."

"Chris?" Danny asked. "Why you wantin' to know about him?"

"Because I need to know ... I wouldn't be asking if it wasn't important," Darcy pushed. "So, have you seen him or not?"

"Yeah, we've seen him, but it's been a while," Danny answered. "He was down at the pool hall, and he was fucking wasted, even more than usual, and from what I can remember, I'm pretty sure he had his fucking kid waiting out in the car for him."

Darcy winced as she glanced over at me. She was clearly thinking the same thing I was as she listened to her brother's recollection of their last meeting with Chris.

Hoping for clarification, I looked over to Danny and asked, "What do you mean by it's been a while? Was it a few days ago ... a few weeks?"

"About two weeks ago, I guess." Danny looked over at Eddie. "Isn't that about right?"

Eddie glanced up at the ceiling as he tried to recall the exact night, then a goofy grin crossed his face as he answered, "Yeah, it was the same night that you got into with Big Tony over that chick in the short mini-skirt and the big tits so, yeah, I'd say two weeks ago is about right."

"No need to bring that shit up, dickhead," Danny fussed.

Trying to get them both back on track, I asked, "And you haven't seen him since that night?"

"Nah ... We used to see him all the time, but he don't come around as often since his ol' lady ran out on him and left him with the kid. Now, he just shows up when he needs to blow off some steam." Danny's eyes narrowed as he studied me for a moment. "Seriously ... What's this all about? He in trouble or something?"

"Yeah, you could say that," I scoffed. "Last night, he kidnapped his daughter."

"What the fuck?" Eddie grumbled with a disgusted look on his face. "How can you kidnap your own goddamn kid?"

"She was removed from the home by the courts and was staying in foster care." I normally wouldn't have revealed such private information, but since it was plastered all over the news, I didn't see any point in keeping it from them. "He broke into their home last night and took Katie at gunpoint."

"Holy shit. I had no idea," Danny replied, seeming

completely caught off guard by my response. "So, he's on the run with the kid?"

"He's hiding out somewhere, and we were hoping you might be able to tell us where we could possibly find him." Darcy crossed her arms as she continued, "We really need to figure out where he's taken her, so if there's anything you could tell us, I'd really appreciate it."

"His brother is a president of some MC. If he's trying to hide out, I'd bet money that he's there." He thought for a moment, then Danny turned to Eddie as he asked, "What was the name of Kory's MC? The Rebels something?"

"The Fallen Rebels," Eddie answered. "It's not a big club. Just ten or twelve of them, but they don't take no shit. If he's taken the kid there, they won't make it easy to get to them."

"Well, we've got to at least try," I replied. "Where is this clubhouse?"

"It's out East ... about forty minutes from here," Rider answered. "I'll talk it over with Gus. If he gives the okay, we'll gather up a few of the guys and go over and check it out."

"No," I argued. "You can't do that. I have to follow protocol, and having Satan's Fury getting involved is definitely not following protocol."

"You're not going over there alone," Rider growled. "It's too fucking dangerous."

"I won't go alone. I'll call and get a police escort," I assured him. "I just need an address, so I can tell him where we're going."

"I don't have a good feeling about this," Rider replied.

"This is my job, Rider. That little girl is my responsibility, and god only knows what Coburn has done to her over the past twelve hours." I knew Rider meant well, but I simply couldn't risk letting the club getting involved—at least not unless there was no other option. "I hope you understand."

"Yeah, I get it, but I'm gonna tell you now ... Clay isn't gonna be happy about this. Not one bit," Rider warned.

"I'll handle Clay. For now, I need that address."

After I got the address from Rider, I gathered my things and rushed out to the parking lot. Once I was in my car, I took out my phone and called Danny, letting him know what I'd found out about Coburn and the Fallen Rebels. As soon as I was done telling him everything I knew, I pleaded, "We have to get over there and check it out."

"Hold up," Danny huffed. "You want to go check out some biker club?"

"From what I understand, it's just a small club... just a few guys, and..."

He cut me off before I could finish by saying, "I don't think that's a good idea, Landry. Not without backup, especially since it was Coburn who broke into your apartment."

"What?"

"That's why I've been trying to call you all morning," he explained. "I was checking the security footage I got from the guard, and sure enough ... it was him. I'm guessing he broke in to get the Hopkin's address so he could get to Katie."

"You've got to be kidding me!"

"It was him. Plain as day."

"I can't believe it. I thought it was someone else altogether."

"You thought it was the guy from the coffee shop?"

"Yeah, I thought for sure it was him, especially after the way he kept threatening me, but it all makes sense now." I thought for a moment, then asked, "Do you think that's why Coburn wanted the continuance, and that he was planning to take her all along?"

"There's no way of knowing for sure." He cleared his throat before asking, "So, what's the name of this biker group again?"

"The Fallen Rebels." I explained the situation a little further, then fussed, "I'm not wanting to bust up in there and cause trouble, Danny. I just want us to go check it out and see if there's any sign Katie... If they give us any trouble, we'll call in backup."

"Fine. Meet me at the gas station across the street, and don't even think about going in there without me," he demanded.

"Okay, I'm heading that way now."

As soon as we hung up, I drove over to the address Rider had given me. When I got there, I was pleased to see that Danny's patrol car was already parked at the gas station. I pulled over next to him and parked. As I got out of my car, an uneasy feeling washed over me the second I caught sight of the Fallen Rebel's clubhouse. It was nothing like Satan's Fury's. Instead of it being a large, guarded building with a high fence and gate, it was a rundown building that was once a bar. The red exterior paint had faded, leaving the wood exposed, and there were bars on each of the windows and the name *Rebels* spray-painted on the side of the building. There were eight or nine bikes parked out front, but there wasn't a soul anywhere to be seen. I was still staring at it when Danny came up beside me and asked, "You sure you want to go in there?"

"No, but I don't have a choice. I have to find out if Katie's there."

"I can go check it out on my own. There's no reason for you to—"

"Danny, I need to do this."

"Fine, but stay close and let me do the talking."

I nodded, then followed him across the street. As we got closer, I could hear the low rumble of country music coming from inside the building, and it only got louder as we got closer to the door. I glanced over at Danny as I asked, "So, do we knock or just walk on in?"

He shrugged. "Your guess is as good as mine."

Fearing the worst if we just barged in, I reached up and pounded on the door. Seconds later, it flew open and revealed an older man wearing a red bandana and a leather vest much like the one the men in Satan's Fury wore, but not nearly as intricate. He had a long gray beard, and his wrinkled eyes narrowed as he gave Danny a quick-once over. Clearly not happy to have a uniformed officer knocking at their door, he growled, "What in the hell do you two want?"

"I'm Landry Dawson from the Department of Child Services, and this is Officer Michaels," I answered. "We're looking for Chris Coburn and his daughter, Katie. We were told they might be here."

"Hmph ... You were told *wrong*. They ain't here."

"Would you mind if we came in and had a look around?"

He crossed his arms with an intimidating glare as he growled, "You got a warrant?"

"No, sir. We were hoping we wouldn't need one," I answered calmly. "Maybe we could just have a quick chat with Chris's brother, Kory. He's the president of the Rebels, right?"

"Yeah, but I can tell you now ... he ain't gonna let no pig in here. Not for nothing."

"Maybe, maybe not, but we won't know unless you go let him know we're here. Besides, if we leave now, we're just gonna get that court order, and instead of one cop being here, there'll be twenty or more. The choice is yours."

"Goddammit." He flung the door open wider and motioned us forward. As we stepped inside, he ordered, "Don't move. I'll be right back."

With that, he turned and walked out of the room, leaving Danny and me to wait for his return. I took a quick glance around the bar, noting how dim it was. It seemed eerie for it to be so dark with the sun shining so bright outside, but the two small windows weren't letting in much light. There were a couple of neon signs hanging on the wall, each looked like they'd been there for years on end, and the ceiling fans were wobbling like they could fall at any second. The red leather on the stools were worn and ripped, and the place smelled of dust and feet. I was still soaking everything in when six burly bikers stepped into the room, glaring at us both as they scattered around us. These men seemed to be much older than Clay's brothers, graying and weathered, not by the natural course of life, but most likely from years of hard living and substance abuse, and there was something about each of them that screamed danger—which didn't make my nervous jitters any better. Danny leaned over and whispered, "You see Coburn anywhere?"

"No, but that doesn't mean he's not here."

I'd just turned my attention back to the other men in the room when I heard a loud *thud* followed by Danny dropping to the floor. Before I could register what was happening, everything went black.

HYDE

*P*atience had never come easily to me, especially when I was struggling to keep my anger under wraps. After seeing the way that Strayhorn motherfucker had put his hands on not only his wife, but his kids, too, I was ready to rip his fucking head off. It only enraged me more to think about him threatening Landry and breaking into her apartment, rummaging through all her stuff. I couldn't wait to give him a taste of his own fucking medicine. Thankfully, I wouldn't have to wait long. After about thirty minutes of sitting out in the truck, the piece of shit came back out of the house and got in his truck. I waited for him as he backed out, and when he started to drive away, I followed.

It wasn't long before he made his first stop. I pulled over a few yards back, watching as he got out of his truck and went over to some guy standing on the curb. They spoke for a moment, then the guy reached into his pocket and pulled out a bag of something. They made a quick exchange, and then Strayhorn quickly turned and headed back to his truck, speeding off to his next destination. Just when I thought the guy couldn't be a bigger piece of shit, I followed him up to a twenty-four-hour strip club. The place was a total dive with prostitutes lingering by the front door. With so many people around, I was worried that I might not be able to get to him without being seen, so I was relieved when he decided to park in the rear of the building, away from any onlookers. His need to keep his location hidden from his wife gave me the opportunity I was hoping for.

Once he was parked, I whipped in behind him. Leaving Duchess locked inside, I jumped out of the truck just as he'd gotten out of his. He was so busy shoving his coke or meth or whatever-the-fuck into his back pocket, he hadn't noticed that I'd come up on him. I gave him a hard shove as I snarled, "Going somewhere, Strayhorn?"

"Who the fuck are you?"

"Who I am isn't important." I reached up and grabbed him by the collar, shoving him against his truck. "But what I've gotta say is very, very important."

"I don't give a damn about what you gotta say, so you best back the fuck off, asshole."

"Don't wanna listen? That's fine. We'll go about this another way."

I reared my fist back and slammed it into the side of his face, jarring his head back against the door of his truck. Before he had a chance to recover, I plowed into him again and again. Losing his footing, he stumbled to the ground. I was about to go at him again, when he lifted his leg and kicked me backwards, forcing me to flail to my back. Next thing I knew, the guy was on top of me, punching me in the face and head. I could hear Duchess going crazy in the truck. I knew she didn't like what Strayhorn was doing to me, but I wasn't done with him yet. After he got in a couple of good blows, I managed to pull my arm free and rammed my fist into his throat, leaving him gasping for air. When he started to falter back, I heaved him off me, and with him still trying to catch his breath, I started in on him again. "You have a thing for preying on the weak ... your wife ... your kids. You think that makes you a real man?"

He grumbled and gargled, but couldn't manage a clear answer. "It doesn't! It makes you nothing. You're worse than fucking nothing, you piece of shit!"

I kept pounding into him until I struck the side of his face just right, and a shooting pain radiated through my hand. I knew right away I'd broken at least one knuckle, if not two. Pissed that I couldn't keep going, I wrapped the fingers of my good hand around his throat, and as I tightened them, I growled, "You lay one finger on those kids or your wife again, and I'll be back to finish you off. You got that?"

When he didn't answer, I tightened my grip and shouted, "You got that?"

With his eyes almost swollen shut and blood covering his face, he managed to nod. I was still choking him when I ordered, "If you have any sense at all, you'll pack up your shit and get the fuck out of town."

With that, I stood up and got back in the truck. Duchess quickly made her way over to me, licking my face and wagging her tail. It was clear that she was pleased to have me back safe and sound. I gave her a quick rub across the head, then ordered, "All right. I'm fine. Get back in your spot."

Like always, she quickly followed my command. As soon as she was settled, I put the truck in gear and backed out of the parking lot. I had every intention of heading straight to the garage, but then my hand started throbbing. I studied the swelling and bruising around my knuckles and knew I needed to get it checked out. Hoping that Mack would be able to do something with it, I changed direction and drove back to the clubhouse. I tried to make a fist with my aching hand but couldn't, leaving no doubt that I'd broken something. I silently cursed myself for getting carried away. While I might've taken things too far with Strayhorn, I had no doubt that our encounter wouldn't be something he'd soon forget.

When I pulled through the gate, it was after ten, so I was surprised to see that so many of the guys were at the clubhouse instead of the garage. Curious if something was up, I quickly parked, then Duchess and I rushed inside. The guys were gathered in the bar, watching the news and talking amongst themselves, and for some reason, I had an uneasy feeling as I made my way over to Rider. His brows furrowed as he looked at the cuts and scratches on my face and hands. "What the fuck happened to you?"

"Nothing. Just had a little conversation with Strayhorn." Before he could respond, I glanced around the room and asked, "What's going on?"

"You get that Amber alert on your phone?"

"Yeah, but I didn't really have a chance to look at it, why?"

He cocked his eyebrow as he suggested, "Best look at it again."

I reached into my pocket and pulled out my phone. I did a quick search, and once I spotted the Amber alert, I opened it. Seconds later, a girl's face popped up on my screen. There was something familiar about her, but I couldn't place her. I quickly scanned the page, and when I saw the picture of her father, it hit me. We'd seen them both the night before when we'd hacked into Landry's files. "Holy shit."

"Yeah, it's fucked up." Rider shook his head. "You reckon he was the one who broke in Landry's apartment?"

"What makes you ask that?"

"It makes sense." Rider shrugged. "If he'd gone through her files, I bet he would've been able to find the address of where she was staying."

"Damn." I took a quick glance around the room, and when I didn't see her, I asked, "Where's Landry?"

"About that …" He grimaced. "You're not gonna like what I'm about to tell ya."

I stood there, listening in utter disbelief as he told me about Darcy's brothers coming to the club and proposing that Coburn might've taken his daughter to a local MC clubhouse. That disbelief quickly turned into horror when he explained that Landry had gone there with her cop friend to see if they were right about their suspicions. A mix of anger and concern washed over me as I growled, "Who the fuck are the Fallen Rebels?"

"An older MC. They're a smaller club … been around for decades, but never hear much about them."

"So, are these guys dangerous?"

"I guess they could be." He gave me a slight shrug. "It'd depend on the situation. Regardless, Landry has the cop with her. She should be fine."

"Yeah, like that fucking cop is gonna be any help at all." I let out a frustrated breath. "You and I both know he won't be able to do shit if those guys decide to take matters into their own hands."

"I tried to talk her out of it, but Landry had her mind set on going over there."

I wanted to give him hell, tell him that he should've tried fucking harder to talk Landry out of it, but I was in no position to lose my temper with Rider, or any of the brothers for that matter. I was just a fucking prospect, and if I didn't want to lose my chance at earning my patch, I had to bite my tongue. Unfortunately, that only made it harder to keep from completely losing my shit. My mind started racing, and with everything that had went down that morning with Strayhorn, I was hanging by a thread. As I tapped in her number, I asked, "How long has she been gone?"

"An hour ... maybe two."

"Fuck!"

The phone rang and rang, but Landry never answered. I sent her a slew of texts and tried calling several more times, but no response. As I stared down at the unanswered messages, I completely lost it. "She's not answering. It's not like her not to answer!"

Consumed with anger and concern, I lifted my already wounded hand and slammed it into the brick wall. An intense pain shot through me like a dagger, and I immediately regretted my impulsive reaction. A stream of curses flew from my mouth as I looked down at my bleeding hand. Rider shook his head and said, "What the fuck, Clay? Breaking your fucking hand isn't gonna help a goddamn thing!"

"Don't you get it? Something's wrong. I can feel it in my gut."

The words had barely left my mouth when Gus came up behind me and said, "Easy there, Hyde. Rein it in."

"How am I supposed to do that?" I let out a breath and tried to pull it together. "It's been over an hour since she headed over there, and now she's not answering her phone!"

"First of all, we don't even know if she's still there. For all we know, she's back at her office or down at the station with the cop."

"And if she isn't?" I pushed. "What if they've done something to her? What if that Coburn asshole hurt her?"

"No sense jumping to conclusions, Hyde. Let's gather the facts, and then we'll see where we stand." Gus turned to Riggs. "Gonna need you to track Landry's phone and get me her location."

"You got it." I watched as Riggs rushed out of the room, only to return moments later with his laptop. He placed it down on the counter. We all gathered around and watched him work his magic. After just a few seconds, he looked over to Gus with a blank expression. "Looks like she's still there."

"Dammit."

The room fell silent, and I knew the brothers were thinking the same thing I was. Something wasn't right. I turned to Gus, waiting for his next move. He ran his hand over his thick beard as he turned to speak to Moose, the club's VP. They spoke quietly amongst themselves for a moment, then Gus reached into his pocket and took out his burner cell. After tapping in a number, he put the call on speaker where we could all listen to it ring. When a man finally answered, Gus said, "Buck ... This is Gus."

"Hey, brother. It's been a while."

"It has." Gus paused for a moment, then continued, "We've got a problem, and I was hoping you might be able to help me out."

"All right." There was no missing the concern in his voice when he asked, "What's the problem?"

"Your brother, Chris. He there with you?"

"Yeah. Got here last night."

"He got the kid with him?"

"As a matter of fact, he does." Buck's previously friendly tone changed inquisitive as he asked, "What concern you got with him and his kid?"

"Besides the fact that he kidnapped her ... I got a problem that the woman who came to your club looking for her this morning is one of *ours*."

"The lady with the cop?" he asked, sounding surprised.

"That'd be her."

"Fuck, man. I didn't know."

"Didn't figure you did. Is she still there?"

"Yeah, they both are." After a brief pause, Buck continued, "Got 'em locked up out back."

Gus wasted no time getting to the point. "Well, if you don't want to go toe to toe with Satan's Fury, I'd strongly suggest you let 'em go."

"You know I don't want that shit, brother. Never had no qualms with you boys, and I certainly don't wanna start nothing now, especially over my goddamn brother. The guy's a fuckup. Always has been. Not gonna let his shit blowback on my club, so come on and get 'em ... *all of 'em*, including my piece-of-shit brother."

"We're on our way."

After Gus hung up the phone, he turned and looked at me with one of those expressions that could only come from Gus. I knew exactly what was on his mind as he sat there ... silently studying me. He wanted me to see that it doesn't always take a fist or a gun to solve problems in our world. He'd kept a level head, hadn't even raised his fucking voice and still managed to solve the problem without going to war. But then again, that was Gus—cool, calm, and collected. He reached over and gave my shoulder a pat as he told me, "All right, Hyde. Go get some ice for that hand, then let's go get your girl."

Minutes later, I was sitting in the truck with a bag of ice on my hand, and Rider and I were following the others over to the Fallen Rebels' clubhouse. We hadn't been riding long when Rider started mumbling to himself. "Hmm ... *Hyde*. I would've never thought of it, but yeah, I'd say it fits."

"What?"

"Your road name," he answered like it was no big deal. "I'm guessing it has something to do with Jekyll and Hyde, right?"

I nodded. "Yeah, Gus used the reference once or twice."

"Well, there ya have it," Rider announced proudly. "You've got yourself an official road name which makes you one step closer to earning your Fury patch."

Any other time, those words would've meant the world to me, but at that moment, I was too focused on Landry to let it sink in. I needed to get to her, to see that she was really okay, and then, and *only then*, could I appreciate the fact that I'd finally earned my very own road name. When we pulled up to the Fallen Rebels' clubhouse, I spotted Landry's car parked across the street next to a squad car. We all pulled in next to them, and as we got out and walked across the street, I was surprised to see that their clubhouse was just a rundown old bar. Seeing the state of the place made it easier to understand why the president of the club hadn't wanted to throw down with Satan's Fury. It wouldn't have taken much to wipe the entire place out.

We all followed Gus and Moose to the door, and when we all walked in, the Rebels were all sitting there waiting for us. The Rebels were all older, at least in their sixties, and the years hadn't done any of them much kindness. One of the bigger men of the group made his way over to Gus and extended his hand. "Good to see ya, Gus... Moose. Wish it was under better circumstances."

Gus nodded as he shook his hand. "Looks like you and the boys have been doing well."

"We're making it all right." He shook his head as he looked to the ground. "Sure am sorry about all this, Gus. I knew it was bad news when he showed up here with Katie. Probably would've sent him away from the start, but I got a soft spot for the girl."

"I understand, Buck. You were looking out for your family."

"Yeah ... Looks like I saved his sorry ass one time too many." Buck turned to one of the others. "It's time to bring him in."

The guy nodded, then walked out of the room, only to return seconds later with Buck's brother, Chris. The blood drained from Chris's face, leaving him looking like he'd seen a fucking ghost when he said, "What the fuck do you motherfuckers want?"

A spark flashed through Gus's eyes, but he didn't move. Instead, he remained completely calm as he said, "Where's the woman and the cop?"

"Like I'd fucking tell you." He turned back and looked at his brother, then spat out, "You gonna tell them to get the fuck out of here or what?"

"That's not gonna happen," Buck answered. "Not gonna have your back on this one."

"What? You're actually gonna turn your back on your own flesh and blood?"

"You heard me. I'm out on this. We all are." Buck crossed his arms as he said, "You gone too far this time, brother. Katie deserves better than this shit."

"Shut your goddamn mouth!" He reached into his back pocket and took out his gun, pointing it at his brother as he shouted, "You don't know shit!"

"Put the gun down, Chris," Buck warned, but Chris didn't listen. Instead, he kept it aimed directly at his brother's head. "Don't make this thing worse than it already is."

"You're so full of shit. Always have been. Acting like you're some big deal because you run this club full of losers, and now—"

Before he could finish his sentence, Shadow charged towards Chris, grabbing him from behind. He pinned his arms tightly against Chris's chest, and with firm jolt, the gun fell from his hand. Chris tried to break free, but Shadow was simply too strong. Buck stepped towards his brother and shook his head as he said, "We're done here, little brother."

"You're gonna regret this!"

"Doubt it." Buck looked to Shadow as he said, "Just get him the hell out of here."

Shadow nodded, then pulled out a zip-tie from his pocket and bound Chris's hands behind his back. After he had him secured, he and Gauge led him out of the bar. The door had barely closed behind them when Gus asked, "So, where's the girl ... and the cop?"

Buck motioned us to follow as he led us out of the bar and down a short hallway. When we reached a door, he quickly opened it and revealed an old, dingy supply closet filled with dirty mops and brooms, as well as a dazed and confused looking Landry and Danny, sitting on the floor next to Katie. As soon as she spotted me, Landry quickly stood up and threw herself at me, wrapping her arms around my neck. "I knew you'd come. I just knew it."

"Of course, I would. Nothing could've kept me away." I held her close as I whispered, "Are you okay?"

"I've got a little bit of headache, but yeah, I'm fine." She leaned back to get a better look at me, and when she noticed the cuts and bruises on my face, she asked, "What about you? Are you okay?"

"Yes, beautiful. I'm fine."

"Good." She clung to me once again, then asked, "Where's Coburn?"

"We got him. Don't worry," I assured her.

"And the others? His brother ..." her voice trailed off when she spotted Buck standing in the doorway. She took a step back, standing protectively in front of Katie as she asked, "What's going on?"

"It's over, Landry. You're safe."

She glared at Buck with apprehension, and clearly

unsure if she could trust him, she reached for Katie's hand, helping the girl to her feet. "Come on, sweetie. Let's get you out of here."

Without saying a word, Katie took a hold of Landry's hand and looked completely terrified as Landry and I led her out of the small storage room. When we returned to the front of the bar, they both watched silently as Gus and Moose took a moment to thank Buck. Neither Landry nor Danny seemed to understand what was going on. I couldn't blame them for being confused by the exchange, especially after they'd found themselves locked in a fucking storage closet for hours. As soon as the pleasantries were over, we headed outside and across the street. Danny looked surprised when he found Shadow standing by his squad car with Chris. He glanced over at Gus and said, "Damn, you guys don't mess around, do you?"

"Can't say that we do," Gus answered with a chuckle. "I trust that you'll take care of him?"

"Yes, sir. Absolutely."

"And I also trust that you'll keep Satan's Fury out of all this."

Danny nodded. "You have my word."

We all watched as Danny opened the back door of his squad car and helped Shadow get Coburn settled in the back seat. Once he'd closed the door, Danny turned his attention back to Landry and Katie. They were both standing by my side as they stared over at the Rebels' clubhouse. Their facial expressions left no doubt that they'd both been rattled by what had transpired there. Danny grimaced as he stepped towards me and said, "I hate to rush you off, but you guys should probably get going. As soon as I put a call into the station to let them know we found Katie, cops will be swarming the place."

Gus nodded, and the guys started making their way back to their bikes, while Landry led Katie over to her car. Landry took a moment to warn Katie about what would occur over the next couple of hours, then closed the door and walked back in my direction. Tears filled her eyes as she reached up and wound her arms around me, hugging me tightly. I knew she needed the moment to collect herself, and to be honest, I needed it just as much as she did. I'd never felt more relieved than I did the second I saw her sitting in that fucking storage room alive and well. It was like I'd been given a second chance, and there was no way in hell I was going to fuck it up. After several long moments, Landry looked up at me and said, "I love you, Clay. I really do."

"And I love you." I kissed her briefly, then said, "The cops will be here soon. We better get going."

With a quick sigh, she released her hold on me and said, "I know."

"When will I see you?"

"It's probably going to be a while. Once we're done here, I'll have to get Katie down to the station and complete a mountain of paperwork there. Then, after I'm done there, I need to head over to the office and fill out even more paperwork, but I'll try to be as quick as I can," she promised.

"I'll be waiting."

She gave me another quick kiss, then I made my way over to the truck and got in with Rider. I never took my eyes off Landry as Rider pulled out of the parking lot. I didn't like leaving her, but with the cops on their way, I didn't have a choice. At least I could find comfort in knowing that it was over. Landry was safe, and it wouldn't be long until Katie was returned to her foster parents. I didn't want to think about what might've happened if Gus and the brothers hadn't come through for us. Once again, they showed me what it meant to wear the Satan's Fury patch, and I couldn't wait for the day when I could actually call them my brothers. As Rider drove out of the parking lot, I turned to him and asked, "We going on to the garage?"

"Maybe later, but for now, we're going to let Mack have a look at the hand."

I'd almost forgotten about it until he mentioned it. I lifted it and wiggled my fingers so he could see all the swelling and bruising. "You think it's broken?"

"Definitely."

"You think Mack will be able to fix me up?"

"Yeah, but it's gonna hurt like a motherfucker," Rider scoffed.

"I'll be all right. Nothing a few beers won't take care of."

When we made it back to the clubhouse, I went down to the infirmary so Mack could have a look at my hand. Rider was right. He was able to patch me up, but it hurt like a sonofabitch. Not only did he have to set the damn thing, he had to put my hand in a fucking cast. By the time he was done fixing me up, it was well into the afternoon and too late to bother with going to the garage. I hadn't gotten much sleep the night before, so I decided to go back to my room for a quick break. I took a couple of the pain relievers Mack had given me and lay across the bed.

The next thing I knew, Landry was crawling into bed next to me. "Hey, handsome."

"Hey, beautiful. Did you get everything sorted with Katie?"

She nodded with a smile. "I did. Thanks to you and the guys."

"I'm just glad it all worked out."

When I went to reach for her, Landry's eyes widened with a gasp as she noticed the cast on my hand. "What happened?"

"It's nothing. I'm fine."

"No, it's not nothing!" she fussed.

"I had a little run in with a wall." I smiled as I told her, "It won."

"So, it's broken?"

"Yeah, but it could've been worse. Now, stop with the inquisition. I'm fine."

"I don't think so. Why did you have a run in with the wall?"

Before I could answer, her phone dinged with a text message. With a huff, she rolled over and grabbed it out of her purse, quickly scanning the screen. Seconds later, she was reaching for the remote. "We need to turn on the news!"

The TV came on, and seconds later, Katie's face crossed the screen. We both watched quietly as the reporter announced the cancelation of Katie's previous Amber alert, stating that she'd been found unharmed and had been returned to her foster home, and just as Gus had hoped, there was no mention of Satan's Fury. As soon as it was over, Landry turned off the TV and lay down next to me. She curled up to my side, she said, "Now, about the hand ..."

"It's fine, Landry. Really."

Her brows furrowed as she pushed, "So, you're not going to tell me what happened?"

"Already told you, there's nothing to tell." It meant a great deal to me that she was so concerned, but at the same time, it was a conversation I'd hoped to avoid. I had no intention of telling her about the visit I'd had with Strayhorn. As far as I was concerned, I'd dealt with him, and if all went as planned, he would no longer be a problem for either Landry or his wife and kids. Hoping to distract her from her line of questioning, I rolled over and faced her as I asked, "You remember that house we went to look at?"

"Yeah, what about it?"

"What would you think if I made an offer on it?"

"Seriously?" She eased up on her elbow. "Why the sudden interest in it?"

"Not exactly sudden," I answered casually. There wasn't anything particularly special about the house. It was just a simple three-bedroom painted brick house with all the basic necessities, but when I thought about Landry being in that house with me, nothing about it seemed simple or basic. Instead, it couldn't have felt more perfect. "It's close to work and has that big backyard for Duchess, and there's plenty of room for you to have an office."

"For me?"

"Yeah, *you*." When our eyes met, I told her, "If I buy the house, I'd be buying it for us."

"But—"

I could see the wheels turning in her head as she considered what I'd said. I knew it was early, that we were still getting to know one another, but I knew without a doubt that Landry was the one for me. Hell, I was pretty sure I knew it from the moment I spotted her out on the street with Duchess. I just hoped she felt the same. "It's a simple question, Landry. Should I get the house or not?"

LANDRY

The days after Katie's kidnapping were a complete blur. Between filling out all the paperwork, answering questions from both Mrs. Hawkins and the police department, and getting Katie settled back in with her foster family, it seemed like I could barely catch my breath. But at the end of the day, it was all worth it. Knowing that he was facing substantial jail time, Christopher Coburn relinquished his parental rights, giving the Hopkins family the opportunity to take her on permanently. I was worried that Katie might not be ready for such a big leap, but when I told her the news, she couldn't have been more pleased. She loved being with the Hopkins, and it meant a great deal to her that she'd be able to stay with them indefinitely. I couldn't deny that it did my heart good to see her so happy. It made me feel like I had some small part in making her life a little better, and I liked the feeling. It was one of the very reasons I'd found myself driving out to the Strayhorn home to check in on Aniya and the kids.

It had been just over two weeks since I'd had the encounter with Aniya's husband at the coffee shop. Considering how that had turned out, I'd decided to back off for a little while, give it some time to settle down, but that didn't mean I hadn't tried to reach out to Aniya. I simply wanted to make sure that she and the kids were okay, but I couldn't get her to answer her cell. Hoping to avoid her husband, I'd tried calling her at the coffee shop, but she wasn't working today. I'd just have to see for myself if Mr. Strayhorn had ruined everything we'd worked so hard to accomplish.

I was feeling a little uneasy as I pulled up to the house but felt slightly better when I didn't spot the Ford pickup in the driveway. I parked and kept my eyes open for any sign of the husband, then made my way up to the porch. A wave of nervousness washed over me as I lifted my hand to knock. My mind was suddenly bombarded with thoughts of Strayhorn yelling at me and threatening to slit my throat. Those memories combined with the fear of having been locked in the storage closet with Danny and Katie were enough to give me second thoughts about my impromptu visit. I was just about to turn and leave when the front door opened and Fiona appeared with a bright smile. The tightness in my chest quickly faded when I saw that Fiona was no longer scared to see me. In fact, she actually looked happy as she announced, "You're back."

"I am." I knelt down, so I could look her in the eye as I spoke. "I wanted to come by and see how you were doing."

"I'm doing 'weally good. I gots a gold star today in Missus Tatum's class."

"A gold star? That's wonderful!"

She nodded. "Momma gots me a treat for it."

"That's really great, Fiona. I'm very proud of you." Seeing her so pleased warmed my heart. I had no doubt that her mother felt the same. Curious as to where she might be, I peered through the crack of the door. "Is your mom at work?"

"She's in da kitchen." Fiona reached for my hand and tugged me inside, leading me straight to her mother. As we entered the room, Fiona excitedly announced, "Momma ... it's Missus Daw-sun."

When Aniya turned to face me, I was thrilled to see that her black eye was almost gone, and there were no other signs of bruises anywhere to be seen. A bright smile crossed her face as she said, "I was wondering if you would be back!"

"I had to come check on my favorite crew." As I stepped further into the room, I spotted Joseph sitting at the table. He was eating a bowl of cereal, and from what I could tell, he seemed bruise free and perfectly content as he shoved a big spoon-full of cereal into his mouth. He continued to chomp away as I told Aniya, "I tried calling, but I haven't been able to reach you on your cell."

"That would be because Stephen busted it all to hell that day in the coffee shop," she grumbled. "But I've got new one. I'll get you the number before you go."

I'd been there several minutes, and from what I could tell there was no sign of Aniya's husband anywhere—no truck, no clothes, and no booming voice, screaming for me to leave. "Since you mentioned him ... Where is your husband now?"

"Hell if I know." She shrugged. "I haven't seen him since the day he packed up and left."

"What are you talking about?"

"I honestly don't know what happened. One day, he was set on staying here and trying to make things work, which would've never been a good thing, and then the next thing I know, he comes to the house all black and blue, covered in blood, and barely able to walk. Somebody got him real good. He hardly said two words to me ... just packed his crap and left. Told me and the kids good riddance." She rolled her eyes with a heckle. "If you ask me, him getting his ass kicked was some kind of divine intervention."

"And how long ago was it that he left?"

"I don't know. About two weeks ago?" I was trying to think back to what was going on two weeks ago when she said, "It was the same morning that little girl went missing."

While I was baffled by what had happened with Aniya's husband, it was easy to see that she was relieved that he was gone, and if Fiona and Joseph's moods were any indication, they felt the same way. "So, things are going okay?"

"Things are going better than okay." She glanced over at her children with a soft smile as she said, "The kids are doing good in school and really like the new daycare, and I just got extra hours at work ... even managed to pay off the water bill balance and part of the electric."

"That's fantastic, Aniya. I'm really excited to hear that." I could've spent the entire day sitting there and listening to her tell me about how well things were going, but sadly, I simply didn't have the time. I'd invited my parents over for dinner, and since it was going to be the first time they'd met Clay, I wanted everything to be perfect. After checking the time, I told her, "I've really enjoyed seeing you guys, but I should get going."

"Okay. I'm glad you were able to stop by." She showed me to the door, and I was just about to walk out when she said, "Ms. Dawson?"

"Yes?"

"Thank you for everything. It's really meant a lot to me." Before I had a chance to respond, she reached out and hugged me. "I couldn't have done any of this without you."

Her words brought tears to my eyes. It wasn't often that I was thanked for the work I'd done, and it meant a lot to me that she'd said them to me. I hugged her back as I whispered, "I'm really glad I could help."

As soon as we said our goodbyes, I rushed back to my car and started towards my apartment to get ready for my parents' arrival. I spent the better half of the afternoon cleaning and cooking, and I had to admit, everything was looking pretty good. That didn't mean I wasn't still freaking out. While I would've never admitted it to her, my mother's opinion meant a lot to me, and I really wanted her to like Clay, especially since I'd agreed to move in with him. I was trying to think of the perfect way to break the news to her when Clay came up behind me and wrapped his arms around my waist, hugging me with my back against his chest. "Hey, beautiful. It smells great."

"You think so?"

"Yep! Can't wait to dig in." He lowered his mouth to my neck, and I started to giggle when his lips brushed across the sensitive flesh. I pushed him back with my hip, causing his cast to bump against the counter. "Easy there, killer."

"Your own fault." I teased. "You know how ticklish I am."

When I turned to face him, he smiled and said, "You're right. I just can't seem to help myself."

"Mm-hmm." My eyes dropped down to his cast, and I suddenly found myself thinking about the conversation I'd had with Aniya. She mentioned that it had happened the same morning that Katie had been kidnapped, the same exact morning that Clay appeared at the Rebels' clubhouse with not only a broken hand, but numerous bruises and scratches. When I'd asked him about it, he was vague at best, so I decided to ask again. "You know, you never really told me how you broke your hand."

An uneasy expression crossed his face as he glanced down at his cast and sighed. "Let's just say I had something I needed to handle, and I handled it."

"Was this something you had 'to handle' club related or something more personal?"

"Landry," he protested.

"Okay, I'll leave it," I lied. I turned my attention back to the stove, and as I started to stir the noodles, I told him, "You know that guy who threatened me at the coffee shop?"

"Uh-huh."

"I talked to his soon-to-be *ex-wife* today." Not giving him a chance to respond, I continued, "She told me that he came to the house a couple of weeks ago and packed all his stuff. Told her that he wouldn't be coming back."

"Oh, really?" he asked casually. "You believe that?"

"I don't know. She said someone had beaten him up pretty bad. He was barely able to walk, so maybe whoever it was talked some sense into him."

I glanced over my shoulder, and when I saw the slight smile on his face, I knew that one way or another, Clay had been involved in getting rid of Stephen Strayhorn. I should've been upset with him for meddling, but when I thought back to how happy Aniya and Fiona seemed during my visit, it was impossible to be angry. Doing his best to play it off, he cleared his throat and said, "Sounds like the guy got some sense knocked into him."

"Apparently so."

With a mischievous smirk, he reached over and stole a bite of bread as he asked, "When are your folks gonna get here?"

"Any minute." I motioned my hand towards the cabinet. "Would you mind getting out a few glasses?"

"Sure thing."

He'd barely taken a step when there was a knock at the door. My breath caught as I watched him go over and open it, smiling kindly as he greeted both of my parents and welcomed them inside. I listened to them banter back and forth with small talk about the weather while Clay took their coats. As he turned to carry them into the living room, my mother looked at me with a big smile. "He's so handsome, and very charming."

"I think so too."

I walked over and gave her a quick hug, then turned my attention to my father. It had been weeks since I'd spoken to him, but I knew that Mom had kept him up to date on everything that was going on in my life. When I reached up to hug him, he squeezed me tight and whispered, "You look wonderful, Landry. I can't remember the last time I've seen you so happy."

"Thanks, Dad. I am happy. In fact, I'm very happy."

"Good." He was still hugging me when Duchess came trotting over and started sniffing at his feet. A big smile crossed his face as he asked, "Is this the dog you hit with your car?"

"Yes! This is Duchess."

Mom's mouth dropped when she saw her. "My goodness, Landry. That dog is enormous. It's a wonder you didn't make a mess of your car."

"I didn't hit her that hard, Mom. It was more of a bump or a hard nudge."

Clay chuckled as he added, "I'm not sure Duchess would agree with that."

"Well, she's just fine, and now that it's all said and done, she's got a good home."

Dad looked over at Clay as he asked, "You decide to keep her?"

Clay knelt down and rubbed Duchess on the head as he answered, "Yes, sir. She kind of grew on me, and I couldn't see letting her go."

"Well, that's great. I'm glad to see that it all worked out." I headed over to the oven and pulled out the casserole as Dad asked, "So, how are things at work?"

"Believe it or not, they're finally starting to settle down."

While I set the table, I told them what I could about what'd happened with Katie, and the promotion I was up for, and while they both seemed very pleased, my mother was much more interested in my relationship with Clay than she was with my work. As soon as we sat down to eat, she watched his every move and listened intently to everything he said. I knew she was trying to size him up when she asked, "So, Clay ... What do you do?"

"I work down at the club's garage." He took a sip of his tea and continued, "We do restorations ... classic cars and bikes mostly."

"That sounds interesting." I could tell by her tone that she wasn't exactly impressed, especially when her eyes dropped to his leather vest. It was moments like these when I wished my mother was more like my father. I didn't have to worry about what he was thinking. As long as I was happy, he was happy. Unfortunately, she didn't feel the same. She'd always felt the need to push my brother and I, so I wasn't surprised when she said, "Is this something you plan to do long term?"

"Yeah, it's good money, and I enjoy the work." His expression softened as he said, "I don't know how to explain it ... There's just something about taking something that's endured years of neglect and bringing it back to life."

My mother smiled as she replied, "I'd say you explained it quite well, actually. It's always nice to see someone genuinely enjoy the work they do, and from the sounds of it, you certainly do."

"Yes, ma'am. I do."

"And what about your family? Are you close?"

"Mom," I fussed. "Enough of the twenty questions."

"I'm just trying to get to know your friend better, Landry."

"It's fine. She can ask anything she likes." Clay placed his hand on mine as he said, "To answer your question ... My father died a while back, but I'm still close with my mother and sister. Since I moved to Memphis, I haven't gotten to see them as much as I'd like to, but I plan on changing that in the near future."

"I'm sorry to hear about your father. I'm sure that was very difficult for all of you."

"It was, but time has helped."

"I'm glad to hear that." A warm smile crossed her face as Mom replied, "You seem like a really special man, Clay."

"He is," I replied. "He really is."

By the time we finished dinner and cleared the table, it was getting late, so Mom and Dad decided it was time for them to head back home. I gave them a moment to say their goodbyes to Clay, then I followed them outside. Once we'd gotten out to their car, I asked, "Sooo ... what did you think of him?"

"It's hard to say for sure, Landry. We've only had a few minutes with him," Mom scoffed.

"Personally, I thought he seemed like a fine young man." My father gave me a wink. "He certainly seems to be crazy about you. I'd say that makes him a pretty smart guy in my book."

"Thanks, Daddy." I gave him a quick hug before turning my attention back to Mom. I didn't want to push, so I simply told her, "Well, you'll get a better feel for him next time."

When I reached over to give her a hug, she clung to me, squeezing me tight as she whispered, "I love you, sweetheart, and if you love this boy, we will love him too."

"And that's why I love you like I do."

I gave them both another hug, and moments later, they were in their car and headed home. I went back to my apartment feeling even better than I had before, and over the next few weeks, Clay and I started making plans to move my things into his new house. It seemed crazy that so much had changed in such a short amount of time.

People would probably think I was crazy for believing that things between us could ever work, especially when our lives were so vastly different, but there was so much good in Clay. I'd seen it with my own eyes when he helped me with Duchess, and again when my apartment was broken into. He was loving and protective, and there was a tenderness in his touch that I'd never felt with any man. We might've been from two completely different worlds, but somehow it just seemed to work, and I had no intention of walking away.

I pointed over to the flat-screen TV as I suggested, "We could always put it in the guest room, and hang the bigger one in the living room."

"Um-hmm," he mumbled as he placed a stack of books into one of the many boxes scattered in the room. "Sounds good."

"My sofa is okay, but I'm not sure if it's big enough. Maybe we should get another one, and put this one in the office."

"Okay," he replied, steadily packing away. "Whatever you think."

"And what about the bed? Do you think it's big enough?" I glanced over at him, watching as he continued to fill the box with odds and ends. I stood there waiting for his response, but it never came, so I pushed, "*Clay?*"

"Yeah, sounds good."

"You aren't listening to a word I'm saying, are you?"

He immediately stopped what he was doing and looked over to me. When he saw my expression, he walked over to me, slipped his hand around my waist, and tugged me towards him, and said, "Let me make this clear. I don't care what sofa we sit on or which TV we watch as long as you're there with me. So, you don't have to ask. Do whatever makes you happy."

"But I want you to be happy with it too."

"I've got you ... That's all I'll ever need to be happy."

I knew he was about to kiss me. I could see it in his eyes. Just as I'd hoped, he pressed his lips against mine. As soon as our mouths touched, I instantly became putty in his hands. It was always like that with him. He got to me like no man ever had. His tongue drifted over my bottom lip, and with a slight whimper, I opened my mouth, giving him access to delve deeper. Instinctively, I leaned towards him, and in a matter of seconds, we were both consumed in the moment. My hands drifted up to his chest, and I could feel his heart pounding as fast as mine underneath his hard muscles. He trailed kisses along my neck, sending chills throughout my entire body as he led me over to the bed. His eyes locked on mine as he whispered, "You're mine, Landry Dawson. All mine."

He was absolutely right. I was his—heart and soul. Without another word, he tilted my chin up and touched his lips to mine. That one gentle kiss was enough to make my entire body hum with anticipation. The kiss quickly became more passionate, his tongue skillfully mingling with mine, seducing all my senses. I could feel the haze of desire overtaking me, and I craved more. I eagerly removed my tank top, tossing it behind me, and his eyes followed my hands as they lowered my pants down my legs. I felt the heat of his stare as his eyes slowly roamed over me, and a longing ache burned inside of me as he growled, "I've never seen a woman as beautiful as you."

"When you say it like that, I almost believe it."

I smiled as he pulled me in for another kiss. I didn't

know how he did it, but when I was in his arms, he made me feel beautiful and wanted, erasing any and all doubts that might have been lingering in the back of my mind. His hands slid up my back, unhooking and gently removing my satin bra. As he took my breasts in his hands, gently caressing each with the pad of this thumb, I became completely consumed with need. My head fell back as he lowered his mouth to my nipple and began nipping and sucking the sensitive flesh, sending jolts of pleasure down my spine. The warmth of his breath caressed my skin as he whispered, "Can't wait, Landry. Gonna need you now."

I nodded as his thumbs hooked in my red satin thong, sliding it down my legs as he trailed kisses down my navel. I stood naked before him, brazenly letting his eyes wander before stepping toward him to help remove his clothes. He slipped off his t-shirt and dropped it to the floor. As I stared at his tan, taut muscles, I couldn't help pressing my palms against the hot skin of his torso. My fingers roamed, caressing his chest before trailing down his abdomen. I could feel the muscles tremble ever so slightly beneath my touch, and I smiled inwardly, hoping I was making him feel as intoxicated as I was. I made quick work of his jeans and boxers, becoming more aroused with each passing second. With all his clothes on the floor alongside mine, I took a step back. My eyes drifted down his perfectly chiseled chest to his long, hard shaft. Damn. The man was beautiful from head to toe. As I stood there staring at him, I found myself wanting to taste him and give him pleasure like he'd given me many times before. I raked my teeth over my bottom lip as he took a step forward. When he reached for me, I placed the palms of my hands on his chest, stopping him as I whispered, "Wait."

A brief look of confusion crossed his face as I gently pushed him back, guiding him to sit down on the edge of the bed. I took his face in my hands and kissed him deep and hard before kneeling between his legs. He froze with anticipation as he watched me reach for him. He sucked in a deep breath, holding it in his chest as I wrapped my fingers around him. I leaned forward, and the second I brushed my tongue across the tip of his cock, he let out a deep-seated groan.

Spurred on by his response, I slowly licked from base to tip, glancing up at him for his reaction. His eyes were locked on me, brows furrowed and jaw clenched. I took him in my mouth, sliding down as I continued to watch him. His head tilted back and his eyes squeezed shut when I began to gently suck and swirl my tongue around him. Seeing his pleasure stoked my confidence and made me feel powerful. I wanted to watch him lose himself in waves of ecstasy as I took him over the edge. I wrapped my hand around him as I began to stroke, slowly at first, but gradually picking up my pace. I sucked and licked him, rocking my head up and down in rhythm with my strokes. As I gently twisted my hand, he let out a deep, gravely moan and gripped the sheets. I picked up my pace, tightening my lips around his shaft and taking him deeper into my mouth. I could feel his muscles starting to tense and his hands wound in my hair and he groaned, "Fuck!"

Suddenly, he grabbed me from underneath my arms and threw me onto the bed. His body quickly covered mine, pinning my hands over my head. As he grazed my soaking wet center with his hard cock, he growled, "See what you do to me?"

Without giving me a chance to respond, he showed me exactly what I had done to him. In fact, he spent the entire night showing me, over and over again.

EPILOGUE

SIX MONTHS LATER

*I*t had been a year since I'd started prospecting for Satan's Fury, and during that time I'd learned a great deal—not only about myself, but also what it meant to be a brother. This wasn't something that had come to me in a moment's revelation. It took time and a great deal of work. I had to admit, there were times when I thought I didn't have it in me to see it through, especially when the long hours started to catch up with me. Thankfully I never gave up, and after so many months of busting my ass, I was now about to be faced with my last task as a prospect.

I'd actually had a quiet morning, and Landry and I had used it to our advantage, spending the early hours tangled up in bed. I'd just gotten up to get us both a cup of coffee when I received a text from Rider. The message was cryptic at best, but it was enough to have me rushing to the garage.

When I opened the door, I was surprised to find that my entire bike had been disassembled, and the parts had been dispersed throughout the garage. Having no clue what to think, I stepped inside for a better look. That's when I noticed a note hanging from the handlebars.

THE CLOCK STARTS NOW–

You have ten hours to reassemble your bike, get to J&T's Diner in Little Rock on the corner of East and Main. There will be a package waiting for you there. Get it and bring it back to the clubhouse by six o'clock sharp.

I TOOK a moment to try to figure out how much time I had on my hands. It'd take me at least two and half hours to get to Little Rock and find J&T's, so that only left me with a few hours to get my bike put back together or I'd never make it on time. Determined not to fail, I sprang into action, quickly gathering all the different parts of my bike and placing them in the center of the room. I was rushing around like a mad person when Landry walked in. She was still in her robe and looking absolutely beautiful with her hair pulled up into a messy bun. Duchess was at her side, and she had her cup of coffee in hand as she looked around the garage and gasped, "Whoa! What is all this?"

"Umm ... my bike."

"Yeah, I can see that. Who took it apart?"

"The brothers."

"The brothers? Why did they do that?" There was no missing the surprise in her voice when she asked, "And how did they get in here without us hearing anything?"

"Babe ... it's Fury." I grabbed a few tools out of my toolbox as I continued, "Nothing they can't do."

Finally piecing together that something was up, Landry's eyes widened as she whispered, "Wait ... *Do you think—?*"

"I won't know until I get it done."

"Okay, I'll leave you to it." As she headed back inside, she shouted, "I love you! Good luck!"

Once she was gone, I started searching for my bike's owner's manual. While I knew how to put the basic components back together, I wanted to make sure I didn't waste time by rushing it. After I found it, I skimmed through the pages, making sure I had everything sorted in my head. Thankfully, I wasn't starting from scratch. They'd removed the gas tank, brakes, wheels, and various other parts, but they'd left the engine intact. As I started remounting the front wheel, I started chuckling to myself just thinking about what kind of crazy motherfucker would've come up with the idea of taking apart someone's bike. If I had to guess, I'd say it was T-bone, but it was impossible to know for sure. In all honesty, it could've been any one of the brothers.

Over the past few months, I'd learned to expect the unexpected where they were concerned. Each of their backgrounds, senses of humor, and interests were so totally different. It was those differences that made each of them unique, but at the end of the day, they all shared the same core values and ambitions which made the club even stronger. I glanced over at the clock, checking my time as I finished putting on the back tire and moved to the gas tank. I'd been at it for at least an hour when Landry came out of the house carrying a cup of coffee in one hand and a pair of jeans and a t-shirt in the other. As she laid them down on the counter, she smiled and said, "I thought you could use these."

I looked down, and for the first time since I came out to the garage, I realized I was still in my fucking boxers. "Thanks, babe."

"No problem." I grabbed my clothes and started to get dressed when Landry asked, "How's it going?"

"It's going." I pulled my t-shirt over my head, then leaned towards her and gave her a quick kiss. "Gotta get back at it."

"Okay." She turned and started back towards the house. Then she stepped through the door and shouted, "Let me know if you need anything!"

As I glanced down at my bare feet, I hollered back, "I could use some socks and my boots when you get a chance."

"You got it!"

I turned my focus back to my bike, only stopping long enough to put on my boots, and after four hours in, I'd finally managed to get my bike back together. I hopped on, turned the key, and was beyond relieved when she started up without a hitch. I revved the engine a few times, just enough to draw Landry's attention. She stuck her head out the door with a proud smile. "You got it!

"That I did." I reached for my helmet and prospect cut, and as I put them both on, I told her, "I'll be back as soon as I can."

"Be careful."

I nodded, then coasted out of the driveway and rolled towards Arkansas. I couldn't deny that I was feeling pretty pumped that I'd managed to get my bike back together so quickly. When I first came to Memphis, I didn't know shit about cars or motorcycle engines. Hell, I could barely change my own oil, but I learned. The brothers gave me no choice. That's how they were with everything. They continuously challenged me to not be just another prospect, but to make a name for myself, take risks, and rise to each and every occasion—all while remaining true to the man I was when I first walked through their clubhouse doors. As I continued towards Little Rock, I thought about all the things these men had taught me, how they'd changed my life in ways I could've never imagined, and I knew, patch or not, these men would always mean a great deal to me.

When I got to Little Rock, it took me a bit to find J&T's diner. It was small and rundown, but the place was packed. Even though I had plenty of time, I was beyond curious about the package I was supposed to pick up, so I quickly parked and rushed inside. The entire place smelled like greasy burgers and fries with a hint of baked apple pie. I was already hungry and beyond tempted with all the delicious smells that it was almost more than I could take as I made my way through the crowd. As soon as I reached the counter, an older lady came up to greet me. "Afternoon. What can I get ya today?"

It was at that moment—it hit me. I had no idea what I was supposed to say to this chick, so I just stood there looking like a complete idiot. I was trying to think of what the hell I should say to her when a soft smile crossed her face. "You one of Gus's boys?"

"Yes, ma'am, I am."

"Thought so. I have something for you." She reached behind the counter and pulled out a small box, then offered it to me. "Here ya go. You be careful heading back home, ya hear?"

"Yes, ma'am." I took it in my hand and said, "Thanks."

I waved goodbye and rushed back outside to the parking lot. After I'd put the box in one of my saddlebags, I jumped on my bike, and a rush of adrenaline surged through me as I started up my engine. I honestly didn't know if this was my final task as a prospect. It could've just been another chance to prove myself, but either way, I was eager to get back home to find out. I was wound up tighter than a two-dollar watch as I headed back onto the Interstate. I kept expecting for something to go wrong—a flat tire, traffic, or even a fucking natural disaster—but it was easy-sailing all the way back to the clubhouse. When I pulled through the gate, it was just a few minutes before six and the entire lot was packed full of bikes and cars—some familiar, others not so much. I quickly parked, and my stomach was knotted up in a nervous, tangled mess as I grabbed the box out of my saddlebag and headed into the bar.

When I opened the door, the entire club was there, along with Landry, Viper and his brothers, my mother, and my little sister. I stood in the doorway, looking at all the people who meant so much to me, and I felt my throat tighten. The last thing I wanted to do was get all choked up, but I knew there was only one reason they'd all be there and the thought had me biting back my emotions. I was still standing there in awe when Gus and Moose walked up to me. A smile crossed Gus's face as he asked, "What about it, Hyde? You got something for me?"

I couldn't muster the words, so I simply nodded as I reached into my pocket and pulled out the small box. A proud smile crept across Gus's face as he glanced over to Rider and gave him a quick nod. Rider was all business as he reached behind him and took a new Satan's Fury cut from the counter and brought it over to us. Gus took it from his hand, and as he offered it to me, he said, "Well done, brother. Welcome to the Fury family."

After removing my prospect cut, I pulled it on, and pride washed over me as I ran my fingers across the brightly colored embroidery. I'd spent months thinking about this very moment, and now that it was actually here, I was in complete fucking awe. I remembered the looks on Dane and Gash's faces the night they'd received their cuts. I'd seen how proud they were. I could see it in their eyes, hear it in their voices, but I never could've imagined those feelings ran so deep. Hell, they ran all the way to my very core. Trying my best to collect myself, I glanced over and spotted Landry at the bar with Viper and Hawk. They were all sitting with my mother and sister, smiling proudly as they watched Gus say, "Open the box."

"What is it?"

"You'll see. Open it," Gus pushed. Quickly, I tore the small box apart and was surprised to find a Guardian Bell attached to a small keychain. Gus smiled as he said, "I know your dad is already up there keeping an eye on you, but we can all use a little extra protection."

"Thanks, brother."

Gus reached over and gave me bear hug. Once Moose had done the same, Rider stepped up and grabbed me, then slapped me on the back. "Never doubted you for a second."

"Thanks, brother. Couldn't have done it without you."

My brothers had started to line up, so Rider quickly stepped out of the way, giving each of them their chance to welcome me into the brotherhood. With each congratulatory hug, they offered me a shot of tequila. I gladly accepted each and every one. At the time, I was too caught up in the moment to remember that I hadn't eaten a damn thing, but I didn't care. I just kept downing shot after shot until I'd spoken to each and every brother. By the time Viper made his way over with my mother and sister, I was feeling pretty fucking good. Viper couldn't have looked prouder as he wrapped his arms around me in a fierce hug. He still had a hold on me when he asked, "Well, you gonna say it?"

Even though I knew exactly what he was talking about, I asked him anyway, "Say what?"

"You know damn well *what*." He stepped back and looked at me with narrowed eyes. "Come on. You know I'm not gonna let it go until you say it."

"Fine." I chuckled as I told him, "You were right."

"Damn right," he boasted. "Always am."

"I don't know about that," my mother scoffed before turning her attention to me. By the way she was studying me, I half expected her to fuss that I hadn't been eating enough or needed to get more rest, so I was surprised when she smiled and said, "You look good, Clay. I wish your father was here. He would've been so proud."

Lyssa could sense Mom was about to cry and slipped her arm around her, giving her a comforting hug as she replied, "He is here, Mom. There's no way he'd miss this."

"She's right." Hoping to take her mind off Dad, I stepped towards them and hugged them both. "I'm glad you both made it."

"You know we wouldn't have missed it." Lyssa took a step back, quickly glancing over her shoulder before asking, "Who's he?"

"Who?"

Her eyes rolled as she stepped towards me and whispered, "The bald guy in the corner?"

I turned my head and when I realized she was talking about T-Bone, I shook my head and snickered to myself. "You gotta be fucking kidding me."

"What?" she pushed. "He's hot—"

"Lyssa, *no*," I warned.

"Well, I happen to think he—"

"Nope! Not gonna happen, Lyssa."

I hadn't realized that T-Bone had come up behind me until I heard him ask, "What's not gonna happen?"

My normally confident sister inhaled a quick, nervous breath and turned to look at the floor, seeming almost bashful as she replied, "Nothing. Clay is just being Clay."

"Oh, really."

T-Bone gave her a goofy smirk as he motioned his head towards the bar. "Why don't you let me get you a drink, and you can tell me all about it."

"Okay."

Lyssa gave me a quick shrug, then followed T-Bone. Before I could protest, Landry came rushing over with Hawk. She waited patiently as Hawk leaned towards me, hugging me briefly before saying, "You did good, brother."

"Thanks, man."

"You know, there's not many who can say that they have it all ... a loyal group of men you can call your brothers ... and a good woman." Hawk glanced over at

Landry with his eyebrow cocked high. "But you most certainly can."

"You're right about that." I stepped towards her, slipping my arms around her waist as I told him, "Might be time for you to consider doing the same."

His eyes never left Landry's as he replied, "If I found a woman like her, I just might."

Hawk gave us both a wink, and then strolled over to sit down with the rest of the Sinners. His words were still hanging in the air when Landry reached up and gave me a hug. "Congratulations, babe. I knew you could do it."

As I held her in my arms, I knew Hawk was right. I truly had it all. I lowered my mouth to that sensitive spot just below her ear, softly kissing her as I whispered, "You know what this means, right?"

"What?"

I looked down at her and smiled as I told her, "You're officially one of Satan's Fury's ol' ladies."

"I don't care what my title is as long as I'm yours."

"Now and forever, baby. Now and forever."

ACKNOWLEDGMENTS

I am blessed to have so many wonderful people who are willing to give their time and effort to making my books the best they can be. Without them, I wouldn't't be able to breathe life into my characters and share their stories with you. To the people I've listed below and so many others, I want to say thank you for taking this journey with me. Your support means the world to me, and I truly mean it when I say appreciate everything you do. I love you all!

PA: Natalie Weston
Editing/Proofing: Lisa Cullinan-Editor, Rose Holub-Proofer, Honey Palomino-Proofer
Promoting: Amy Jones, Veronica Ines Garcia, Neringa Neringiukas, Whynter M. Raven
BETAS/Early Readers: Kaci Stewart, Tanya Skaggs, Jo Lynn, and Jessey Elliott
Street Team: All the wonderful members of Wilder's Women (You rock!)

Best Friend and biggest supporter: My mother (Love you to the moon and back.)

A short excerpt of Rider: Satan's Fury MC-Memphis Book 7 is included in the following pages. Blaze, Shadow, Riggs, Murphy, Gunner, Gus and Rider are also included in this Memphis series, and you can find them all on Amazon. They are all free with KU.

RIDER: SATAN'S FURY MC-MEMPHIS EXCERPT

PROLOGUE

 was born and raised in Oakland, Tennessee, a small town where life revolved around farming and Friday night football. Hell, it didn't matter if you were rich or poor, young or old—everyone came out to the game on Friday night. It's what folks lived for. They'd pack the stands and cheer like there was no tomorrow, silently praying for a big win with each new play. It was those big wins that would help distract them from the crops that weren't coming in or the bills that were piling up. As the team's quarterback, I was one of the many players the crowd was shouting for, but I never heard their screams. As soon as I stepped out on that field, I was in the zone, not thinking about anything except getting that ball from point A to point B.

There was no greater feeling than standing there waiting for the snap. As soon as the ball was in my hands, I was ready. A rush of adrenaline would surge through me as I'd watch the opposing team make their advance. I could hear the sounds of helmets and shoulder pads slamming against each other as my offensive line held off the defense. I'd take a three-step drop, and once I was in the pocket, I'd quickly scan the field for my receiver. Knowing exactly where I was tossing the ball, it wouldn't be long before we were hanging a half dozen on the board. I was good, one of the best, and even when we didn't win the game, I always gave the fans something to talk about. My latest game was no different. I threw a pass that was risky. Some might even say it was too risky. My receiver was completely covered by the opposing team and it could've easily been picked off, but I saw a sliver of opportunity and took it. Just as I knew it would, the ball went straight into his hands, and he made the winning touchdown. The crowd went wild, and I left the field knowing I'd done what I'd set out to do.

I was feeling on top of the world when I'd left the locker room that night. Everything was going exactly as planned. After a few more great plays, I'd get that scholarship to play ball at UT and finally have my way out, because once I was gone, I'd never look back. I was headed out to my truck when my best friend, Bryce, shouted across the parking lot. "Yo, Caleb! You coming with us or what?"

He was standing next to Emmet's truck, another one of my good friends, and when I answered, "Yeah, I'm coming, but I'll have to drive. I gotta help my dad out in the morning," a look of disappointment crept over his face.

"Damn, man," Bryce complained. "After that game, you'd think your dad would give ya the day off or something!"

"Yeah, right. We both know that's never gonna

happen." My father was a cotton farmer, and I'd been helping him bring in the crops since the time my feet could reach the pedals on the tractor. When I wasn't helping with the plowing, planting, or picking, I was doing what I could to help prepare to plow, plant, or pick. I'd work on the farm equipment, haul trailers back and forth from the gin, and whatever else he needed me to do. While my dad loved everything about farming, it just wasn't my thing, and I was always relieved when football season rolled around. It was the only time he didn't complain about me not being out in the fields.

I could hear the others calling out to Bryce, telling him to hurry, so I said, "You guys go ahead. I'll see you over at Landon's in a few minutes."

"You know, Janey Thompson was asking about ya earlier."

"Yeah?"

"Sure was." A smile crossed his face as he opened the door to Emmet's truck. "She's gonna be there tonight. If you play your cards right, you might just get you some of that."

"I can have Janey Thompson any day of the week," I boasted, then murmured under my breath, "and so can every other football player in town."

"Guess we'll see about that tonight!"

Before I could respond, he'd climbed into the truck with the rest of the gang and closed the door. Clearly eager to get to the party, Emmet slammed his foot on the accelerator, hurling loose gravel from his rear tires. Unimpressed by his redneck display, I went over to my truck and tossed my stuff in the backend, then got inside and cranked the engine. By the time I started to pull out of the parking lot, most everyone had already gone. The only ones left were the coach and the cleaning crew, or so I thought.

I was just about to pull out onto the main road when I noticed Darcy Harrington's beat-up pickup truck parked across the street. The hood was up with the taillights flashing, so I assumed it had broken down on her. As I sat there staring at her flashing lights, a battle ensued between my ears. I'd always been the kind of guy who'd lend a hand whenever someone needed it, especially when it came to women, but Darcy wasn't like most women.

When we were kids, Darcy and I were actually pretty good friends. We'd hang out on the school playground during recess, eat lunch together, and even run around at football games, but things were simpler then. There was no judging one another by the clothes we wore or the houses we lived in, but as we grew older that changed. Like a slow turn of the wind, we started talking less and less, and it wasn't long before we didn't say a word to one another, even in the hallway. That didn't mean I stopped noticing her. Hell, there wasn't a soul around who didn't pay attention when Darcy Harrington walked by. The tomboy with pigtails and freckles sprinkled across the bridge of her nose had turned into a beautiful girl with long auburn hair and curves that would give a *Playboy* model a run for her money.

Darcy's looks weren't the only thing that changed over the years. Where she was once sweet and funny, she'd become cold and detached—never letting anyone get too close. Her strong persona made her come off as unapproachable, so everyone kept their distance, fearing if they crossed her there'd be hell to pay. It was no wonder why Darcy acted the way she did. Her family was rough. They were the kind of folks you didn't want to cross in a dark alley—mean and mouthy, and didn't think twice about breaking the law. I didn't know their whole story, but from what I'd heard, you didn't mess with the Harringtons—especially Darcy.

I sat there a few more minutes, listening to my engine idle and the monotonous tick of my blinker as I questioned my next move: I could head on over to the party, toss back a few beers, and spend some *quality time* with Janey Thompson, or risk getting my balls handed to me by the very girl who'd starred in every one of my fucking wet dreams since middle school. Before I even realized what I was doing, I'd pulled out onto the road and was headed in Darcy's direction. When I parked behind her truck, she peeked her head around the hood and watched with a blank expression as I got out and started towards her. "Is everything okay?"

"Take a look around, Sport." Her words dripped with sarcasm as she barked, "I'm out here alone in the dark, parked on the side of the road with my flashers on, and my hood up. I'd say those are pretty good signs that things are *not* okay."

Ignoring her sour tone, I continued towards the front of the truck. When I reached her, I asked, "You got any idea what's wrong with it?"

"The battery cable's loose," she grumbled.

Even in the dark, I could see that Darcy looked fucking incredible. She was wearing a pair of tight-fitting jeans with a low-cut tank top, showing just a hint of cleavage, and the silver bangles around her wrist jingled when she reached into her back pocket for her cigarettes.

After lighting one up, she announced, "My numb-nut brother snatched my tools, and now I don't have a way to fix the stupid thing."

I leaned in to take a closer look, and even though I already knew the answer, I asked, "Would a crescent wrench do the trick?"

"Yeah, it would." A hopeful expression crossed her face. "Do you have one?"

"Hold on, let me see." I rushed back over to the truck and grabbed my tools. Once I found the wrench, I brought it over to her. "Got it."

"Well, how about that." After tossing her cigarette to the ground, she took the wrench from my hand, then handed me a flashlight. "You mind holding this?"

"Sure." I pointed the light at the battery. "This good?"

"Perfect."

She leaned forward with her phenomenal ass perched in the air, and I had to fight the urge to readjust myself as I stood there watching her reconnect the cables. Damn, I'd never seen anything so fucking hot in my entire life, and it took all I had not to reach out and grab her into my arms. Once she'd adjusted the bolt, she walked over to the driver's side of the truck and got inside. When she turned the ignition and pressed the gas several times, the truck sputtered a bit, then finally roared to life. Darcy turned to me with a smile. "Looks like Sport saves the day again."

"Again?"

"Yeah…that pass you threw to win the game. It was really something."

She walked back to the front of her truck and closed the hood. As she handed me my wrench, I asked, "You saw that, huh?"

"I did." She gave me a slight smirk. "You made the good folks of Oakland very proud tonight. I'm sure they'll be talking about it for weeks."

"I got lucky."

"We both know that play took a lot more than just luck. Besides, I don't put much value in luck. Either you have it or you don't. Simple as that." She walked by me and got inside her truck. "Thanks for giving me a hand tonight. I appreciate it."

"Anytime." It was the most we'd spoken in the last couple of years, and I wasn't ready for her to go. Trying to play it cool, I told her, "Landon Creasey's having a party out at his place."

"Doesn't he have a party every Friday night?" she scoffed.

"He does." I knew it was a reach, but I had to try. "You should stop by."

"Thanks for the invite, Sport, but I don't think so. High school parties and I just don't mix." She closed her door and leaned her head out the window. "So, you working with your dad tomorrow or whatever?"

Surprised she knew anything about me, my brows furrowed. "Yeah, why?"

"What time will you get done?"

"Some time after dark…maybe eight."

She studied me for a moment, then said, "You know the old racetrack down by Eastman's grocery?"

"Yeah?"

"Meet me there tomorrow night at nine."

I nodded and replied, "I'll be there."

"Good." A soft smile crossed her face, and the whole world stopped spinning. Damn, I'd always thought that

Darcy was beautiful, but when she smiled, she was absolutely stunning. I couldn't take my eyes off her as she shifted the truck into drive. Before pulling away, she waved and said, "See ya tomorrow night."

She was already out of earshot when I shouted, "Looking forward to it!"

I was in a complete daze while I stood there and watched her taillights fade into the night. I couldn't believe Darcy Harrington had just asked me on a date, or at least, I thought it was a date. At that moment, I didn't really care; it was enough to put a smile on my face. I headed back to my truck, and when I started the engine, I saw that it was almost midnight. Knowing I had to get up early in the morning, I decided to skip the party and head home. When I got to the house, I wasn't surprised to find that the lights were out and everyone had already gone to bed. I went into the kitchen and grabbed a quick bite to eat, then started up to my room. Just as I topped the stairs, my mother called out to me. "Caleb?"

I turned back and found her standing in her doorway with a concerned expression. "Yeah?"

"You're home early. Is everything okay?"

"Yeah, everything's good."

"Okay, good." She smiled as she said, "You played a great game tonight."

"We did all right."

"You did more than all right, Caleb." When I didn't respond, she asked, "You going to set your alarm, or do you want me to wake you?"

"I've got it, Mom," I assured her. "Go back to bed."

"Okay. Good night."

"Night."

I went on to my room and crawled into bed. As I lay there, a smile crept over my face when my mind drifted back to Darcy. Our brief encounter had made quite an impression on me, and I found myself looking forward to the following night when I'd get the chance to know her even better. I was feeling pretty damn positive about things. My chances to play at UT were looking good, and I had a date with none other than Darcy Harrington. As I drifted off to sleep, I couldn't imagine things being any better. Sadly, the following morning, my life took a drastic turn.

With one fleeting moment—one stupid, careless mistake, I lost everything. My chance with Darcy. My football scholarship at UT. My friends. My family. Hell, I'd lost my entire life as I knew it, and to make matters worse, I'd done it all to myself.

RIDER

I was busy working in the garage when I heard Blaze ask, "Everything all right there?"

I glanced over my shoulder and found him pacing back and forth in his office as he held his cellphone up to his ear. I could tell by the tone in his voice and the expression on his face that he was talking to his ol' lady, Kenadee. The poor guy had been worried sick about her for days, calling her job every few hours to make sure she was okay, even though he knew one of the prospects was there at the hospital watching over her. I could hear the relief in his voice when he continued, "Good. So, no sign of the Disciples?"

He paused, giving Kenadee a chance to respond, then told her, "I'm aware I asked you that two hours ago, and I got news for you…I'm gonna ask you again and again until I'm sure those motherfuckers'll be leaving you alone."

Kenadee is a triage nurse at Regional Hospital. If she was working anywhere else, it might not have been so bad, but being an emergency room nurse at one of the biggest hospitals in the city of Memphis was tough. Night after night, she dealt with gunshot wounds, stabbings, overdoses, and God knows what else, but Kenadee loved her job. Blaze, on the other hand, didn't feel the same way. He believed that it was too dangerous for her to work there, and the other night we all realized just how right he was. Kenadee was working the graveyard shift when a kid came in with multiple gunshot wounds and was barely hanging on. They did everything they could to save him, but he was simply too far gone. His father immediately lost it, shouting and tossing shit everywhere. When the cops came to escort him out, he threatened Kenadee, warning her that he was going to make her pay for letting his boy die.

It wasn't the first time she'd gotten threats, but this time it was different. This time, it was Keshawn Lewis. He was known by the name "Slayer" and was the leader of the Inner Disciples' gang. When he threatened Kenadee's life, Blaze was understandably troubled that he'd make good on his promise. Because of that concern, Blaze brought Kenadee and his son, Kevin, to stay at the clubhouse. He knew we'd do everything in our power to ensure her safety.

Before he ended the call, he told her, "Love you, too, babe. I'll be there at six when you get off."

Blaze shoved his phone in his back pocket, then turned his attention back to the stack of paperwork on his desk. He was in charge of the garage and took his job very seriously, always making sure everything ran smoothly. After several minutes, he stepped out into the main garage and shouted, "Hey, Murph? How much longer on the Chief?"

"I'll be done on my end in an hour or so," he answered from the back of the garage. "I've got everything broken down. Just need to finish prepping for paint."

"Good. Maybe we can have it all wrapped up by the end of the week."

"You know, it'd go a lot faster if we were able to get the painting done here," Murphy complained.

"I know. I'm working on it. Hope to know something this afternoon."

"What happens this afternoon?"

"Riggs is doing a background check on that girl T-Bone suggested hiring. If everything checks out, I'm going over to see if she's interested in taking the position."

"We could really use the help around here," Murphy complained. "Do what you gotta do to get her ass over here."

"You know I will." Blaze assured him. "Just let me know when you're done, and I'll get everything across town."

"You taking the Honda, too?"

"I would, but Rider just started on it two days ago. No way he's done with her yet."

"Actually, she's ready when you are," I told him.

"What?" Blaze looked over at me, surprised. "You're done?"

"Yep." I nodded. "Finished everything up last night."

"Damn, brother. You didn't have to go and do that."

"I know. I just wanted to do what I could to help out."

When I started prospecting for the club, I quickly realized I'd been given a second chance. It wasn't something I thought I deserved, not after all I'd done, but Gus, the president of Satan's Fury, didn't agree. He saw something in me that no one else did. Without even asking anything in return, he and the brothers helped me turn my life around. That in itself was enough to make me forever grateful, so I always tried to do more than what was expected. It was the only way I knew how to show my appreciation. I motioned my hand over to the Ford pickup I'd been working. "A few more minutes, I'll have Mr. Pruitt's water pump sorted."

"You trying to make the rest of us look bad or some-thing?" T-Bone taunted.

Before I could answer, Gunner looked over to him and snickered. "Not like you make that too hard for him."

"He's right," Blaze added. "Hell, we've been waiting on you to finish that fucking gas tank for two days."

"Hold up. I can't help it that the damn thing had a fucking leak," T-Bone complained. "With all this damn humidity, it took forever for the fucking epoxy to cure."

Gunner chuckled as he mumbled, "Excuses. Excuses."

T-Bone was about to argue further when Blaze cut him off. "Look, we don't have time to be fucking around here, guys. We have a lot of shit to finish up, and Gus wants us over at the clubhouse at seven for church."

"You got any idea why?" I asked. "Is something up?"

"Got no idea. Guess we'll all find out together."

I nodded, then got back to work installing the water pump on Pruitt's truck. After I finished, I went over and helped Tank finish with the gas tank and rear fender. By the time we had everything sandblasted and ready for paint, it was almost five and time to close up shop. We had just enough time to grab a hot shower and a bite to eat before we had to meet up with Gus for church. Once we'd locked up the garage, I followed T-Bone and Gunner back to the clubhouse, while Blaze and Murphy took the bike parts over to the paint shop and picked up Kenadee from the hospital. As soon as I got back to the clubhouse, I went to my room and took a shower. Once I threw on some fresh clothes, I headed down the hall to the kitchen to find something to eat. Several of the hang-arounds were busy making lasagna with all the fixings. Gunner, and Shadow, the club's enforcer, were already sitting at the table eating with our VP, Moose, and his ol' lady, Louise. I was about to make myself a plate when Jasmine, one of the hang-arounds, came up to me. "Hey there, good lookin'. You want me to make you a plate?"

I wasn't one to let others do for me what I could do myself, so I shook my head. "No. I'll get it, but thanks."

"You sure? I don't mind."

"I'm sure."

I made my way over to the stove, and after I fixed myself a plate of lasagna and garlic bread, I went over and sat down at the table next to Gunner. Just as I was about to start eating, he looked over to me and said, "You should've told me you were going back to the garage to work last night. I would've given you a hand."

"I know. That's why I didn't mention it." Gunner was a good guy—one of the best. He'd have to be, otherwise Gus would've raised all kinds of hell when he found out about Gunner and his daughter, August. After she showed up at the clubhouse looking for help with finding her daughter, Harper, Gus ordered Gunner to watch after her and keep her safe. Gunner did what he could to fight the pull he felt towards her, but from early on, he knew she was the one for him. Once Harper was returned and the issues with August's ex were resolved, Gunner and August started planning their future together. After all they'd been through, I knew he needed to be spending time with them, not helping me at the garage. "With the move and all, I'm sure August and Harper want you home with them."

"Yeah, but they'd understand if you needed me," he pushed.

"Maybe so, but it wasn't a big deal." Before I took a bite of my lasagna, I added, "Besides, I managed fine on my own."

"You know, you're gonna have to stop doing that at some point."

"Doing what?"

"That thing where you keep trying to prove yourself." He smacked my shoulder. "You've already done that, brother. Otherwise, you wouldn't be sportin' that patch."

"Not about that," I started. "I'm just trying to do my part."

"We both know it's more than that."

He was right. It was so much more than that, but I found it doubtful that he'd understand. Hell, there were times when I didn't understand the shit that was going through my head, so there was no sense talking about it. Thankfully, Blaze came over and sat down next to us, drawing Gunner's attention away from me and over to him. "Kenadee make it okay today?"

"Yeah. No sign of any trouble."

"Good. Maybe this thing with the Disciples will just blow over, and Kenadee can put this shit behind her."

"Damn, I hope so, but I got a feeling that ain't gonna happen." Before Blaze took a bite of lasagna, he said, "But on a good note, I think we've got ourselves a new painter for the garage."

"That chick from Thompson's garage?" Gunner questioned.

"Yeah. Everything checked out on the background check Riggs did on her. Grew up in Oakland, and since she left there, she keeps pretty much to herself. No boyfriend or husband to speak of, just a couple of brothers who give her shit from time to time, so I offered her the job." Blaze was clearly pleased as he said, "She's agreed to come down to the shop tomorrow and look things over, which is great cause this chick's got real talent. Since she started working with Thompson, his business has almost doubled. If she takes us up on our offer, Thompson's gonna be pissed."

I didn't have to ask who they were talking about. I already knew it was Darcy Harrington. I could still remember the day T-Bone suggested that the club offer her the job; I shouldn't have been surprised that her name came up though. Darcy was extremely talented. In fact, she was one of the best custom painters around, but it didn't change the fact that I hoped they wouldn't hire her. It wasn't her fault that I felt the way I did. She was simply a part of my past, and any time I thought about her, the memories of that morning and the months thereafter would come flooding back. I'd spent the last couple of years trying to forget them, but I was slowly learning that I could no more avoid them than the beating of my own heart.

Blaze looked over to me as he asked, "You grew up in Oakland, right?"

"Yeah. I did."

"So, did you know her?"

"I did," I admitted. "It was a small town. We all knew each other, but that was a long time ago." Without even realizing it, I'd started rubbing my right arm, trying to ease the dull ache that had started to throb deep within the muscles and old scar tissue. Concerned, Gunner leaned towards me and asked, "You all right, brother?"

"Yeah," I lied. "My arm's just acting up."

"You should see if Doc can give you something for it," Blaze suggested.

Unfortunately, there was no drug and no amount of alcohol on this earth that could ease the pain I was feeling. I'd already tried. Damn near killed myself searching for something to numb the ache. It wasn't until I started prospecting for Fury that I discovered something that'd give me any relief and that was riding my Harley. My bike gave me an even greater rush than I'd felt when I was playing ball. I needed that distraction right now, but it would have to wait. We had church in a few minutes, so I released the hold on my arm and replied, "No need for that. I'll be fine."

"You sure?"

"Absolutely."

When I turned my attention back to my food, Gunner did the same, and by the time we were all done, it was time for church. I followed Gunner and Blaze into the conference room, and we joined the others at the table. As soon as we were all seated, Gus turned to us and said, "You all know, the leader of the Inner Disciples made a threat against Kenadee a couple of weeks ago. Riggs has been doing what he can to monitor the situation, watching the security feed at all their hangouts, and we both have our concerns about Lewis's current behavior."

"Why? What the fuck is he doing?" Blaze asked.

"Lewis doesn't run his crew like most of the gangs around here. He's been a loose cannon, driven by the ownership of his turf and vengeance, but for the most part, he's stayed clean. Recently, he's been cracked out on coke, involved in shootouts with neighboring gangs, and the other night, a few of his boys robbed a downtown pawnshop. They got a pretty damn good take on AR15s and Glocks. If I didn't know better, I'd say they were making preparations."

Murphy leaned forward and asked, "Preparations for what?"

"No way to know for sure. Just be on high alert," Gus warned. "If this guy tries to make good on his threats, I want you ready."

"Understood," we all replied.

"Good. Church is dismissed."

We all stood and started to disperse. Like most nights, some of the brothers went to the bar to toss back a few beers, while others went home to their ol' ladies. I didn't have a woman and wasn't in the mood for drinking, so I started towards the parking lot. I was just about to walk out the back door when I overheard Blaze talking to Gus. I could hear the mix of relief and excitement in his voice as Blaze told him, "We'll have to see how it goes. She's coming first thing tomorrow morning to check it out and see if she's interested in working with us."

"You sure it's a good idea to bring a woman into the garage?"

"This Darcy chick has real talent, Gus, and Thompson hasn't had any problems with her working at his place."

Gus's tone grew harsh as he replied, "Yeah, well... Thompson isn't using his garage as a front for his club."

Blaze ran his hand over his beard. "I don't know what to tell you, Prez. There's a lot I don't know about this chick, but I've got a good feeling about her."

"We'll have Riggs look into her and make sure she's not someone we'll need to be concerned about."

Damn. From the sounds of it, Blaze had his mind set on hiring Darcy Harrington. The thought didn't set well with me as I headed out to the parking lot. I got on my bike, turned the ignition, and seconds later, I was pulling out of the gate. As soon as I hit the open road, I turned back the throttle and disappeared into the night. It's hard to explain how alive I felt at that moment, like I was completely in tune with the world around me. When I was on my bike, I could see things more clearly, smell every scent, feel the wind against my skin, and hear the sounds of the city echoing around me. As I leaned my bike into a winding turn, it was just me and the road ahead. I wasn't thinking about Darcy Harrington or my past, and in no time, the tension I'd been carrying all night started to fade. I rode for several hours, and when exhaustion started to set in, I went back to the clubhouse to crash for the night. By the time I walked into my room, I could barely keep my eyes open. I thought for sure I'd go straight to sleep, but unfortunately, that didn't happen. Instead, I spent the entire night tossing and turning as I thought about coming face to face with Darcy Harrington again. I had a feeling that it wouldn't be a happy reunion for either of us.

Made in the USA
Middletown, DE
19 March 2021